WAKING LAZARUS

A GUARDIAN NOVEL

D.J. WILLIAMS

LOS ANGELES

Copyright ©2016 by Forgotten Stories, LLC

ISBN-13: 978-0692677186
ISBN-10: 0692677186

Printed in the United States

www.djwilliamsbooks.com

A GUARDIAN NOVEL

WAKING LAZARUS

Official Soundtrack

WWW.DJWILLIAMSBOOKS.COM

Composed by Jené Nicole Johnson

ALSO BY D.J. WILLIAMS

THE DISILLUSIONED

"ONE SPARK SETS THE STORY ABLAZE."

PROLOGUE

S he stared at her reflection for a long time.

Her bloodied hands cupped together as she splashed water on the open wounds on her face and arms. The coolness lasted only a few seconds and did little to revive her senses. Though she'd spent a few hours safely inside the dilapidated house, she still struggled to grasp reality.

Crawling. Stumbling. Digging her way through the desert for hours had been more than a physical test of endurance. Her five-foot-three, one-hundred-pound frame was broken in other ways. By the time she stumbled into town, she wasn't sure where she was or how she ended up there.

She gazed into the mirror at her ragged clothes and bony cheeks. Her eyes, once fiery with determination, were now sunken and empty. Dried blood caked her filthy hands. Proof that what happened was real. She ran her fingers through her sweaty, blondish-brown hair, which was normally a perfectly styled bob. She desperately wanted to scream. Her signature voice had garnered the world's stage with a booming tone that pronounced every syllable with passion and conviction. Now that passion and conviction had devolved into survival and anguish.

Glimpses of what happened flashed in her mind. Her body shook and she squeezed her eyes so tightly she could see the blood pulse with every heartbeat. She longed to rid herself—not of the woman, Alice, who called her *Sister*—but of the man known as Adler. The pounding in her chest

1

intensified as she slowed her breathing. She dug her face into her palms and whispered under her breath, "God give me strength."

Barefoot, she shuffled across the wood floor toward the edge of the bed. It was as far as she could go as she slumped face down on the mattress. Nicotine seeped from the covers, floorboards, walls, and curtains — suffocating her in the darkness as she warned herself of what was ahead.

You will not return an adulterer but as God's messenger.

A heavy fog seemed to engulf the room as she closed her eyes and found herself in a familiar place in the backseat of a Pontiac Coupe driving alone through every town and ghetto from New York to California. She stepped from the Pontiac and found herself on a street corner surrounded by hundreds of onlookers. Dozens of coffins lined the sidewalk. She stood as God's chosen messenger amidst an epidemic that swept through the nation. Her words were light amidst the darkness. She believed and held on to them as her refrain, her passion, her driving force, and her pulpit.

Fearlessly, she reached out her hand and prayed. A blind man stepped forward and laughed with excitement as vibrant colors illuminated all around him. A woman jumped for joy as she listened to the man's laughter, her world of silence forever changed. A mother wheeled her boy into the center of the crowd. With one touch, the boy jumped to his feet and walked. Cheers from the crowds grew louder in each town until there were thousands who followed, believing they had found their salvation.

She turned from the crowd and found herself knee-deep in the Mississippi River. Thousands stood along the banks ready to be baptized. Another flash and she was inside a tent surrounded by coloreds. Her voice rang with gospel lyrics as she played bluesy chords on a piano. All eyes watched as she turned her attention toward a young deaf girl. The music faded and the anticipation thickened. She casually walked up to the girl and whispered in her ear. The crowd gasped as the girl began to sing. Her angelic voice cut through the humid night and engulfed them. Hundreds stepped forward, weeping with eyes fixed toward the heavens. The young girl sang softly as God's messenger gazed out on the faces of her followers.

Then she turned her attention to a man who was brought forward.

"Brother, rise upon His promise now!" Her words were loud enough for all to hear.

The man nodded as she rested her hands on him. A surge of energy shot through the crowd like lightening. Instantly, the man stood from his wheelchair and walked across the stage, tears rolling down his cheeks.

She wasted no time as she turned and lifted another woman out of a chair.

CRACK...CRACK...CRACK...

Bones snapped into place as the woman's curved spine straightened. Voices rose even louder as the young girl's singing was drowned out by a burst of celebration and applause.

When she opened her eyes she expected to see the multitudes that flooded the tent. Instead, she was alone in the room. Her vivid memories of the Pontiac, the wooden pulpit, the evangelistic meetings, and the street-corner sermons with megaphone in hand seemed like a lifetime ago.

She had shouted the salvation message to the drunks outside the bars. She stood alongside the Negroes in the cotton fields and sang with them during her revivals. She embraced the undesirables. Black and white immersed as one. No segregation. No condemnation. Only a message of hope, love, and unity. Proclaiming the Good News was her way to fight against the demons that lurked in the deep corners of her faith. But pursuing her calling came with a heavy price.

A ray of light pierced the gap between the curtains as the sun rose on the horizon. She rolled slowly from the bed and winced in pain. She mustered up enough strength from the prayers she poured out on the lost, broken, and hurting. Then she breathed in deep and sensed the Holy Spirit energize her being.

Quietly, she walked down the hall from the bedroom toward the front door. In that moment she was eager to return home, to continue her calling, and to leave the events of the last thirty days behind. She squinted as the morning flooded through the doorway where a shadow waited patiently.

1

I found the house in a cul-de-sac in La Cañada, nestled in the foothills, twenty minutes north of the City of Angels. A wrought iron fence surrounded a concrete driveway lined with large oak trees that covered a perfectly groomed lawn leading to a two-story, white brick house.

In a city where every waiter, car salesman, and Starbucks barista perceived him or herself as a struggling actor or writer, I was no different. I spent countless nights feverishly typing away in coffee houses all over town, but Rachel's pregnancy was a game changer. I needed to put my dream aside. Becoming a bestselling author was no longer in the cards.

Eight years after Samantha was born, I snapped. Not the kind that made everyone think I'd gone crazy, but the kind that was reckless to those around me. I was convinced my book was my...no...it was our salvation. I mailed dozens of manuscripts to random agents, waited anxiously for the phone to ring, and prayed for a sign from heaven that I hadn't wasted my life and sacrificed my marriage for nothing. The silence was deafening. Time passed, and the guilt weighed heavily. Rachel stood by me for as long as she could, but when our savings bled dry so did our marriage.

Then yesterday, the phone rang. The call was a sign with a thirty-day deadline. Seven hundred hours. Forty-four thousand six hundred and forty minutes. Tick tock. The clock started that Tuesday morning at 8:37 AM when I climbed from my Chevy Tacoma, pulled my duffle bag from the bed, and strolled up the sidewalk in time to see the front door swing open. In the doorway stood a man with thinning gray hair, slender, with a familiar face more wrinkled than I remembered.

Doc Warren, an old friend of my father's, asked me to ghostwrite a memoir. I barely remembered the man. I didn't know how he found me. I didn't ask how much he was going to pay. I didn't care. I told him I'd do it. This was my last chance. Maybe my string of bad luck had finally ended. I hoped it was an open door to get back together with Rachel and our daughter Samantha.

Selfishly, I wanted this more than anything. And I needed the cash no matter how little it might be. My heart pounded as I pictured his memoir on the NYT bestseller list. Of course, it wouldn't be my name on the cover, but I would know who penned the story. Once publishers knew of my skills, the floodgates would open wide and I'd get my shot to sign a six-figure deal and write my own works of fiction.

Maybe then I'd feel forgiven.

"You're early!" He announced as he stepped forward, grabbed my shoulder, and eyed me from head to toe. "God, you look just like Frank. Come on in. Breakfast is almost ready."

I stepped inside and closed the door. He was already halfway down the hall. He moved quickly for a man in his sixties. I paused for a moment and stared at the black and white photos on the walls. A much older photo of him aboard a canoe in a remote jungle. Standing in an African village beside a mud hut. Kneeling with a group of children posing for the camera in a nondescript slum in the Orient. Then there were the headlining newspaper photos of him outside City Hall surrounded by reporters and shaking hands with the Mayor. It was like two extremes: compassion and law.

I wondered if these were the stories I'd be writing about. A thrill rushed through me for the first time in ages. I hurried to the kitchen where he hovered over the stove.

"I was surprised you called," I slid onto a barstool. "How'd you know where to find me?"

"I played golf at Brookside with your dad." He reached for two plates and forks from a granite counter. "Sounded like you're trying to break into the publishing world. I thought you'd be perfect for what I have in mind."

"Well, I'm ready to work."

"Don't worry, we'll get started soon enough. First, let's eat."

I watched him from across the island. I was never much of a cook, but it was clear he was an old pro. He grabbed a pan from the stove and dished a pile of scrambled eggs and a few strips of bacon. He poured a glass of freshly squeezed orange juice and set it all on the granite countertop. The aroma filled my nostrils as my stomach rumbled. I couldn't remember the last time I'd eaten a home-cooked meal. Lately, take-out and drive-thru were my food of choice, evidenced by the extra twenty pounds around my waist.

Minutes passed as we ate in silence.

"There's a few things I need to attend to before we start." He nodded towards the backyard. "You can get settled in the pool house."

"Mr. Warren..."

"Call me Doc."

"Okay. Doc, I just wanted to say thank you for giving me this opportunity."

Doc finished his last bite of eggs and left his plate on the counter. "Tell you what...you do the dishes and we'll call it even."

"Deal."

Life as a ghostwriter had officially begun. I was willing to do whatever it took and if that meant doing dishes then so be it. I rinsed the plates, stacked them in the dishwasher, and then headed out to the bungalow directly across from a saltwater pool.

From inside, the glass doors offered a clear view of the backyard and main house. The rooms were furnished with top-of-the-line furniture. Leather chairs in the living room, a down comforter spread across a queen-sized bed, off-white walls, and dark hardwood floors accented the thousand-square-foot hideaway. The showpiece was a restored stone fireplace in the center of the living room. The whole place was like stepping inside the pages of *Architectural Digest*. One thing was for sure: Doc was a man of good taste.

I dumped my duffle bag in the corner, set my backpack next to the fireplace then slumped into the nearest chair. I needed to set some ground rules for the next thirty days. No working at a desk. No email. Cell phone only in an emergency. No distractions from Facebook or Twitter. I was going to unplug from the outside world. All I needed was my iPad and a little something to ease the tension.

For a moment, I was like a kid outside the gates of Disneyland, waiting for the guy in the yellow windbreaker to let the crowd into the Magic Kingdom. I had tried to pick the lock for an eternity, but now here I was about to run through the park. It was a glimmer of hope in what had been a sea of brokenness. Of course, it could all fall apart if I failed to write the memoir. Maybe Doc wouldn't think I was good enough. I'd never been published. Maybe he'd fire me after the first week. I couldn't help but wonder why he chose me...and what else Frank had told him.

I tried to rid myself of my nemesis—failure. It seemed to follow me everywhere. It messed with my head, and it squeezed the last ounce of confidence from my veins.

I reached for my backpack and retrieved a bottle of JD. I needed a drop of liquid courage. With the bottle pressed against my lips, I convinced myself this time would be different. The Scotch warmed my chest and calmed my nerves. I glanced towards the far wall filled with rows of hardcover books placed perfectly in a custom bookshelf that reached to the ceiling. Not only did Doc cook and have good taste in decor, but he was also a bookworm. Definitely not a tree hugger.

My cell rang and Rachel's name appeared on the screen. I purposefully waited until the third ring before I answered.

"Rache?"

"It's been three weeks, Jake!"

"Uh...right...I was going to drop it in the..."

"You haven't returned my calls. You can't keep avoiding this."

"I've been working around the clock."

"Really? Where?"

"I can't tell you. I signed a confidentiality agreement."

"Whatever. I just need you to sign the papers."

"Well, I'm over in La Cañada. I can meet you tomorrow."

"Fine. Starbucks off of Verdugo. Three o'clock. Bring the papers and don't be late."

"Got it. Is Sam there?"

"Jake, not now."

The line went dead. Our conversations were always a whirlwind. I never had a chance. Rachel had hounded me for months to sign the divorce papers. I stalled for as long as I could, but now that my luck was turning I had no intention of signing them. I was out of excuses, but I refused to believe I was out of time. I'd worry about how I was going to handle her later.

I almost didn't hear Doc enter. I quickly slipped the bottle into my duffle bag. I didn't know him well enough to label him as a drinking man. I didn't want my first impression to be a shot of Scotch after breakfast. I noticed he had changed into blue sweats, a UCLA sweatshirt, and a brand new pair of Nike cross trainers.

"I hope you'll be comfortable out here." Doc surveyed the space. "No one's stayed in the pool house in years. I don't get many visitors these days."

"This is great, really." If he only knew where I'd slept the night before. I set my cell on the coffee table and checked my watch. "So, where do you want to start?"

"Let's go for a walk. At my age, the doctor says I need to stay active."

"Uh...okay."

It never dawned on me that exercise was part of the plan. I hadn't packed any workout clothes. Honestly, I hadn't seen the inside of a gym in over a year. I looked at Doc and figured we were going on a leisurely stroll so the chances of me having a heart attack were fifty-fifty. If I paced myself, I might survive.

La Cañada Flintridge was sandwiched between the 2 and 210 freeways, hiding a virtual melting pot of doctors, lawyers, Hollywood elite, bankers, international movers and shakers, and generations of families who inherited old money from ancestors who moved West in search of the American Dream. For those who could afford the multimillion-dollar price tag, this was the perfect getaway from the insanity of the city while staying close enough to the action.

A few blocks from the house, we climbed a windy road through a neighborhood lined with Victorians, Craftsman, and Cape-Cod inspired homes. Doc had the pace of a twenty-year-old, and by the time we reached the top of the hill, I was winded. I crouched over and tried to catch my breath, while cursing myself over how out of shape I'd gotten since my college days.

"Five minutes?"

"We still have another mile and a half to go." Doc laughed.

"Wow. It must be the smog that's slowing me down."

"How about we start every morning like this? It'll get the juices flowing."

"Sure...great...I can't wait. How early?"

"Six thirty...AM." Doc chuckled, obviously amused. "It'll be good for you."

"Right." The pain in my chest intensified. "Doc, I gotta ask...why me?"

For a few seconds Doc gazed down the hill. Had he heard me?

"You know I've never been married. Never had kids of my own. My life has always been about trying to protect others. Now that I'm retired, I've realized how much of a fool I've been. I've left things undone. This is my chance to set the record straight. Frankly, I needed someone who had nothing to lose."

"Then you picked the right guy. So, where does your story begin?"

Doc turned and headed back down the hill. He shouted over his shoulder.

"Ghosts of the Flaming Cross...that's where it all started."

9

2

God's guardians on the earth of new and old
Protect a secret more powerful than altars of gold
A power unleashed through a covenant of light
Defends a faith that will not go gently into the fight

Blind unbelief ushers in trouble, war, and fear
A battle of profound love offers courage to all who hear
Yet when the skies are filled with smoke and fire
The end draws near, and faith becomes dire

After an hour of carrying boxes from the study into the pool house, I was ready for a break, but I was anxious to get the writing process going. It seemed Doc wasn't in as much of a hurry. He struck a match and lit the fireplace. I watched as the logs slowly burned and the flames glowed. Then Doc read the poem, and we were on our way.

He explained that it was a piece of a poem penned by a woman evangelist, Evelyn Shaw. At the time, she was believed to have drowned in the waves off Santa Monica. I tried to piece together how the poem fit with her drowning while Doc paced back and forth.

"Thousands flooded the shores, day and night, hoping for a miracle. The *LA Reporter* fueled the media frenzy by suggesting she hadn't drowned at all. Instead, the headlines were filled with accusations that she slipped away with Sunset Pictures leading man, Arthur Elliott, who had also gone missing. Evelyn's husband, Bernard, even held a press conference to announce that he would take over the church immediately following the memorial."

"Doc, did she drown or have an affair? And what exactly does the poem mean?" I had a sudden urge to know. Before he could answer, I rattled off one more. "Why was her husband talking about a memorial if they didn't know what happened to her?"

"Sister Evelyn was walking along the boardwalk in Santa Monica when she was approached by a man asking if she would pray for his sick wife. Of course, she never hesitated. She followed the man toward a parked Model T where a woman was hunched over inside, seemingly quite ill. Before Sister Evelyn realized what was happening, she was pushed into the backseat with a Colt 1908 inches from her face. She was blindfolded and for hours listened as the sound of the city disappeared until there was only the hum of the engine and a cool breeze."

"Sounds like you know this story well. So, she *was* kidnapped?"

Doc poked at the fire. The glow reflected off his eyes as he turned and faced me. The story was captivating, and I couldn't help but lean forward to hear what he said next.

"Everyone believed she either drowned or was hiding away with Elliott. Hollywood was flooded with rumors and sightings. Reporters drove north to Santa Barbara to find the love shack. Sister Evelyn's devoted followers lined the beach in Santa Monica and prayed to find her miraculously alive. No one believed she was kidnapped. It was scandalous from the very beginning. Being one of the few woman evangelists in that era, she was known for controversy, whether it be public disputes with local politicians, religious leaders, or organizations that wanted to control or destroy her ministry."

"What about her husband?"

"Bernard did what he always did."

"Which was?"

"He put the ministry first, starting with writing her eulogy."

"Wait a minute. You lost me. So she died?"

Doc shook his head slowly. "She was taken to an old shack with boarded windows and locked inside. For days, she endured the sweltering heat of the desert, on her knees, digging until her hands were bloodied. Her body was worn from hunger, clothes ragged, and her spirit fought against the voices that swirled in her mind. Every few days, the man she called Adler returned with little food and a jug of water. Nearly a month passed before she seized her opportunity.

"One morning Adler entered and she caught him by surprise. She attacked like a wild animal and clawed at his face. They stumbled to the dirt as fists punched in all directions. Sister Evelyn gripped his black hair and with every ounce of strength, she pounded his skull into the ground until he stopped moving. Everything grew silent."

"She killed him?" The thought that a prominent preacher murdered the kidnapper took the story to a new level. "And who was Adler?"

Doc ignored my questions. "She was lost in the desert below the moonlight. For hours, she stumbled past Joshua trees and cactus until sunrise. Her golden hair was soaked with blood and sweat. Her hazel eyes, once filled with fire, were sunken and dazed. Blisters from her face burned as morning turned into a sweltering afternoon. She prayed, 'Lord, you have not brought me this far to die.' And then she walked out of the desert of Agua Prieta, Mexico, and crossed the border into Arizona.

"A local farmer watched her from a distance until she collapsed outside of town. He ran to her, picked her up, and carried her to his home. '¿Qué te pasado?' he asked as he poured her a glass of water."

"What happened to you?" I mumbled, surprised I remembered my C-level Spanish.

"She struggled to lift her head. Her eyes dazed. Her hands shook as she held the glass. The farmer barely heard her whisper, 'I am Evelyn Shaw...and I have been kidnapped.'"

I was on the edge of my seat. I needed the last act. Doc didn't continue. "That's the whole story?"

"One version of it anyway."

"I don't get it. Was she kidnapped or not?"

"That's what she told the world when she stepped behind the pulpit."

"She said it happened exactly how you described?"

"Exactly."

"She didn't drown, she could've had an affair with Arthur Elliott, but she says she was kidnapped."

"Books have been written, newspaper headlines plastered the events, hundreds of articles are available online, and her own testimony is documented in five thousand pages of court records." With a glint in his eyes, Doc sat across from me only a few feet away. "But the truth always lies in who is telling the story."

Doc pulled himself up and walked towards the bookcase. He ran his fingers across the spines until he landed on a leather-bound book about an inch thick. With his back turned, he pulled it from the shelf and flipped through the pages.

"If this is where it starts, what does this have to do with you?"

"Everything." Doc closed the book and handed it to me. "It is the genesis."

I noticed a rusted nameplate stuck to the front cover with the engraved initials, N.S. I listened to Doc recite the story as if he had crafted the words a hundred times. It was as if he had lived it time and time again. A dozen more questions flashed in my mind. I tried to wrap my head around Doc's last statement. Did he mean it was the genesis of *his* story? How was that possible when it happened in 1925? I snapped out of it when Doc patted my shoulder.

"We'll continue this afternoon."

I watched him leave the bungalow and cross the backyard. Once he was inside the main house, I pulled the curtains closed, grabbed the bottle from my duffle, and poured myself another glass.

"Last one." I sipped slowly, and then set the glass down on a coffee table. I picked up the book, ran my index finger along the smoothness of the worn leather, and rested my thumbs on the corner edges. I slowly exhaled as I turned to the first page.

3

Pacific Empress, June 26, 1910

The rain has stopped after three monsoons. It is hard to imagine one month ago standing at the keel of the Titanic as Evelyn preached to the workers. What a magnificent vessel it will be. I have tried to make her rest but continue to find her in the saloon sharing about the Savior. Now I lay here tonight as my bride sleeps, knowing tomorrow we arrive in Kowloon to begin the mission God has set before us. I pray we will find the right path. God protect us and give us strength to do your will. Amen.

July 3, 1910

We leave Kowloon in the morning and will travel by sampan to Macau to preach in the villages. I am burdened by the sickness all around us. Evelyn's determined spirit to preach and pray for healing only increases my love for her. God, you have blessed us greatly in the midst of the suffering here. I pray for your protection in the days ahead. Lord, show us the way.

July 21, 1910

My body is broken yet my spirit remains strong. Lord, I cannot strike this peculiar feeling that when you come back again, I shall rise to meet you from this soil. You have allowed me to see what others cannot. I shall bring with me the souls that I have won. Save this nation! Send a revival to this land.

August 19, 1910

How can this be? Lord I have followed your word. I have spoken about you to all who will hear. Yet this day is filled with death greater than I can bear. You have healed many through my hands, yet in his sickness a miracle was not your will. Pure love has been ripped from my soul. Now I am alone. God help me understand.

I stood and stretched my aching back, which had stiffened considerably since the three-mile walk. I paced the room and wondered why after two months of entries, the pages were blank. I flipped through them all and noticed the edges of a torn page no longer there. I also thought it was odd that the handwriting in the last entry was different than the ones before. The room spun as it struck me. I caught my balance and glanced down at the empty bottle. I closed the diary and set it on the mantle. The blank pages were pieces of Evelyn's story that would never be written.

My body relaxed as I thought of the first time I laid eyes on Rachel from across the movie theater. It was the longest two hours as I mounted up the courage to get her name once the credits rolled. I don't know if she felt sorry for me, or if my awkwardness was somehow endearing. From that night on she captured my heart. I loved her to the core of my soul, much like NS loved his bride, Evelyn.

That love only grew stronger when we found out Rachel was pregnant. I never imagined loving someone as much as her, but Samantha had equally captured my heart. Bringing a newborn into the world was scary, exciting, stressful, exhausting, and rewarding. I never imagined Rachel raising our daughter without me. I exhaled slowly and admitted for the thousandth time that I had wanted my dream so badly that I pushed their dreams aside.

I shook off a blanket of depression that wrapped itself around me. It was hard enough to think about the divorce without wallowing in self-pity. I turned my attention back to NS.

I paced the room and Googled on my iPad. Finding Evelyn Shaw was done with only a few taps. I scrolled down the page until I found the identity of the mystery man, Nathan Shaw. He was Evelyn's first husband. With the iPad in one hand, I picked up the diary from the mantle and compared the entries with a timeline in Wikipedia. A perfect match.

In 1910, Evelyn and Nathan traveled to China as missionaries. Two months after arriving Nathan contracted malaria, an epidemic at the time, which took the lives of many missionaries. Nathan died only days later, leaving Evelyn alone in a foreign land in a culture that refused to accept her beliefs.

I continued reading and recognized pieces of Doc's dramatic version of the kidnapping. A few more websites revealed similar stories. But there were slight variances in Doc's version. I chalked that up to him embellishing the tale or to retirement.

The stack of boxes in the corner called out to me. If Evelyn's story was the genesis of Doc's memoir, then maybe the first chapter was somewhere inside one of them. A seed of curiosity was planted, and that meant once I opened the first box there was no turning back from falling into this rabbit hole.

Finishing off the bottle left me woozy. But that's what writers did, right? They drank. It was as good of an excuse as any. I pulled a lid off the box and wondered if inside I'd find the truth about the evangelist. I lost my balance and stumbled backward. The box crashed to the floor. Dazed, I slumped back into a chair and let the Scotch knock me out cold.

4

A sprawling estate tucked behind the iconic Bel-Air gates was packed with Hollywood royalty, Century City moguls, and a host of special interest groups who each paid thirty grand a head to eat beef Wellington in the same room as President Palmer. From the home's owner—Oscar-winning producer, Miles Bay—to the staff of Uptown Catering to the minimum wage valets, each person was meticulously and thoroughly vetted by the Secret Service.

Alan Leung, one of the wealthiest bachelors in Asia, was on the list. He mingled with the crowd who were doused in Chanel No. 5, Marc Jacobs, and enough Botox to float the Titanic. He greeted acquaintances, nodded to those he'd never met but recognized, and smiled as they reminisced over parties he never attended. He graciously excused himself, cut through a kitchen in utter chaos, and then strolled down a long hallway lined with triptych art.

Secret Service guarded a door to a private study. Leung showed his credentials, waited as they ran a wand over his body, and followed an agent who motioned him inside. He was ushered across a two-story library toward a row of books that swung backward to reveal a hidden room. After a firm handshake, Leung sat across from President Palmer, who relaxed in an oversized leather chair smoking a Cuban cigar.

"Malcolm speaks highly of you."

"He is a good man," Leung replied. "It is truly an honor to meet you,

Mr. President."

"He believes you're the favorite to win the election."

"You cannot believe what the polls say, but I am optimistic."

"Ain't that the truth." Palmer chuckled. "Malcolm is not as keen about your opponent."

"Xu Li Ma is … controversial."

"Her heritage is concerning."

"Corruption exists in all forms of government. She has very powerful supporters within the PRC, who have much to gain if she is elected CEO of Hong Kong."

"Do you believe, if elected, her first act will be to reopen the Golden Triangle?"

"She has alluded to it in recent weeks as a way to boost import and export of goods."

"I thought the exact route was kept secret by the Triads."

"You might say she holds a family secret."

"Well, I appreciate the information you passed on to Malcolm. I assure you, we will look into it closely."

"Mr. President, I must admit that was not my only reason for meeting with you." Leung leaned in closer, even though they were the only two in the room. "I am sure you are aware of the exclusive contract that Mulfira Mining has signed with the PRC and Argentina to revolutionize the shale gas industry."

"And I'm sure you're aware of my stance on shale fracking." President Palmer set the Cuban on the edge of an ashtray. "Unlike my predecessor— who some might suggest was responsible for the Halliburton Loophole—I believe that without strict regulations, it is too risky."

"I understand your position," Leung said. "However, I see this as an opportunity to build an alliance between the PRC, Argentina, and the United States to reduce oil dependency. Perhaps if you were to lend your voice to such an alliance, the PRC will view that as an olive branch for the debt negotiations. In fact, I have already been approached by the State Council to mediate such a discussion once I am elected into office."

"What makes Mulfira Mining a better alternative than Exxon or Royal Dutch?"

"Trademarked technology that limits the risk of contamination or tremors."

"You can guarantee no groundwater pollution or earthquakes?"

"Of course, there are no bulletproof scenarios. But the United States is already fracking, which means you are already in the game."

"You are as well, correct?"

"Full disclosure, Mr. President. I am a shareholder. However, I can assure you that unlike the loss encountered with the rare earth monopoly, this is an opportunity to not only bridge the gap with the PRC but to achieve a successful and profitable energy shift." Leung paused, knowing that he was walking a thin line. "We are projecting sixty to one hundred billion cubic meters of shale gas by 2020. Record high oil and gas prices have made fracking a viable alternative—not to mention highly profitable. The State Council in the PRC has approved shale gas as an independent mineral source with nearly thirty-one trillion cubic meters trapped, which is fifty percent more than the United States. From Sichuan to Eagle Ford, Texas, you will have unlimited access."

"I understand that shale gas is an alternative source." President Palmer picked up the cigar. "However, I am not prepared to fight Congress until more research is done. While I appreciate your insight on Xu Li Ma, I'm afraid I will have to pass on your offer."

Leung eyed him steadily as he handed over a sealed envelope. "Perhaps you might reconsider."

5

As a young ambitious attorney in the DA's office, Doc bent the rules to work his way up the ranks. He closed more cases than his peers. He aggressively pursued stiff penalties for all offenders. He made a name for himself and pushed the boundaries to convict rapists, murderers, thieves, and corrupt politicians. In a career that spanned thirty-two years and countless cases, he still found himself haunted by the ones he was never able to solve.

Perhaps the one that stayed with him the longest was the murder of an Asian woman, believed to be a prostitute, when he was Assistant District Attorney. She was murdered in an alley off of Hollywood Boulevard. No DNA or fingerprint matches. A single GSW to the head, execution style. Even without enough evidence to officially proceed, Doc chased that cold case for years before he caught a break.

An inmate in the Twin Towers claimed to know the identity of the killer. Doc listened as the snitch described, in detail, a man he referred to as the Cleaner. Doc promised the snitch a reduced sentence if the information led to an arrest and conviction. Two days later the inmate was found stabbed twenty-six times in the prison shower.

"You have something that doesn't belong to you."

Doc turned cautiously away from his bedroom window towards the voice and stared directly at a man standing in the corner of the room. Peppered hair. Slender build. Piercing dark eyes.

"I'm afraid you're mistaken," Doc said. "I'm an old man with nothing more than memories."

"Return what belongs to them, and I will make this quick."

"What if it is not here?"

"Then tell me where it is, or you will not be the only one who dies today."

He had made himself right with God, so he wasn't as afraid as he thought he would be. He was going to die, but he refused to allow anyone else to endure the same fate, especially Jake Harris. He exhaled slowly. What was life like on the other side? A brilliant light? Endless darkness? He feared this day would come. Pandora's Box had been opened, and he held the key. His greatest regret was failing to tell the others who he had found.

"It's in a safe," Doc said. "Downstairs in the study."

"Combination?"

"I must have your word this will end here."

"You are in no position to negotiate."

"I have told no one. There is no evidence. Do you understand?"

"Give me the combination."

Doc paused for a moment and then surrendered. "Twenty-three...thirty-two...nine."

"On your knees."

Silence brought a few more seconds of peace. He knew there was no way to save himself. Perhaps he'd known since the beginning. He only hoped Jake would find the truth. He closed his eyes and quietly prayed. The woman in the alley flashed in his mind as he felt the silencer pressed against his skull.

***

Neco Rimoldi pulled the trigger. No hesitation. No emotion. The old man slumped forward, his eyes closed as if he were still in prayer.

Rimoldi used the barrel of the gun to nudge the man back against the nightstand. With a pocketknife, he removed the slug from the wall, and then left silently.

6

Flames from the fireplace turned to ash by the time I opened my eyes. Instinctively, I reached for my cell and checked the time. I cursed under my breath, shocked at how long I'd dozed off. Finishing the bottle was a mistake in a growing list of questionable choices. I wasted the afternoon, which was not how I planned to spend the first day living out my dream. Everything was riding on this. Everything.

I rubbed the sleep from my eyes and stretched my cramped muscles. My joints cracked as I hobbled to the refrigerator. I hoped it wasn't a sign of the days ahead. Maybe the early morning hikes with Doc would be my greatest challenge. Still a bit groggy, I reached into the refrigerator and grabbed a soda. I glanced around the room and tried to remember what I was dreaming about. That part of my life was never clear.

In high school, my teachers thought I had ADHD. In college, I chalked it up to partying way too much. As I got older, it was embarrassing to admit that I couldn't remember anything before my sixteenth birthday. It had always been a mystery why I blocked out that part of my life. Drinking was how I dealt with the unknown.

I turned my attention back to Doc's beautiful home, a successful career, good health, and how all of that equaled years of dedicated service and the fruits of retirement. I couldn't deny a twinge of envy flowed through my veins. I always dreamed of carrying Rachel over the threshold and raising Samantha in a place like this. Instead, I was here as a guest. I didn't even have enough cash to rent a place of my own or to buy groceries. I hadn't given Rachel a dime in months like I'd promised in every conversation since being kicked out of the house.

I once believed there was greatness within me, but that diminished the more I was trapped in a nine-to-five, mounting credit card debt, and a haunting feeling that greatness would always be out of reach. Rachel was the one who made the sacrifices I was too afraid to make. Life was too hard and happened too fast.

I drowned my self-pity one drink at a time. It was a way to deal with the pain. I never saw it as an addiction. I promised myself I'd turn it around. Maybe instead of dreading the early morning hikes, I would embrace them. Instead of reliving the ways I'd failed, I'd focus on making the right decisions moving forward. Instead of trying to relive my childhood, I would leave it locked away where it belonged. Doc offered me a second chance. It was a wake up call. I wasn't about to blow it this time.

I chalked the first day up to a rookie mistake, and then exhaled the lost opportunities and inhaled a renewed sense of optimism. Hiding away for a few months, writing around the clock, and getting paid was the perfect recipe to get back on track.

Feeling a bit more clearheaded, I turned my attention to the pool outside. I thought maybe Doc would be there reading a Grisham novel, smoking a stogie, or possibly waiting for his ghostwriter to emerge with a barrage of questions. Instead, the backyard was empty and quiet.

I glanced up at the blue sky and then back to the crystal pool. I had two choices. Bury myself in a mountain of research hidden somewhere in the stack of boxes, or find Doc and get some sense of where to begin. My body ached and the slight hangover was growing into a migraine that squeezed behind my pupils. It was an easy decision as I headed outside.

The French doors leading into the kitchen were unlocked. I walked down the hall, directly past the photos I'd seen earlier. I listened closely. No footsteps. No television. No voices. It was as if the house were asleep. Maybe Doc was taking a nap. Isn't that what you do when you're retired?

It wasn't like he needed to check in with me, this was his house.

I stopped at the edge of the formal living room. I hadn't paid much attention to it when I first arrived. With antique furniture much older than the rest of the house, the room looked like it had never been used. Artifacts from other countries displayed on the walls and in every nook and crevice of the room. Directly behind me was a closed door. For a few seconds, I paused and considered calling out for Doc. I decided against it. Instead, I faced the door and knocked softly. I waited a few seconds before I turned the knob and pushed it open.

7

Burgundy walls and paisley furniture surrounded the study. A large oak desk pushed against an even larger bay window overlooking the front yard. It was possible Doc stood in that exact spot earlier that morning waiting for me to arrive. A piece of me knew I crossed the line sneaking into his study, but curiosity won that battle.

With one eye on the door, I scanned the room. Photos, plaques, and numerous awards hung on the walls. Even more were scattered on end tables and shelves of a floor-to-ceiling bookcase. Years of loyalty to the city of Los Angeles captured in one place, like a museum, to commemorate the legacy of one of the most decorated head DAs in the city's history. Doc's words echoed in my ears. *I never married. I never had kids.* Those were two things I had that he never experienced. Putting all of his success aside, I wondered who he celebrated life with.

A sense of being alone struck me hard. I fought the instinct to go to the nearest liquor store and drown myself in another bottle. Everything in the study reminded me of how far I had to dig for a grain of success. My heart sank the more I stared at his accolades. A lump lodged in my throat at the thought of signing a piece of paper that ended any chance of hanging onto the two people I couldn't live without. Reconciling with Rachel was a long shot. Being left out of Samantha's life was unthinkable. I wasn't ready to leave the rest of those pages blank.

"Pull yourself together," I whispered.

I reached for one of the desk drawers. I almost didn't hear the creaking noise. I froze. Panic shot through me. It was bad enough that I'd snuck into the study. Now I was going to get caught prying into Doc's private drawers.

Without thinking, I darted across the room and hopped over a chair large enough to hide behind. Cautiously, I peeked around the corner of the armrest and waited for Doc to enter. I only caught a glimpse of the gun before I ducked back against the chair. Curled up tight, adrenaline pumped through my veins.

A strange instinct overwhelmed me. Attack. Be the aggressor. Completely contrary to any logic. I gripped the side of the chair to keep myself from jumping up and listened as drawers slammed, followed by what sounded like books hitting the floor. A few seconds of silence only heightened the tension. I held my breath and fought the urge to leap up and attack. I could almost see the action in my mind's eye. I broke out in a cold sweat, nausea bit the back of my throat.

A clicking noise caught my attention. I heard what sounded like a lever being pulled. Then the footsteps faded and a door closed.

I reached for my cell and realized I'd left it in the pool house. What an idiot. I checked my watch and counted. It took another five minutes before I emerged from my hiding place. As the adrenaline faded and left me shaking in its wake, so did the aggressiveness. I was uncertain what was happening to me. A weird primal instinct?

Standing in the study, I noticed the desk drawers were now opened and books were scattered on the floor. I stepped towards the bay window, but there was no sign of anyone outside. When I turned around there was something else. A wall safe, hidden behind a painting, was opened. I looked inside. It was empty.

"Doc." Where was he? Had anything happened to him?

I snatched a poker from the fireplace, headed out into the hall, and climbed the stairs to the second floor. With each creak, I stopped and wished I'd never answered Doc's call. At the top of the stairs was a hallway with bedrooms on each side. I gripped the poker tight, glanced in each room, before entering the last one. Bed made. Blinds closed. It looked undisturbed.

I whispered, "Doc, are you in here?"

Slowly, I stepped around the side of the bed and gasped at the sight of Doc slumped against the nightstand. A bullet wound cratered the center of his forehead. Blood splattered the walls. I hunched over, grabbed my knees, and vomited.

Running down the stairs and out into the backyard, I burst into the pool house and scrambled to find my cell. The throbbing in my head intensified as I pushed a pile of papers aside on the coffee table before rifling through the mess from the box I'd left sideways on the floor. Frantically I dug my hand deep into the side of a leather chair and felt between the cushions. Bingo. My hands shook and my body buzzed as I punched in numbers.

8

Detective Mitchell Lane strolled up the driveway far from the media frenzy at the end of the block. News vans parked one behind the other. Reporters hovered like vultures.

As a twenty-five-year veteran, he knew better than to get stuck in front of the cameras. He avoided the press whenever possible. During his mildly decorated career, he'd only had a handful of run-ins with the press. Only one ever filed a formal complaint. He was the model officer who respected the badge, obeyed his superiors, and avoided getting himself shot. He learned early on that life was about self-preservation. It was also about knowing how to keep out of the spotlight.

A black Suburban pulled up to the curb near the yellow taped barricade. Reporters shoved, bumped, and nudged for position. National networks garnered the front row, while the local stations fought for over-the-shoulder shots.

Two hours after his office was notified, Mayor Osoria, emerged from the backseat of the SUV dressed in a dark suit and bright red silk tie. Cameras and microphones pointed directly at him as if he were the one under arrest. Everyone knew the drill. A brief statement. No questions. Then the mayor would be whisked away to another fundraising dinner while the reporters promised to stay on the scene for further developments.

The whole routine took less than ten minutes.

Osoria was a street-savvy politicalite who was also the frontrunner to win reelection. Mitch had only spoken to him briefly once before a medal ceremony at the academy. Word within the department was that Osoria had his own demons beneath his charismatic exterior. The verdict was still out on whether he was a man who could be trusted. It was only natural to be leery of anyone who had the ability to abuse authority or power.

Now, what they both shared in common was their claim to be true Angelenos who bled Dodger Blue.

As a rookie, Mitch patrolled the beat in Lincoln Heights and worked his way up the ranks to detective at the Glendale Division, one of the safest cities in the nation. He paid his dues. He closed his quota of cases. He put offenders behind bars. He stayed away from the politics of the department.

At times it was exhilarating, but in recent years he was satisfied with investigating domestic disputes, warrants, and the occasional drugstore robbery. And for the last eight years, he worked cold cases. It had been a long time since his name was called to lead a homicide.

Warren's death was a high profile case. Not only was the man a legend in the DA's office, but in the rank and file of the LAPD as well. Mitch was ordered to find the truth, and that's exactly what he intended to do.

He made a quick sweep of the house, including the upstairs bedroom and downstairs study, and he spoke with several officers and CSI investigators to get up to speed. At first glance, it seemed like the crime scene might be a botched home invasion. There was an empty safe, some fingerprints and blood splatter, but no shell casings or footprints. But the fact that Warren was found deceased upstairs in the bedroom made Mitch question that theory. Rolling that over in his mind, he entered the living room, found a seat, and introduced himself to his number one suspect.

"Mr. Harris, I'm Detective Lane. I know this has been a difficult few hours, but I was hoping you'd walk me through what happened here today."

"I already told the other officer all I know."

"Sometimes it helps to go over the details a few times, in case you missed something."

"Okay. Well, uh, I got here this morning a little after eight, spent a few hours with Doc, and then the rest of the afternoon I was out in the pool house."

"How well did you know Mr. Warren?"

"I don't—I mean I didn't know him that well. He's a family friend who played golf with my dad. He called a few days ago and asked me to work on a project."

"What kind of project?"

"Ghostwriting a memoir."

"Before that, how long had it been since you'd seen him?"

"I think I was sixteen or seventeen. I don't remember exactly."

"Okay." Mitch scribbled a few notes. "So, you arrived around eight o'clock. Walk me through the timeline of the day in as much detail as possible."

"We ate breakfast. I got settled in the pool house, and then went for a walk with Doc. When we got back, he had some stuff to do in the main house, so I worked out in the pool house. Around four o'clock, I decided to check in since I hadn't seen him all afternoon."

"You never left the pool house before four?"

"I was researching and sorting through some of his papers. I flipped through a few books and then I dozed off."

"How did you enter the house?"

"Through the kitchen. I didn't hear or see anything out of place so I figured he was asleep or maybe he'd gone out. I took a look in his study."

"That's when you saw the suspect."

"All I saw was a gun."

"Where were you in the study?"

"I heard a noise so I ducked behind a chair in the corner. I didn't know whether I was supposed to be in the study or not. I panicked. I only saw the gun for a second. I didn't see who it was.

"How long was the intruder in the study?"

"Only a few minutes."

"Did you call 911 right away?"

"No." Jake's cheeks flushed. "I wasn't sure who else was in the house.

I waited a few minutes. When I got up, I saw the mess..."

"And the opened safe," Mitch said.

"Right." He rubbed his hands against his thighs. "That's when I ran upstairs and found Doc."

Mitch tried to gauge whether Jake Harris was telling the truth. His body language showed obvious trauma and shock. It was clear he was shaken up, but that didn't mean he was innocent.

Mitch pushed him a bit harder. "Mr. Harris, do you own a firearm?"

"Absolutely not. Your guys already wiped my hands for gun residue. You'll see I'm clean."

"I'd like for you to come down to the station."

"Am I under arrest?"

"No, I'd just like for you to write down your statement so it's official."

"Can I get my stuff from the pool house?"

"I'm afraid that won't be possible."

"Everything I own is in there."

"All of it is considered evidence. We'll also need to keep your truck for a few days. Standard procedure."

"Do I need a lawyer?"

"I don't know," Mitch replied. "Do you?"

"Detective, I'm telling the truth. You have to believe me."

Mitch leaned forward. "Mr. Harris, how much have you had to drink today?"

9

The ride over to the Glendale Division took less than twenty minutes. I stayed quiet, mainly because I was afraid I might say something that would get me in deeper trouble. All Detective Lane did was ask questions. I wondered if my answers were believable, not because I was lying, but because he knew my secret. I watched enough crime dramas to know that riding down to the station meant I was either a witness or a suspect. Since I hadn't seen anything worth writing down, I worried it was the latter.

I cursed myself for being so irresponsible. Maybe if I was sober, I might've heard or seen something helpful. I hardly knew Doc, but now I felt responsible for the man's death. I shrugged off the thought. I was in the wrong place at the wrong time. Enough guilt already weighed on my shoulders.

After I dialed 911, I was struck by flashes of blurred visions so intense they caused me to drop to my knees and shake uncontrollably. It lasted less than a minute, but it scared me as much as seeing Doc's lifeless body. As usual, they dissipated, leaving confusion in their wake.

I pulled myself together before the first officers arrived on scene. As I sat in the passenger seat, I tried hard to picture those flashes in slow motion, but they were gone along with the sudden rush of emotions.

Only one thing was on my mind. Call Frank. It seemed absurd.

When we reached the station, Detective Lane ushered me through a back entrance to avoid the press who were already jockeying for position out front. I followed him down a long hallway, past several offices encased in glass, and into a room with a table and two facing chairs. I noticed a mirror against the wall, which I assumed was a two-way. It seemed big brother would be watching this part of the interview.

A woman entered and swabbed my hands a second time. Then she asked me to breathe into a Breathalyzer. Detective Lane waited until she was gone to resume. For the next three hours, he interrogated me with the same questions asked in slightly different ways. I repeated the details I'd given him at the house, only this time I brought up Evelyn Shaw. He didn't seem too interested in that part of the story. Whenever I veered off course, he brought me back to what happened inside the house, my connection to Doc, and how much I'd been drinking.

"Enough to ease my nerves," I admitted. "I've waited a long time for an opportunity to write. It wasn't like I…"

"One glass. Two glasses. Be specific."

"There wasn't much left in the bottle." I clasped my hands together under the table.

"But enough for you to pass out."

"I wasn't wasted, if that's what you're getting at. I finished it off and fell asleep."

As the clock ticked, it was like riding a merry-go-round. Right when I thought I was getting off, we went around one more time. Finally, Detective Lane handed me a yellow legal pad and asked me to write my statement in as much detail as possible. That exercise took thirty minutes. Then I left the room and followed him down the same hallway out to the parking lot where we climbed into his Crown Vic.

I gazed out the passenger window as we cut over to Broadway and headed towards Eagle Rock. I eyed him closely. His tie hung loosely around his neck, and his holstered .45 peeked out from his wrinkled suit coat. This wasn't his first rodeo. He'd probably seen hundreds of witnesses who hadn't actually seen the crime being committed.

"Jake, you'll need to stay in town."

"I'm not going anywhere. You've got my cell number and the address where I'll be." I thought about the address I'd given him and decided it was too late to change my mind. "Detective Lane, I have nothing to hide. I swear everything I've told you is the truth."

He pulled over and parked at the curb beneath the glowing gold, red, and white letters of the world famous burger joint, Tommy's Burgers. At eleven thirty in the evening, the line was long. Artsy twenty-somethings. Nightshift city workers. Teenagers out past curfew. And now a potential suspect to murder.

"There is one thing..." Detective Lane draped his arm over the seat back. "What does Evelyn Shaw have to do with Doc's memoir?"

"I've been asking myself that question all day. Honestly, I have no clue."

"You're sure this is where you want to be dropped off?"

"Yessir. I'll be fine. Thanks."

I climbed out and stood on the sidewalk as the Crown Vic pulled away and headed down Colorado Boulevard. With the cool night seeping into my bones, I zipped my hoodie tight, dug my hands into my pockets, and joined the end of the line. All I'd eaten since breakfast was a Snickers and a Coke courtesy of the Glendale PD.

Even though my stomach was in knots, I was starving. Eating was a way to ease the angst after a day that left me running on empty. I checked my pockets and counted ten bucks. I stepped up to the counter and ordered a double chili cheeseburger, chili fries, and a Pepsi.

So much for shedding the extra twenty.

I picked up my order from the window and found a spot away from the other late nighters. I inhaled the grease-filled, calorie-busting combo meal in a matter of minutes. All that was left was the stained chili sauce that refused to wipe from my fingers.

A black Mercedes pulled up to the curb. The license plate read HARRISINC.

I slipped into the backseat. Without a word, the driver pulled a U-turn and headed east on Colorado. I closed my eyes. Exhausted. I thought about how the day started out with such promise but had ended so tragically. Doc was dead and so was my dream. I dialed my cell and waited for the beep.

"Rache, sorry to call so late. I, uh, I'm just confirming that we're still on for tomorrow. And um, well, I just want you to know that I'm sorry—for everything."

As the clock neared midnight, reality sunk in. I was headed back to where my childhood memories were locked away from my consciousness, where I remembered being raised by strangers, and where I promised I'd never return. Now it was the only place I had left to go.

10

The alarm sounded at 7:00 AM.

After a restless night, I rolled out from under the covers, sat on the edge of the bed, and tried to shake the fog of the last twenty-four hours.

When I was a teenager, this was my refuge. After being gone for so long it felt empty and cold. I was surprised to find a few of my old UCLA shirts hanging in the closet. I grabbed one, pulled it over my head, and tugged at the sides. It fit a little too snug, but I wasn't making a fashion statement. I slipped on a pair of jeans and headed out the French doors to the backyard.

Frank always believed someday I would take over the family business. But I had no intention of running a multi-million dollar consulting firm. I was a free spirit who longed to travel the world in search of adventure. I thought being an author was one way to live out that dream.

Spending my life in a high-rise, being a corporate monkey under his supervision, wasn't what excited me. And I refused to give my loyalty, or sacrifice years of my life, to a man who was more an outsider than flesh and blood.

Being back here, I thought of those first memories. The clearest one was as a freshman in high school shooting baskets in a gym. Then there was the day I accepted a full-ride scholarship to UCLA as a shooting guard for the Bruins. I started out with visions of the NBA but soon realized I wasn't disciplined or skilled enough. That disappointment faded when I met

Rachel. I traded my dreams to play pro ball for the love of my life.

Distancing myself from Frank didn't stop him from reaching out. Emails. Phone calls. I ignored them all. I even ignored Rachel's advice: "Put your pride aside and call your dad." I wanted nothing to do with a man who kept my past from me. Why wouldn't he tell me about my mother? What was he hiding? Whenever I asked, he stayed silent, and then we argued.

Tall, square hedges lined both sides of a perfectly manicured lawn that led directly towards an infinity pool at the edge of the property. I felt the moist grass between my toes. I stopped at the pool and gazed down on Brookside Golf Course and the Rose Bowl stadium.

Music rang in my ears from the night I held Rachel's hand amidst a hundred thousand fans singing along as Bono belted, "You broke the bonds and you loosed the chains. Carried the cross of my shame." We had never been closer, but those feelings faded over time.

To the right, in the distance, was Suicide Bridge.

A few weeks earlier, I heard the story of a preacher's wife who jumped from that exact spot. It was all over the news. At the time, I wondered how anyone could make such a selfish choice. But who was I to judge? I had my own chains and shame to bear.

My mind felt scattered. One moment I was reliving the thousands who sang *Amazing Grace* as Bono dropped to his knees with hands raised. Another minute I was back in Doc's study fighting the urge to attack an intruder. I tried to envision anything I might've missed. It was a pointless exercise. Doc's life was taken from him and that piece of the binding chain would stay with me for a long time. Perhaps it would never be broken.

If I was awake I might have been killed too. More shame washed over me. I reached to the sky, stretched my aching muscles, and reassured myself that if I tried to stop the intruder there would be two graves instead of one.

But I couldn't shake a familiar rush of adrenaline that made me feel alive before it vanished like a wisp of smoke.

I breathed in deeply and filled my lungs with the brisk air. Yesterday was gone. I needed to focus on today. Right now. This moment. What was I going to do next?

"Beautiful morning, isn't it?"

I turned towards Frank as he approached. Blondish-graying hair cut close to the skull. His slender build exaggerated by broad shoulders. He wore a custom-tailored royal blue suit with no tie. Even though he was sixty, it looked as if he hadn't aged since I saw him last.

"I'll only be here a few days." I concentrated on looking him in the eyes. I felt him size me up, knowing I had failed to live up to his standards. "I needed a place to crash, that's all."

"I'm leaving town in a few hours. You can stay as long as you need."

"Listen, me being here doesn't change anything. If that's a problem then I'll leave right now." I broke eye contact for a second. "How much do you know?"

"Not much evidence was found in the house. No broken windows or forced locks. They're not sure how the suspect got inside. Initial report is that it was a botched robbery. Jake, you should've called me sooner."

"I can handle it myself."

"Do you know you're a suspect?"

I straightened. "I gave them my statement and told the truth."

"It's standard protocol until you're officially cleared." He stepped closer. "Listen, neither of us wants to be dragged through the press."

"So this is about saving your—"

"It's about stopping you from screwing up. Again."

I shoved my hands in my pockets. "How do you know all this anyway?"

"I called in a few favors. If they want to ask more questions, call Mark Watson." Frank reached into his coat pocket and removed a business card. "He's been my attorney for years. I've already briefed him on the situation. He'll handle everything from here. Don't talk to anyone unless he is with you, understood? I've been assured your name will be kept private as long as you keep your mouth shut."

"That must've been a big favor."

He glanced at his watch. "Jake, I need to go. I left some cash on the kitchen counter. Should be enough to get you through the next few weeks.

Cars are in the garage with the keys inside." He offered a half-smile, patted me on the back, which made me cringe, and then headed towards the house. He took a few steps before turning around. "When I get back we should—"

"You know all Doc talked about was Evelyn Shaw."

"I'm not surprised." Frank paused. Then he turned and started walking. "He's been obsessed with her for years."

11

Mitch was six months away from sipping margaritas and smoking cigars with his feet in the sand. Working until he croaked was never part of the plan; retirement had never been a dirty word. He was ready to toss his suits, memories of every case that still haunted him, and relax into the sunset. He had survived a long career in the department, and that was something to be proud of. He followed three simple rules. Keep your head down. Always wear a vest. Know when to walk away.

For twenty-five years, he followed the rules and stuck to the plan. Now there was enough in his pension to buy a one-bedroom condo with a partial ocean view and a convertible with enough muscle to cruise Ambergris Caye. He already pictured himself strolling along the shore as the waves rolled in.

After a career hardly recognized by the suits at City Hall, he deserved to turn in his badge and find some peace. He had accepted living in the gray of justice, following the letter of the law, most of the time. But there were far too many sleepless nights, as well as two divorces, as a result. He hit a wall chasing cold cases the last few years and knew it was time. With one foot out the door, no rounds of drinks at O'Shanty's were necessary.

Warren's murder landing on his desk was a major glitch. Being the lead investigator on the biggest case since OJ meant his six-month timeline to paradise was in jeopardy. The case could drag on for months, if not years. It wasn't like he needed to see it through, it's just that he had never walked away from a case, and he didn't plan on starting now.

After dropping Jake Harris in Eagle Rock, he headed back to the station. He thought about swinging by the house to change clothes, but since there was no one to go home to, it didn't make much sense. By the time he reached his desk, the initial report from the evidence gathered on scene was waiting.

By 3:00 AM, he had compiled everything into a manila envelope. It was another few hours before forensics and the coroner submitted their reports. Everything was expedited because Warren was one of them. Jolts of caffeine from enough black coffee to wake a tranquilized rhino energized him to push through to daylight.

By 8:30 AM, other officers and detectives arrived for their shift and the place took on new life. But everyone knew better than to bother him while he was working a case.

Around 9:00 AM, he received an email from a friend within the DA's office. It contained a list of Doc Warren's most publicized cases. He printed it out and tucked it into the manila envelope. While there might be a possible suspect on the list, he wasn't ready to go there yet.

He pulled photos from the envelope and spread them out on the desk. A series of shots showed no forced entry. No fingerprints on the safe or in the bedroom. And the only sets of fingerprints in the house, other than Doc Warren's, belonged to Jake Harris and Margaret Johnson.

Mitch dialed Ms Johnson. From her DMV records, he knew she was African American, forty-eight, five foot three, a hundred and twenty pounds, and lived in Atwater Village.

"Ms Johnson, I'm Detective Lane from the Glendale Division."

"I had a feeling someone might be calling me." A raspy voice came through the receiver. "I watched the news last night and couldn't believe it. I'm still in shock."

"When did you last see Mr. Warren?"

"Saturday. I'm his house cleaner."

"How long have you worked for him?"

"Well, I was a clerical assistant at the DA's office for eight years and worked for Doc until he retired. A year after he left, I got laid off due to city cutbacks. I called him for a reference, and he offered me a job. That was about five years ago."

"So you and Mr. Warren knew each other well?"

"He was a kind man. When he found out I had cancer last year, and that I'd lost my insurance, he stepped in and paid my medical bills. He also paid cash for the house cleaning so that I'd have more for myself. He was very generous. Did you know him, Detective Lane?"

"Not personally, but he's been a legend around here for years." Mitch wrote a few notes on a legal pad. "Ms Johnson, were there any strange phone calls or visitors within the last few weeks?"

"Doc didn't have many visitors. He stuck with the same routine. Early breakfast, a walk in the neighborhood, and then he spent the rest of the day in his study. You know he didn't have any family."

"I see that here. What days did you work?"

"Wednesdays and Saturdays mostly. I wish I could be of more help, Detective."

"I appreciate your time. I may call you again with more questions."

"Of course." The line went silent for a few seconds. "It's just so sad. Why anyone would—"

"There is one more thing," Mitch interrupted. "Do you know a Jake Harris?"

"Jake Harris? I can't say that I do."

"Okay, again, thanks for your time."

Mitch hung up and Googled Jake Harris. His brow furrowed and eyes squinted as he stared at a picture of Jake in a Bruins uniform standing next to an older man with a slender build and the same eyes. He scrolled further down the page and stopped at a photo with the caption DOC WARREN AND FRANK HARRIS AT BROOKSIDE CHARITY GOLF TOURNAMENT.

Mitch noted this and then ran Jake through the system. No arrests. Not even a parking ticket. His home address was listed in Sunland where he lived with his wife and daughter. Mitch glanced down at the toxicology report and shook his head.

He scribbled the names on a whiteboard behind his desk. Doc Warren. Margaret Johnson. Frank Harris. Jake Harris. Next, he lined the photos from the crime scene side by side. With a marker, he noted a timeline beneath each photo. Then he moved on to forensics.

The slug exited the back of the skull, evidenced by the mess of flesh and bone, and entered the wall behind Doc's head. Several more photos showed blood splattered against the nightstand. He lined up another row of photos from the study that showed the opened safe, scattered books, and the leather chair with Jake's fingerprints on the armrest. A third row showed random shots outside the house as possible entry points. In one corner of the whiteboard, he posted a report that stated no slug was recovered at the scene.

Mitch sat on the edge of his desk and started to doze off. He rubbed his eyes and finished off the last drop of sludge. He thought about digging into Doc's cases next, but there was something he needed to do first. He grabbed several photos from the board and dropped them back into the envelope along with the DA's list.

On the drive over to La Cañada, Mitch rifled through a mental checklist. At first glance, the crime scene looked like a botched robbery, except for the fact that Doc's body was found in the bedroom instead of in the study. If the perp was going to kill Doc, he would've most likely done it in the study after the safe was opened. The fact that Doc was upstairs changed the motive from robbery to something more calculated. The missing slug was a problem to the theory too.

Fifteen minutes later, Mitch rounded the corner and passed a few straggling reporters hanging on for one last sound bite to keep their faces in front of the camera. The yellow tape was gone and the neighborhood looked undisturbed, except for an LAPD squad car parked out front. Mitch parked across the street and waved at the officers as he passed by.

Entering the house, he expected to find it in the same state as the night before. It was still an active crime scene. He stopped cold when he poked his head into the study. Everything was put back to normal. The framed picture that hid the safe was hung. The books that were tossed had

43

been returned to the shelves. The room was spotless, as if nothing had occurred.

Mitch darted upstairs into the bedroom. He headed straight for the nightstand and found it wiped clean. The hole in the wall from the missing slug was now smooth and the wall freshly painted. The carpet was gone. In its place was a distressed wood floor. Mitch knelt where Doc's body was found to search for bloodstains. His nostrils filled with a mixture of bleach and wood cleaner.

Mitch ran towards both officers who casually climbed out of their squad car. "How long have you been here? Who else has been in the house?"

"We started our shift at six thirty." One officer stood by the hood. "Cleaning crew arrived around seven. We called it in to confirm."

"Who'd you speak to?"

"Detective Lane."

"That's not possible." Mitch poked his finger into his chest. "I'm Detective Lane."

12

I grabbed a stack of Franklins from the marble countertop and counted them as I headed towards the garage. Two grand was enough to hold me over until I found a place to stay. I couldn't remember the last time I had that much cash in my hands.

I replayed the conversation with Frank and concluded that I held my ground. But taking the money meant I had allowed him back in my life. While that annoyed me, I was relieved there was an inside source to the investigation. I'd seen stories of innocent men who spent decades behind bars for crimes they never committed. I was innocent, but without a suspect that might not be enough. In a city where everyone had secrets, the one person you wanted in your corner was Frank Harris.

As I stepped into the garage, a row of fluorescent lights blinked on. I stopped and admired the classics, collectibles, and modern status symbols of wealth: '69 Cobra, '59 Ferrari 250 California Spyder, 2016 convertible Mercedes, dual jet black Range Rovers, and a bright red Porsche Carrera. The beautiful, smooth lines, custom rims, shiny chrome, and detailed paint translated into more money than I had made in my lifetime.

I chose one.

The Ferrari Spyder screeched down a long driveway and slowed enough to turn onto Linda Vista. I kept my foot on the accelerator and hugged the curves beneath the overhanging trees that formed a natural tunnel. Hitting each corner, the engine revved and then whipped with precision until I reached Berkshire Avenue.

For a moment, I allowed myself to daydream. Staying in the real world meant I was always going to be second best. Who said money couldn't buy happiness? Being raised in a home where your dad was never around and your mother never existed, meant that money solved most relational caverns. Back then it was enough. I got whatever I wanted, whenever I wanted it, and I didn't have to earn any of it. I never thought of myself as spoiled, just lucky. But in the end, I was the high school jock who partied through college and fizzled out in the real world.

I was on autopilot as I cruised past Descanso Gardens, where I proposed to Rachel, and continued in the direction of the UA Theater. I wanted to get there before she arrived to get my story straight. The last twenty-four hours left my head swimming. How was I going to explain it to her? I hoped not having the divorce papers would buy me another week or two to figure out a Hail Mary. Knowing Rachel, that was a long shot.

I parked away from the moviegoers and caffeine addicts. My cell rang as I climbed out of the Ferrari. I didn't recognize the number so I ignored it. The outside sitting area at Starbucks was empty, but I figured there was safety in numbers so I headed inside.

The space was crowded. On one side, teenagers lounged on stools and texted, while on the other, a communal table was covered with laptops. A line eight deep waited to order their afternoon fix. On my turn, I stepped up to the barista and ordered two soy lattes as a way to break the ice. I found a table that faced the entrance and waited.

I hadn't seen Rachel in months, which meant I hadn't seen Samantha even longer. I felt like I was on a first date. Nervous. Anxious. Sweaty palms. I wanted to say the right thing. Thinking there would never be another chance ate away at me. I had promised to take care of them, and I failed. I couldn't help but wonder when Rachel stopped loving me and if Samantha still did. I'd disappointed them both.

I watched through the window as Rachel walked towards me. My heart raced. Her piercing hazel eyes glanced in my direction as she slipped through the crowd. I stood not knowing whether to hug her or stand there like a tree. I awkwardly handed her the latte. As she sat across from me, I noticed her shorter black hair, slender frame, and tanned skin.

"You look great." After a long pause I added, "We haven't been here in ages."

"Jake, I don't have time to go down memory lane. I need to pick Sam up in twenty minutes. Just tell me you brought the papers."

I turned my cup in circles. "Um...something's happened."

"I should've known." Rachel sighed. "What excuse is it this time?"

"I witnessed a murder."

"C'mon." She slapped her palm on the table.

Everyone from the communal table shot curious stares in our direction.

"A retired District Attorney who's a friend of Frank's." I took a deep breath, relieved that I said it out loud. "He hired me to ghostwrite his memoir. I arrived at his house yesterday, and then— I still can't believe it."

"Well, I don't believe it."

I pulled out a business card and slid it across the table. "Call Detective Lane if you want."

Rachel eyed the card for a moment. "What does this have to do with the papers?"

"Everything I brought with me got snagged up in evidence. I was down at the Glendale PD most of the evening yesterday being questioned. Then I crashed at Frank's place."

"You saw your father?"

"I had nowhere else to go."

"Whatever you've gotten yourself into, I don't want to know any more. I'm done. You made your choice, and I've made mine."

"Are you seeing someone?" I searched her face, looking for—and fearing—confirmation. "Is that why you're pushing for this?"

"That's none of your business." Anger flushed her face. She reached into her oversized purse, retrieved another copy of the divorce papers and a pen. She tossed them on the table. "Sign it so we can move on with our lives."

"What about Sam?"

"Not now, Jake."

"I haven't seen her in months."

"She needs more time." Rachel pushed the papers closer to me. "I think we all do."

"What she needs is both of us in her life."

"We'll talk about it once this is over."

I stared at the document, and then glanced up at the baristas and customers. It was surreal to end our marriage this way, in this place, next door to the theater where it all began. I was out of options without a backup plan. I felt my chest tighten. My cell rang with the same number as before.

"Hello?" I was relieved to be momentarily saved by the bell. Rachel glared out the window as I listened intently, my stomach dropping. "I understand."

I slipped my cell into my pocket and looked at Rachel with a blank stare. I picked up the pen, flipped to the last page, and signed my name. I stood before she had a chance to reach for the papers.

"Rache, I have to go."

With that, I walked out and never looked back.

13

The meeting with Sergeant Chapman was pushed to the end of the day, which gave Mitch a few more hours before another briefing. While the night was long, the day proved to be even longer. He tossed his cell on the desk, and then glanced around the squad room as the place buzzed with activity. He fought the irritation that scratched at his nerves as he wondered who set him up.

He caught himself staring in a daze and went back to reading through the evidence. He felt like all eyes were on him, even though the news about what happened at Warren's house was kept tightlipped. The two officers on scene were sequestered in an interview room, making sure they filed all the reports. Sergeant Chapman had already been informed that the FBI was stepping in to assist. Containment was critical until they found the mole.

Special Agent Kate McNaughton made her entrance around three o'clock. She headed straight into Chapman's office, and for the next hour the door and blinds remained closed. Mitch took advantage of the time to do his own recon. He found out that Kate McNaughton was an eight-year veteran of the Bureau who graduated top of her class at Quantico. Her most recent fugitive collar was Angelo Maldone.

Mitch sized her up as she stepped out of Chapman's office and walked towards him. Early thirties meant she was young enough to be his daughter. Straight brown hair pulled back in a ponytail. Green eyes. Dark pantsuit. White button-down blouse. A holstered .45 on her hip. She looked ambitious, intelligent, and someone who definitely played by the rules. That combination made him nervous.

"Detective Lane, let's take a walk."

In an attempt to break the ice, he said, "You can call me Mitch."

"And you can call me Agent McNaughton." Her voice embodied her strong East Coast roots. When he didn't laugh she added, "Kate'll work too."

They exited the building and walked down Wilson Avenue. With the recent time change, it was getting darker earlier, which meant the rest of the night would feel even longer. The brisk air did little to revive his senses.

Mitch had poured over the evidence a dozen times at the station after being ordered to leave the scene by the Feds. He spent the rest of the afternoon digging through Warren's old case files brought over from the DA's office. It was a list he wasn't ready to share with anyone just yet.

Uneasiness loomed over him at the thought someone in the department was involved, someone who had a score to settle with Doc Warren, and someone who had no problem making him the fall guy.

He squinted at the headlights as they sped by.

"So, you worked the Maldone case?"

"Five years." McNaughton said. "We were lucky. Caught a break through one of our CIs."

"Hard to believe he was living in a one-bedroom in Venice Beach."

"I stayed on the case until the verdict. Thirty-six counts of racketeering, money laundering, and weapons charges. Not to mention sixteen murders. Judge sentenced him to two consecutive life terms plus five years. If you ask me, I think he got off easy."

"I'm sure that boosted your cred at the Bureau."

"Enough to get me reassigned to LA, which is better than another winter in DC."

"That case was two years ago. What've you been doing since?"

Her stride was purposeful and business like, not breaking as she turned to look at him. "You ran a background check on me?"

"Just curious, I guess."

"I took an extended break, courtesy of the Bureau."

"And now you're on this case."

Her step faltered, almost imperceptibly. "Didn't really have a choice."

They turned left on Broadway and headed north. While it seemed his penance for the chaos was a new sidekick courtesy of the FBI, that didn't mean they were going to be partners. It had been a long time since he had partnered with anyone. Seeing as this was most likely his last case, he planned on going out solo.

"I must've missed you by about five minutes at the house." McNaughton broke into his thoughts. "We did another sweep and interviewed the officers. Same story you told Sergeant Chapman. We'll send them both home later tonight and try our best to keep a lid on the details. Any thoughts on who called with the all clear?"

"I know it wasn't me," Mitch said. "I was talking to a contact in the DA's office on my way to Warren's house."

"We checked that already. Time matches. Plus, Chapman vouched for you. Said you're one of the best he's got, and there's no way you'd be involved in something like this. Besides, you'll be retiring in a few months, right?"

"If I can get this wrapped up."

"That's why I wanted to talk." McNaughton hesitated for a moment. "I've been ordered to supervise from here forward."

"So you want me to hand over what I've got so you can run with it?" He dug his hands into his pockets. "You know, I've never walked away from a case, but maybe this time it's for the best."

"Well, I was thinking we'd work together on this one."

"I don't work with partners."

"Chapman mentioned that too." McNaughton stopped walking. "Mitch, I need your help. Believe me, we're after the same thing here. You know the city inside and out, and you know the people inside the Division. I need your help to find the snitch and our suspect. You're already up to speed on the evidence, and I'm sure you've got some thoughts on Warren's cold cases. Whoever was in that house left no fingerprints, no DNA, and no evidence to link us to a suspect. But I might've found something."

She pulled a thumb drive from her pocket.

"I knew it had to be there." Mitch pointed at it. "A guy like Doc would've been extra cautious, especially with some of the dirt bags he's put away. That's why I was headed back there this morning. Where'd you find it?"

"Mounted in between the gutter and roof near the front door. It would've been easy to miss. There was also a second camera mounted to a tree in the backyard. We downloaded the footage from a computer in the study, but haven't had a chance to go through it yet."

"A true pro would've known about the video surveillance."

"Maybe we'll get lucky." McNaughton started walking again. "If we watch it at the station, we might be able to flush out our snitch."

"If that's the plan, what are we doing out in the cold?"

"I need to know what you've got, and we need to check out the van."

"What van?"

"LAFD found it burning near the Tujunga Wash. Matched the officers' description from Warren's house. Might be nothing, but we should check it out before we're buried in paperwork and hours of footage."

"I guess you're already calling the shots."

"Sergeant Chapman fought with the higher ups to keep you in the loop. I want you involved so I've cleared that on my side. If you're not on board then the train is leaving without you."

"Are you always this blunt?" Mitch yawned as a way to downplay his annoyance. He was tired, grumpy, and suddenly not the least bit amused at how eager McNaughton was to flex her authority. The days of chasing murderers, molesters, and snitches were behind him. His pride wanted to finish out his career by closing this final case. It had nothing to do with glory. He planned to cruise into retirement. If McNaughton wanted to be the hero, that was fine with him.

He waited a few more seconds. "Might as well teach you a few tricks before I'm put out to pasture."

"Now you're talking." She smiled. "I told Chapman we'd get along."

"I just hope you don't slow me down."

"We'll head out to Tujunga within the hour and see what we find. You can walk me through the evidence, and then we'll watch the footage. With any luck, we'll find some leads. Maybe our mole will poke his or her head out where it doesn't belong."

"I have one question."

"What's that?"

"Where are we going?"

"IHOP. I figured you could use your senior citizen's discount." McNaughton laughed. "Welcome to government cutbacks, Detective."

14

"What do you know about Jake Harris?"

Mitch was surprised it took McNaughton so long to ask. He thought for a moment as he eyed the patrons who were enjoying breakfast for dinner.

Mitch knew the game all too well to be reeled in by her tactics. He had to admit she was more calculating than he suspected. First, she broke the ice. Second, she took control. Third, she convinced him he was still on the team. Smooth. Sharp. Definitely top of her class.

What she didn't know was that she tipped her hand to an old dog. There was a reason why she needed him, and it had nothing to do with being part of her team. Maybe the Feds found something at Warren's house that he missed. Maybe she thought he was the mole. Whatever it was, Mitch knew one thing for sure, taking an hour to sit and eat dinner was a waste of time unless she was fishing.

"He was hired to write Warren's memoir." Mitch wiped his mouth with a napkin. "His father was close friends with Warren, so that's probably how he got the gig. Sounded like he needed the cash."

"He's an author?"

"Said this was his first ghostwriting job."

"His fingerprints were all over the house. Front and back doors. Study. Kitchen. Living room. Warren's bedroom." She stabbed at her eggs. "You don't think he's involved?"

"His fingerprints weren't found on the safe. Not on the books or desk drawers either."

"He could've wiped them clean."

"If it was him then he'd be long gone. Why stick around as the only suspect?"

"What about the timing?"

"Coincidence, nothing more." Mitch smothered his pancakes with maple syrup. "Kate, rattling off a list of facts as evidence is much easier than interpreting what it all means. I spoke to him at the house, and he was in shock. He puked in the bedroom for God's sake. On the drive over to the station, all I saw was a blank stare. I interviewed him for hours, and his story never changed."

"What about the toxicology report?"

"Yes, he was drunk, but that doesn't mean he pulled the trigger. Whoever killed Warren was a pro, and that's not this guy. Maybe he was down on his luck because he got cut off from the family fortune, or maybe he was just trying to live out a dream. I don't know and I don't care. He's just a guy who was in the wrong place at the wrong time. Trust me when I tell you, he's told us all he knows."

"The GSR report came back clean." McNaughton sipped her coffee. "Okay, so let's put him aside for a minute. What do you think was in the safe?"

"Obviously, something worth killing for. Warren lived in an upscale neighborhood. Ran in high-profile circles. As the DA, he put away the worst in society. If you ask me, there's probably a laundry list. Who knows what he kept hidden?"

McNaughton finished off her eggs, bacon, and hash browns by wiping a piece of toast across the plate. She downed her third cup of coffee as she flagged the waitress for the check. "What about Margaret Johnson?"

"She worked for Warren at the DA. After he retired, she stuck around, got laid off, and then he hired her as his housekeeper."

"That's it?"

"There might be more. She was definitely shaken up by the news. She said Warren was very generous. He even paid her doctor bills after she lost her insurance and was diagnosed with cancer. It's possible they were closer than she admitted on the phone."

"We've subpoenaed his phone records. We'll see if that shows us anything. What do you know about his old cases?"

"I've narrowed them down to the top ten. Mostly high profile."

"How'd you get it down so fast?"

"Look, I'm sure you've already heard that Warren was a legend." The sugar rushed through his veins and spiked his diabetes. "He was a good man with influential friends who want to help. You just have to know who to ask."

McNaughton nodded, paid cash for dinner, and then slipped out from the booth. Mitch grabbed his coat and flipped up his collar as they left.

For a few blocks, they walked in silence. Both dug their hands in their pockets as the night dropped a few more degrees.

"Mitch, what happened to your partner?"

"Chapman didn't tell you?"

"He said it was better not to ask—but I'm asking."

"Dexter and I were partners straight out of the academy." Mitch exhaled as his breath frosted in front of him. "He died eight years ago."

"On the job?"

"April 17, 2008, he called me around ten thirty and left a message. Said he'd found something on an old cold case. The next morning he was floating in the LA River."

"I'm sorry to hear that. What was the case?"

"Homicide. Victim was found in an alley behind the Roosevelt Hotel on Hollywood Boulevard. We picked up the case nearly fifteen years after it happened. We never identified the victim. She was a Jane Doe. Single GSW. No matches on DNA or fingerprints. No signs of sexual assault. The file sat on Dexter's desk for years. No new leads. No witnesses. We went through the evidence dozens of times, but too many years had passed. It was just another cold case gathering dust. Until now."

"What makes you say that?"

"It's one of Warren's top ten."

"It was high profile?"

"Not at all," Mitch replied. "Like I said, you gotta know who to ask. After he retired, it was the only case he ever called the DA's office about so I took another look." They reached the Crown Vic in the parking lot.

As they climbed inside he added, "I think I might've found what got Dexter killed."

15

I stared down the street from where I parked the Ferrari. My nerves spiked at leaving a priceless piece of art unguarded. I already regretted the decision, but it was necessary. Rachel got what she wanted. Whether she knew it or not, I did it to protect them. My head spun from the call. I wanted to believe I did what any loving husband and father would've done. I hoped one day I'd find a place in their lives again. For now, I needed to do what I was told.

A row of black SUVs blocked access to Doc's house. I pulled my hoodie over my head, cussed under my breath, and ducked into the bushes. I found a side gate unlocked and cautiously crossed a neighbor's backyard. My body tensed with each leaf that rustled beneath my feet. Every noise sounded like a Rottweiler ready to attack. I fought the urge to run more than once.

A light inside the house blinked on. I froze. An elderly woman appeared in the window and began washing dishes. Seconds felt like an eternity while I stood exposed in the middle of the yard. *Don't stop, you idiot.* I gingerly stepped through the flowerbeds until I reached the opposite fence. I was a burglar seconds away from being in the crosshairs of a SWAT sharpshooter ready to take me down.

My muscles burned as I struggled to pull my body over a concrete wall. I landed awkwardly between the wall and a metal shed. Pain seared through my left ankle as I nudged myself free. It took more effort and left me winded. I kneeled to catch my breath before limping behind a row of hedges. With gritted teeth, I fought through the pain, scaled another wall, and lowered myself gingerly behind Doc's pool house.

At night, the yard was even more breathtaking. Sparkling pool beneath exterior lights that illuminated the multi-million dollar hideaway. I stayed in the shadows and watched two men and a woman inside the main house. There were several others who milled about between the kitchen and dining room. I recognized the yellow lettering on the back of their windbreakers. FBI. I shuddered as my ankle pain spiked. I hugged the wall like a security blanket. My hands shook as I mustered up enough willpower to move.

Yesterday, I tasted my dream, and it was good. Tonight, I was breaking into a crime scene with the Feds twenty feet away. I was a witness on the verge of becoming a prime suspect. Something about Detective Lane's voice urged me to do it. No questions asked. One murder. One signature. Both ended a life and dream I wanted desperately. My chance at happily ever after vanished. Doc was right, I was someone with nothing left to lose.

Nerves rattled my bones as I stepped from the shadows. I was too afraid to look towards the house so I focused on the door in front of me. It was unlocked. I slipped inside and stood motionless in the center of the room until my eyes adjusted. Lights were off. Blinds shut. Everything was exactly how I'd left it the day before. Boxes were still stacked at one end of the living room. Books filled the shelves. An empty glass and bottle sat next to Evelyn Shaw's diary on the table. The same box I'd dropped was still there with papers and photos scattered on the floor. It seemed the Feds hadn't gone through the place yet.

Staying longer than necessary increased my chances of being caught. My ankle throbbed as I limped into the bedroom and searched for my backpack and duffle. *Gone.* I slipped a backpack I'd found in Frank's garage off my shoulders and went back into the living room. I stood for a moment and listened to the deafening silence.

I'd never snuck through someone else's backyard. I'd never broken into a house. I'd never stolen anything, especially possible evidence to a murder. I'd never been a witness to a crime, or a suspect for that matter. I didn't know how many laws I'd broken. I was sure the Twin Towers were in my future sharing a cell with a guy named Tiny.

Before yesterday, both were inconceivable to me. Even after telling Detective Lane my story, it still sounded crazy. I grabbed the diary and tossed it into the bag. Then I searched the shelves for any other books related to Evelyn Shaw. It was a shot in the dark. I didn't know what I was looking for, but I followed instructions.

The boxes were next. I rifled through the first one and found a stack of handwritten letters. I didn't waste time reading before tossing them into the bag. The next box was filled with old photos and newspaper clippings. I grabbed a handful and stuffed them into the bag as well. Printed sermons typed in an old font were in another box. I closed the lid and set it aside. I took the papers on the floor and stuffed them in with the rest. I hoped there was a nugget in the pile.

Inside the last box, I found a locked bamboo case. I grabbed a knife from a kitchen drawer and struggled to pry it open. I jammed the knife deeper and gripped the edge. With a snap, the lock broke free, and I opened the case to see file folders stamped with red letters, TOP SECRET. The adrenaline pumped hard. I took them all, left the bamboo case behind, and stacked the boxes exactly how they were when I entered.

One glimpse at the empty glass and bottle and I knew how far I had fallen. I zipped the backpack closed and hoisted it onto my shoulders. It was heavier than I expected. I wiped the sweat from my forehead and searched for a way out.

I rummaged through the kitchen drawers again and found some matches. I grabbed the box of sermons and placed it in the center of the room. With a flick of a match, the papers smoldered and started to burn. I opened the door enough to slip out and sneak towards the side of the main house. Each step was a struggle. I reached the front yard and heard a voice from behind.

"We've got a fire out here!"

For a split second, I glanced over my shoulder. An orange glow and gray smoke seeped from the pool house. I hoped the distraction was enough. I crossed into the neighbor's yard, hobbling like a cripple. Another minute and I rounded the corner with the Ferrari in sight. I dropped the bag onto the passenger seat, slid behind the wheel, and turned the ignition. Wiping the sweat from my forehead, I exhaled deeply, and casually drove in the opposite direction. One thing for sure, I was in deeper than I wanted to be.

16

Detective Lane, and a woman I didn't recognize, stood next to the Crown Vic as I drove down the long driveway at Frank's house and pulled into the garage. I grabbed the backpack from the passenger seat and headed inside without a word. Both of them followed. I limped down the hallway and dropped the backpack on the kitchen floor.

"I did what you asked," I snapped.

"I don't know what you're talking about," Detective Lane said.

"You said they were in danger, that I needed to grab all this from the pool house." I opened the refrigerator and found a bag of frozen broccoli. I sat on a barstool, removed my sneaker, slapped the bag on my ankle, and felt the cold seep into my bones. My ankle was already a mosaic of colors. "This isn't normal. Why would you ask me to sneak into a crime scene and steal evidence?" I caught the surprised look between them. "Oh, you didn't tell your partner? Did you know the Feds were there?"

The woman stepped forward. "I'm Special Agent Kate McNaughton. FBI."

Detective Lane turned to McNaughton. "I didn't call him, I swear."

"The Bureau has no knowledge of Detective Lane's actions."

"For God's sake." Detective Lane spread his hands. "I don't know what he's talking about."

"You were at Warren's house earlier?" McNaughton asked.

I nodded.

"I suggest we keep that between us. Now, what was it that you took?"

"Detective Lane said to grab whatever I could find on Evelyn Shaw, including TOP SECRET files inside a bamboo box." I glared at them. "I thought my wife and daughter were in danger. Is that true?"

Detective Lane stared at me. "I never called you."

"Then if you want to talk to me, you can call my lawyer."

"You have a lawyer?" McNaughton asked. "You've been cleared in the investigation."

"That's why we're here." Detective Lane jerked his head towards the front of the house. "Your stuff is in the trunk of my car. We can have an officer drive you down to the Division to pick up your truck if you'd like."

"What number registered on your cell?" McNaughton asked.

I checked my cell. "Private." I tossed the frozen broccoli into the sink. "I need a drink. You have exactly five minutes to tell me what's going on before you'll need to leave."

"Maybe you should hold off on the...nightcap," Detective Lane suggested. "Sounds like we'll all need to be clearheaded to sort this out."

Dark hardwood floors accented a sprawling living room surrounded by priceless Van Goghs and Picassos. A sixty-inch flat screen hung above a white marble fireplace. Black leather furniture wrapped around a coffee table made from an old riveted airplane wing. As sleek and modern as the room looked, it lacked the warmth of a home.

I slumped onto a sofa and perched my foot on the wing. I stared at the mixture of black, blue, and purple that covered the side of my ankle. It wasn't broken, but it was severely sprained. I glanced at the bar and longed for the bottle of Jack Daniels that called out to me. I wanted it badly. I needed it to steady my nerves. But I was too embarrassed to drink in front of them, especially after I'd been caught once already. I fought the urge, even though my will slowly crumbled.

"Tell me why I shouldn't report you?"

"For starters, I wasn't the one who called you." Detective Lane sat in a chair to my right. "Look, Jake, we shouldn't even be telling you this, but earlier today someone impersonated me and tampered with the crime scene."

McNaughton sat across from me. Was she in on it? "Detective Lane returned to Doc's house. When he arrived, the whole place had been wiped clean. We don't know who it was that pretended to be Detective Lane, but we are extremely concerned."

"I don't get it. What does that have to do with me?"

"The place wasn't just wiped clean." Detective Lane leaned forward. "It was as if nothing ever happened. Fingerprints gone. Furniture and books back to exactly how they were before the suspect rifled through the study."

"The bedroom?"

"You never would've known that's where he was killed. I've never seen anything like it."

McNaughton picked up where Detective Lane left off. "Your name's been kept from the press, but whoever called you knows you were in the house. It's possible they altered their voice on the call—to sound like Detective Lane."

"So, they know I was there?"

"Or they swept the house, found your fingerprints, and tracked down your number."

I rubbed my head with the palms of my hands in frustration. "That's great."

"Whoever the mole is might've seen me bring you in for questioning." Detective Lane met my gaze. "They could've run you through the system, found your address, family details, and then placed the call."

"Tell us again what you took from the house?" McNaughton asked.

"I grabbed whatever I could find on Evelyn Shaw."

"You said there were TOP SECRET files?"

"They're in the backpack." I gestured over my shoulder. "What about my wife and daughter?"

"We'll send a unit to monitor your apartment until we figure this out." Detective Lane glanced back towards the kitchen. "You may want to call and let your wife know you won't be home for a few days. I'm assuming you've told her about Warren already."

I shifted on the sofa. "I haven't had a chance to tell her very much."

"We'd like to speak to your father," McNaughton said. "Can you reach him?"

"What's he got to do with this?"

"His expertise might be beneficial in this situation."

"I can try." I was confused as to what kind of expertise Frank would have in this situation. I didn't want him involved any more than he already was. "He's out of town."

McNaughton slid to the edge of the sofa. "It's really important, Jake."

"Until we know who's behind the calls, you'll stay with me," Detective Lane said. "It's not the Ritz, but you'll be comfortable."

"Is this like witness protection?"

"Not exactly," McNaughton replied.

"For how long?"

"A week. Maybe longer."

"We'll keep this off the books." McNaughton shot a quick glance at Detective Lane, then eyed me closely. "If we file any paperwork we risk tipping off the wrong person, and that could put you and your family in more danger."

I leaned back and stared at the ceiling. "I don't want to get involved."

"I'm afraid it's a bit late for that," she said matter of factly. "What were you supposed to do with the backpack once you returned from the house?"

"I was supposed to wait here for you to call," I said to Detective Lane.

"Like I said, it wasn't me."

"Maybe you can help make sense of what you found." McNaughton suggested.

"Will it help find Doc's killer?"

"It might connect the pieces we need to solve the case."

"The list of files from the DA," Detective Lane said to McNaughton. "Maybe there's something that ties the two together."

McNaughton leaned in close. "Your family's safety is our top priority. So, it's up to you. If you decide you don't want our protection, or to assist with the investigation, we'll walk right out the front door. No harm. No foul. We'll take the backpack with us, and no one will know where it came from."

I rested my elbows on my thighs. Signing the papers wasn't enough to protect them. I was a fool to think it was that simple. I swallowed hard and looked McNaughton directly in her eyes. "As long as *you* protect them, I'll do it."

17

Growing up with a single parent meant a lack of parental supervision that offered a broad spectrum of independence. I spent most of my summers playing hoops all over the city. The competition, the ball swishing through the net ingrained in me a love for the game. I learned early on that in order to gain respect you needed to dominate the opposition.

Four high school championships as a Flintridge Spartan, I shattered the all-time scoring record. As a senior, I watched my number raised to the rafters. What I accomplished on the court defined my identity. Points and assists translated into notoriety and popularity, instead of life as a loner.

A pile of recruitment letters fueled my ego. I dreamed of playing for the blue and gold since I first stepped onto the court. The summer before I entered the big show as a Bruin, I honed my skills in South Central, Compton, Long Beach, West LA, and Santa Monica. I showcased my game and made some extra cash. I laced up the Jumpmans and stepped onto the court as a scrawny white kid playing a black man's game. Local ballers knew me strictly as Bird because I never saw a shot I didn't like.

It was addicting. I was a hustler, a gambler who talked trash to demand respect and allowed my skills to crush any opponent. I drained the long-range jumper with the game on the line. Ice was in my veins. I was a stone-cold baller immortalized in the hoods and barrios all over town.

Each night, I returned to the lavish home in Pasadena and pretended that was another life. I didn't belong with the rich and famous. I belonged on the streets where having the skills to survive was all that mattered. When I dribbled up and down the court I wasn't a rich kid living off Frank's money. I was a competitor who demanded respect for my game.

College took that to another level. I excelled against bigger and faster athletes because my desire to win at all cost was greater than theirs. I stood out as one of the elite until my sophomore year. Nights lost in frat parties where beer flowed freely overshadowed shooting drills in the gym. I returned to the streets, played for cash, and ended up owing the wrong people. Frank bailed me out. I lost my scholarship and suspension followed. My game plateaued and my skills faded.

At twenty-one, life peaked when I realized the dream was over.

I thought about this as the Crown Vic headed down Foothill. From the backseat, I watched several youngsters at Sunland Park drain shots under the floodlights. When had I lost my competitive edge? When did mediocrity steal my will to win? Once I was a warrior who battled with passion. Now I had no identity left. I'd never succeeded in a career. I didn't succeed as a husband. Hell, I was barely a father.

Losing drained the life from me while drinking stole my future.

Rachel never knew about my battles off the court. She believed the best in me when no one else did. She held us together because she had faith it would turn around. I wasn't the man she married, not anymore. She deserved better than a washed up collegiate athlete who relived his glory days to find his worth. Shame weighed heavily on me.

We passed one of our favorite joints, Giamela's. Many nights we shared a footlong meatball and provolone.

Across the street a block further up was our apartment. I'd driven past that place dozens of times since Rachel kicked me out. Tonight was different. I didn't want to be anywhere near them. I didn't want them to fall into whatever it was that got Doc killed.

Did they know they were being watched?

I wanted to protect them, but I wondered if the best way to do that was by staying away.

Why did Doc call me? Why did he tell me about Evelyn Shaw? Why did he give me her diary? What was I supposed to do now that he was dead? I hardly knew him, yet we were now forever linked. I knew nothing about Evelyn's secrets. I didn't know if anything I'd grabbed from the pool house was worth the risk.

Swirling questions, impossible to grab, let alone answer. They clouded my mind with uncertainty and doubt.

I snapped out of my thoughts as McNaughton spoke. "Jake, how long've you been married?"

"Eight years." As a way to direct the attention off me, I asked, "How about you?"

"Oh, there's no ring on my finger." McNaughton laughed and splayed her fingers. "Casualty of the job, I guess. How old is your daughter?"

"Samantha will be nine in a few months."

"Must be great to see her grow up."

"Yeah. It happens too fast though."

An awkward silence followed.

"We can arrange for you to see them in a few days if you'd like."

"I think it's better I stay away until this is over. I'll text or call if I need to."

"I've got two of my best heading over there. Another team will alternate every twenty-four hours."

She gave me a sympathetic smile as I turned my face towards the window.

"Thank you."

McNaughton's cell buzzed. She read the text and then said to Detective Lane, "Dead end on the cell trace. Looks like the call was from an encrypted phone. More sophisticated than a burner though."

Detective Lane nodded but stayed silent. He veered to the right and drove parallel to the 210 freeway. Minutes later we passed Angelus National Golf Club before reaching a long stretch of ranch properties. A few more miles, we turned off the main road and parked outside of a wrought iron gate with a sign that read BIG TUJUNGA CREEK.

Detective Lane glanced at me in the rearview. "Wait here, and keep the doors locked."

I cracked the window a few inches and slumped low in my seat. The pungent smell of manure filled my nostrils. It only confirmed how I was feeling.

I watched as they disappeared into the dark.

18

A cool breeze swept through the night.

The dirt path led McNaughton and Lane along the edge of the dry brush that lined a fire road where a year-long drought left the wash empty. It had been the worst drought in nearly a hundred years. At the end of the dirt road, a black and white idled with headlights directed at what was left of a charred van.

Kate strode towards the van. "We should've taken him in."

"Warren chose him for a reason. Whoever is behind this already knows he's involved. We should keep him close until we know why he's so important. Besides, he might be useful."

"You really didn't call him? Look, I'm fine with bending the rules, but breaking every possible regulation in one night must be some kind of record."

"I thought you leaned more towards being a mustang than a donkey." Mitch glanced at her with a smirk. "You didn't bring Maldone in by following the rules, right?"

"You didn't answer my question."

"No. I didn't call him."

"We'll lose our badges."

"I'll take a polygraph."

"If anyone finds out he's with us, we'll be flipping burgers."

"I'll opt for retirement."

An LAPD officer climbed out from the squad car. "Detective Lane?"

"That's right." Mitch glanced at the officer's badge, ANDERSON, and then nodded towards McNaughton. "Feds."

"I was wondering if you were going to show." Anderson bit off the words. "My shift was supposed to end two hours ago."

Mitch watched Anderson glance past them. The officer looked familiar. "You're from Foothill Division?"

"No. Five years in Glendale. I've seen you around."

From his frown, Kate could tell that wasn't the answer Mitch expected. Anderson shifted his weight and scanned the surrounding area.

"You were first on the scene?"

"Dispatch radioed at three fifteen. When I arrived, the van was already on fire. Checked for victims. No one inside. No one in the immediate area. LAFD showed up and took care of business. I figured it was kids fooling around until I was ordered to wait for you."

Mitch stepped toward the van and leaned in through the driver's side window. Kate walked around and gingerly leaned in on the other side. Mitch's flashlight pointed towards the melted steering wheel and dashboard. The entire front windshield was gone. The VIN was unrecognizable. A beam from the flashlight crossed over the hood as a heavy odor of burnt metal, plastic, and rubber lingered.

Mitch tugged at the door until he forced it open. He checked beneath the front seats.

Kate's flashlight scanned the empty cargo area before she turned her attention towards the front of the vehicle. She checked the glove box, but there was only ash. Nothing in the van was worth the thirty-minute drive out to the Valley. Kate joined Mitch at the rear where both stared at the one piece that might prove useful.

"Partial plate." She snapped a photo with her cell.

"Other than that, it looks like a dead end." Mitch glanced over at Anderson. Anderson had kept his distance, constantly scanning the area.

Under his breath, Mitch asked Kate, "What time was the 911 call?"

"Three twenty-seven."

Mitch eyed Anderson closely as he approached the officer.

"Just confirming—you were first on the scene?"

"You just asked me that." Irritation soaked every word. "I got here five minutes after dispatch called."

"So you were nearby?"

"Just down the hill."

"Not your normal patrol." Mitch widened his stance. "Foothill should've handled this."

Anderson stayed silent. Kate sensed the tension rise. She stepped in closer but froze when Anderson reached for his firearm.

Mitch pointed his finger at Anderson. "Why were you in the area?"

"You don't understand. I had no choice."

"Slow down." Mitch held up his hand. Kate locked her eyes on Anderson. Her fingers instinctively gripped her .45. "No one wants to do anything stupid here."

"It's too late. I'm already dead."

Before Mitch or Kate could react, the first shot whizzed by and hit Anderson squarely in the forehead. He fell backward and hit the ground with a thud. A second shot ricocheted less than a foot away as Mitch and Kate dove for cover. Both were pinned against the side of the van as bullets pinged around them.

"We gotta move!" Mitch pulled his .45. "You first."

Kate nodded.

"One...two...three."

Mitch fired several rounds as Kate scrambled on all fours towards the front of the van. When she reached the other side, she turned back around with her .45 pointed across the wash and fired three shots, expecting to see Mitch headed her way. She stopped and waited. At first, all she saw was Anderson's lifeless body. Another barrage of bullets hit the metal and she ducked back.

When she peered around the edge of the bumper, she saw Mitch scrambling in her direction. She fired more rounds as a muzzle flashed from across the wash about two hundred yards away. A few steps from her,

Mitch fell face down in the dirt.

"Mitch!" He didn't move. She frantically dialed her cell. "Officer down. Tujunga Wash. We're under fire. Need immediate response."

Kate pushed her cell in her pocket and then darted toward him. More shots hit around her as she blindly fired back. She skidded to her knees and reached into Anderson's pockets where she grabbed his cell. She shoved her .45 back in the holster, grabbed Mitch under his arms, and pulled with every ounce of strength.

At first, she struggled to move his two-hundred-thirty-pound frame, but the adrenaline pumped harder as she knew the longer she was exposed the greater the risk of being hit.

Another barrage of bullets sent her stumbling to the dirt. For a second, she laid on her stomach behind Mitch's limp body. The impact of a bullet piercing his leg, followed by blood splattered on her arms, jolted her.

"Don't die on me!"

For a moment, the gunfire stopped. Kate heard the sound of an engine. She spun around expecting to be flanked but was surprised to see headlights from the Crown Vic approaching at high speed. Instinctively, she turned toward the wash and emptied her clip towards the last spot she'd seen the muzzle flash.

Dust flew in the air as the Crown Vic skidded sideways around the black and white and stopped directly in the line of fire. Behind the wheel was a wide-eyed Jake Harris, who ducked right as the driver-side window shattered. A second later, the back door flew open.

Kate didn't waste another second. She grabbed Mitch with every ounce of strength left, shoved him into the backseat, and dove in after him. Jake punched the accelerator, sending the Crown Vic lunging forward towards the wrought iron gate.

As quickly as the shots first echoed, the night grew eerily still.

The Crown Vic peeled onto Foothill Boulevard and barreled onto the 210 East.

She removed her torn jacket, ripped a sleeve, and then quickly tied it around Mitch's leg to slow the bleeding. She rolled him over and pressed the rest of her jacket against the bullet wound in his chest. Blood soaked into the material as he moaned in pain, a sign that he was fighting to stay alive.

Keeping pressure on the wound, she pulled Anderson's cell from her pocket and scanned his outgoing calls. Mitch was right. Anderson had been the one who dialed 911.

She glanced up to see Jake staring back at her in the rearview mirror.

19

I checked the clock on the wall, and then stared blankly out the second-story window. Across the street, Goldsteins and Starbucks were closed. I'd forgotten it was the night before Thanksgiving. Fried turkey. Cranberry sauce. Sweet potatoes with marshmallows. Stuffing. Laughter. Love. Family. No matter how much we struggled to keep it together, Rachel and I always made Thanksgiving special for Samantha. Looking out on the night, I wondered if there was anything left to be thankful for.

Regret lingered far longer than reminiscence.

A steady stream of traffic drove up and down Verdugo beneath the 2 and 210 interchange. For the last hour, I watched the glow of lights from inside a white-walled room dense with antiseptic. I survived death for a second time in as many days. But being stuck in this room was suffocating.

Once Detective Lane was wheeled into the ER, McNaughton grabbed my arm and marched me into a vacant room, ordering me to keep the lights off and stay out of sight. I knew better than to argue. Hiding in this room meant I wasn't a witness anymore. I was a target.

For the first thirty minutes, I stood in a fog. My mind pierced with flashes. When I shifted the Crown Vic into gear, something inside shifted too. It wasn't desperation, but more like determination. I'd never been so scared. I'd never felt more alive either. Pure instincts fueled a split-second decision into the crosshairs. Somehow, I knew what to do.

Now, I didn't know if I was more afraid of being a target to some shadow assassin, or being alone without those I loved. At the very least, I hoped when this nightmare ended I'd find a place in Samantha's life again. That was going to be up to Rachel. I was powerless to change the mess I found myself in. The past haunted me, the present broke me, and the hours ahead threatened to destroy me.

McNaughton entered and stood next to me in the dark. "He'll be in surgery for a few more hours." She set my duffle bag on the bed, with all that I owned stuffed inside. "We were supposed to protect you, not the other way around. Most people wouldn't have the courage to do what you did. Thank you."

I wasn't sure what to do with her thanks, so I just studied the floor tiles for a moment. "So, what happens now?"

"First, I need to deal with the firestorm downstairs. Then we'll take it from there."

"Does anyone know I'm here?"

"Jake, someone on the inside is one step ahead of us. Telling anyone you're involved is too dangerous now. You need to trust me."

I ran my fingers through my mop of brown hair and itched my stubbly beard. My mind raced as the pendulum swung. Walk out and risk being the next victim, or trust someone I hardly knew. I wished there was door number three.

"You and me—we live in different worlds. But my deal still stands. You protect Rachel and Samantha, and I'll do whatever you want."

"They've already been moved to a secure location," McNaughton clasped her hands behind her back. "Understandably, your wife has questions."

"I bet she does." I turned and gazed out the window. "You know, just a few hours ago we were across the street at Starbucks signing divorce papers."

"She mentioned that. It's really none of my business."

"I was trying to protect them. Now I've put their lives at greater risk, and I don't even know how that happened." I turned and stared directly at

McNaughton. "I won't allow them to get hurt because of me."

"I'll do everything in my power to keep them safe. You have my word."

"I believe you, Agent McNaughton."

"Listen, with everything we've gone through tonight—why don't you call me Kate."

I paused for a moment. "Kate, why did Doc choose me? I'm nobody."

"I don't know."

"He was a family friend, but I hardly knew the man."

"What about your father? Were the two of them close?"

"Until last night, I hadn't seen my dad in years. I had nowhere else to go so I crashed at his place. I saw him briefly this morning before he headed out of town. We've never really talked much."

"Jake, what do you know about your father's company?"

"Honestly, I never paid much attention. I think it was some kind of consulting firm for the government."

"You never worked for him? Ever go to his office?"

"I stayed as far away as possible. You have to understand, there's never really been a bond between us. I was on my own long before I turned eighteen."

"Doc found you through you father, right?"

"They played golf together at Brookside. I guess that's how Doc got my number."

"We need to talk to your father. He could help answer some questions."

"I've tried calling him."

"Keep trying."

One kidnapping nearly a century earlier, a dead woman in Hollywood, and Doc's murder didn't add up to answers, only more questions. Surely, Doc never thought I'd be the only survivor to tell a story with blank pages. Maybe he hadn't chosen me after all. As we stood side by side, it crossed my mind that beneath Kate's calm demeanor was the one person who would keep me alive.

20

By midnight, Kate joined Sergeant Chapman down in the cafeteria. Both grabbed coffee and waited. A few minutes passed before Commissioner Marcus Powell arrived. Kate knew about the Commissioner through the grapevine. He was a decorated veteran of the force who climbed the ranks with a stellar record. He was also a no-nonsense straight shooter who demanded loyalty and excellence from his officers. He was not one who shied away from facing off with LA's biggest politicalites, including Mayor Osoria, either. He gained the respect of the men and women in uniform and was admired by the Angelenoes who lived across town from Rodeo Drive.

Kate had asked Mitch about the Commissioner on the ride over to see Jake Harris. She was surprised to learn that Chapman, Powell, Dexter Thompson, and Mitch had been long time buddies since the academy. Mitch admitted he was far less ambitious than them, but that never affected their friendship on or off the force. In fact, the Commissioner persuaded him to stick around long enough to collect his full pension.

The security detail took up positions at the entrance of the cafeteria. Kate wasn't surprised both men rushed to the hospital, as evidenced by their casual attire. She was on edge with what she knew must be kept from them. She had orders of her own. Chapman introduced Kate to Commissioner Powell while the three remained standing.

Powell asked, "How is he?"

"Two GSWs," Chapman replied. "One missed his femur by a few inches. The other's more serious. It's lodged in his upper chest. It'll be a few hours before he's out of surgery, and I don't know how long before we can talk to him. Marcus, he owes his life to Agent McNaughton."

"It could've been either one of us," Kate said.

"Thank you for protecting one of our own," Powell said. "Any leads on the shooter?"

"We're canvassing the wash," Chapman answered. "Nothing solid."

"Shots were fired from at least two hundred yards out in the pitch dark." Kate clenched her fists by her sides. "A dozen or more rounds. Commissioner, we were ambushed."

"We think it's connected to the Warren homicide," Chapman said. "Possibly the same suspect."

"Officer Anderson was hit with the first shot, and then Mitch was hit as we ducked for cover. I don't believe it's a coincidence. We're dealing with a pro, sir."

"I never should've talked Mitch out of retiring last year." Powell crossed his arms. "What do we know about Anderson?"

"He was on edge when we arrived," Kate said. "Mitch pushed him with a few questions and then Anderson pulled his firearm. There was no time to calm the situation down. Anderson said we were too late, that he was already dead."

"Chap, I need you to dig up everything you've got on him. We need to know if he's the only one within the Department."

"Anderson was one of mine, so I'll handle it myself," Chapman said. "Agent McNaughton retrieved his cell at the scene and matched the 911 call with dispatch. He's definitely the one who reported the fire. He received a call from what we believe to be a burner phone. A few minutes later he made the call."

Powell turned to Kate. "You don't believe Jake Harris is involved?"

"I don't believe so. He was in the house, but we cleared him as a suspect. His statement is clean. Mitch and I dropped off his belongings earlier tonight. There was nothing out of the ordinary."

"Maybe Anderson was trying to pin the fire on him somehow," Chapman suggested. "I'll see what I can dig up on our end."

"Bring it straight to me." Powell's face pointed towards the floor as he gripped the side of a chair. "We need to know if this is an isolated incident." He turned slowly to Kate. "I'll let the Mayor know that the Bureau will be handling all aspects of the investigation from here forward." He pulled out his phone, read a text, and then said to Chapman, "Call me the minute Mitch is awake."

Kate waited until Commissioner Powell disappeared out an exit through the kitchen. Chapman offered her a reassuring look.

"Mitch is a brother to us. Find the truth no matter where it leads."

"I owe him that much." Kate willed her fingers to uncurl.

"Now, what about Jake Harris?"

"I'm not sure I understand your question."

"You have his wife and daughter in protective custody. But where is he?"

"I'm afraid that's classified."

Chapman nodded and then headed for the door. He paused and glanced over his shoulder. "Do whatever it takes."

Kate waited until she was alone. She checked her watch and thought of how to smuggle Jake out of the hospital. As she headed down the hallway the sound of her boots echoed off the cold walls.

She whispered, "I never should've come back."

21

The 134 freeway was empty as gusts of wind pounded through the shot-out windows. Pieces of glass were scattered on the seats and floor mats. Kate McNaughton avoided staring at the blood stained seat in the rearview. There was a moment when she saw the life leave Mitch as they were exiting the freeway a block from the hospital. That feeling was hard to shake.

As a way to get her mind off the backseat, she double-checked that the thumb drive was still in her pocket. She'd forgotten it was there. Now it was the only piece of evidence in a case that had evolved from homicide to something more sinister. She feared that connecting Doc Warren, Officer Anderson, and the Sunset Boulevard cold case was only the beginning. They were pieces in a puzzle without any edges. Except for one—Jake Harris.

By the time she dropped Jake in Pasadena and exited Glendale Avenue, her body was frozen, which only tightened her stiff muscles. She replayed the seconds leading up to the first shot and tried to slow everything down. What could she have done differently? Was she doing the right thing keeping Jake in play? Mitch believed he was a piece that needed to be placed, but Jake was also the one person she'd been ordered to protect by someone she couldn't say no to. He was the reason why she returned to the Bureau.

At the Glendale Division, she parked the bullet-ridden Crown Vic and dropped the keys with the Desk Sergeant. There were only a few detectives working the early shift so most of the desks in the squad room were empty. Kate ignored the curious stares from several officers. If she hadn't been wearing her badge on her hip, she never would've made it past the front desk. Her dirty, blood-stained blouse was evidence, but she hadn't had a chance to change. There was no time to waste as she pulled reports and photos from the whiteboard behind Mitch's desk and placed them in a box. Before anyone noticed what she was doing, she headed out.

Sunrise was still a few hours away.

She climbed behind the wheel of her Jeep and blasted the heater. A quick shortcut down Wilson landed her in Eagle Rock, a somewhat forgotten neighborhood turned trendy hotspot as property values rebounded after the market collapsed. She slipped in at the right time and fell in love with this unique, culturally blended, and relatively unknown spot fifteen minutes from Skid Row. She needed a place to call home, and this seemed to be a perfect fit.

The Jeep pulled into the driveway of a two-bedroom bungalow tucked away on a dead-end street. Kate had lived in the house for nearly a year but hadn't fully settled. Walking through the front yard, she noticed the patches of brown amidst the blades of grass that needed to be mowed. If the state weren't in a water shortage, she'd take five minutes and water the flowers. She noticed the trim around the entrance needed sanding and a fresh coat of paint. All projects she intended to do once she had the time.

Maybe it was because she always imagined living in a place like this with a family. One day, she'd get married. One day, she'd have kids. One day, she'd deal with what she survived in foster care. One day, she'd settle down to life away from the chase.

From an early age, she never had a sense of being settled, and that feeling only grew stronger after the Maldone case. Once Maldone was captured, she spent her days lost amidst the artsy types who sipped lattes at Swork and the locals who downed *the* best pulled-pork sandwiches in the city at Oinksters. She tried to convince herself that being nothing more than a neighbor, a fellow Angeleno, was a good thing. Being thirty-something, single, without a family, and risking her life for a living tweaked her social life and left her searching for a balance between normalcy and hunting the dark side. Since moving into her bungalow, she'd spent far too many sleepless nights chasing ghosts. She thought taking time away from the Bureau would help deal with the aftermath.

Inside the bungalow, a white sofa and overstuffed chair were the only pieces of furniture in her quaint living room. A flat-screen was set on an old coffee table she found at a yard sale up the street. Framed beach photos lined the walls as a reminder of the peace she longed for once the ghosts were gone. To stand with her toes in the sand, gazing out on an endless ocean, and finally being able to let go of it all was the end game. After eight years on the hunt, she hoped she'd made a difference for the greater good, but on days like this she wondered.

Brad always said to push through to the other side and you'll catch your demon. He was a mentor, and someone she respected. But he was wrong. Evil lurked beneath the surface even after men like Angelo Maldone were locked away. It was an endless cycle. Brad had bought her time away from the grind because she was his best agent. When she denied his request to return to the Bureau, she thought it was over. He needed her back because she was special to Maldone, who insisted on only speaking with her about Doc Warren. But Maldone never mentioned Jake Harris, which at the time didn't seem odd until POTUS ordered her to find and protect him.

What makes Jake so special?

Kate shrugged off the demons and imagined herself back near the ocean. That lasted only a brief moment. She was troubled by the fact that POTUS had kept her in the dark. Even though she trusted Brad to watch her back, she refused to end up like Mitch, bleeding to death in the backseat of a Crown Vic. But the stakes were too high. Until this was over there was no escape.

She shuffled her mail on the dining room table and exhaled. She was a specialist who operated outside the lines. She found those who didn't want to be found. She stopped the worst from happening by pushing men like Maldone to the edge. In many ways, the boundaries of the Bureau didn't pertain to her because she was allowed to make the rules. Faith guided her in the fight, but it was a journey filled with plenty of doubt.

Her cell rang.

Chapman was on the other end. He confirmed the Crown Vic was processed, and a full search of the wash turned up nothing. He prodded about Jake Harris again, but she wasn't giving an inch. Chapman ended the call with a reminder that Commissioner Powell would appreciate being kept in the loop. She reassured him that once there was anything solid, she'd let them know.

Still wearing her blood-stained blouse, she set the coffee pot, entered the bedroom, tossed her cell on the bed, and set her .45 on the dresser. She stripped down and stood in the shower as steam hung in the air. The hot water stung as the cuts on her elbows and hands burned. For a few minutes she blanked out. She turned the water off and stopped cold. A floorboard creaked, and she knew exactly where it was. A second passed before she heard it again. Soaking wet, she wrapped a towel around herself and cautiously opened the door.

Her .45 was still on the dresser. She grabbed it and moved towards the living room. The fresh aroma of coffee sifted in the air. She paused before peering around the corner. A familiar rush spiked her senses. Her heartbeat quickened as she moved. The living room was empty. She braced herself as she entered the kitchen. She was relieved to see the back door was locked. She stepped out into the backyard with her head on a swivel. No one was there. She double-checked the garage to be sure.

It had been a long night. She wondered if she'd overreacted. She paced through the house and checked the second bedroom and the closets. Maybe her lack of sleep caused the sudden paranoia. She breathed in deeply at the thought that someone had invaded her space—her sanctuary. She got dressed, downed a quick cup of java, and holstered her .45 on her hip. She needed to head downtown. She was nearly out the door before she remembered the thumb drive. She entered the bedroom, grabbed her slacks from the floor, and reached into the left pocket.

It was gone.

22

During the early 1920s, the public opinion of Evelyn Shaw wavered between hot and cold. No one was lukewarm to the evangelist. Church leaders blasted her flashy persona, public battles with politicians, publicized alliances with the Ghosts of the Flaming Cross, and aimed their Sunday sermons at the woman they referred to as a trickster. Journalists remained captivated by her soap opera life and descended each week to her extravagant church in the heart of Bel-Air. Sister Evelyn added fuel to the fire when she rubbed shoulders with Hollywood and garnered admiration from the likes of Zukor, Lasky, Goldwyn, and Fox.

Mary Pickford, Jean Harlow, Clara Bow, and other Hollywood bombshells showed up in droves to hear Sister Evelyn's distinctive voice cut through the sanctuary with conviction. Arthur Elliott was a regular who often led the benediction at the end of the service. Rooms backstage overflowed with costumes, props, and scenery to capture the gospel message. Music played to the masses as volunteers prayed in two-hour shifts. The switchboard was overloaded with those ready to offer counsel to the less welcomed in the church. Traffic jammed clear down Sunset Boulevard as Hollywood premiers played second chair to Sunday nights with Sister Evelyn.

Questions swirled on whether her account of the kidnapping was a crime or a hoax. The headlines splashed with the controversy. Sunset Pictures took advantage of the press and released Arthur Elliott's film,

Golden Age, three months early.

On the first day of the trial, Sister Evelyn, in her customary black robe and white cross, marched down Main Street with hundreds of women. Her ministry, her influence, was as white hot as anything the world had ever seen. No one, not even the DA, David Strong, knew how powerful she had become.

What was clear from the pile of newspaper clippings, letters, and photos was that Sister Evelyn's spectacles in Bel-Air reached far beyond the pulpit. Husbands. Wives. Alcoholics. Drug addicts. Rehabilitated mobsters. All were welcomed with open arms. Sister Evelyn distributed food, provided shelter, and became a lightening rod of hope in communities during the Depression.

From coast to coast, thousands arrived at Union Station searching for a new beginning. Sister Evelyn offered them a road to faith they were desperate to travel. She preached to thousand of homeless women and teenagers with illegitimate babies in the midst of a battlefield of the West between oil barons, real estate tycoons, movie moguls, corrupt police, and the mob led by notorious gangster, Mickey Cohen. No matter where she was, even after she returned from Agua Prieta, she seemed to never be afraid to cross the line to care for the poor and offer salvation to the lost. But not everyone in this exclusive community welcomed the inferior of society.

After Kate dropped me at the house, I couldn't sleep. So, for most of the night I crammed everything I could find about Evelyn Shaw into my brain. The French door windows were covered with taped photos, articles, and handwritten letters.

I narrowed down what I'd taken from Doc's house to a cast of characters. Arthur Elliott. Detective Edward Winters. David Strong. Judge Carl Hyde. DC Kasper. Douglas Police Chief Patrick O'Connell. I stared at a handwritten registration slip from a hotel in Santa Barbara. Next to it was a kidnapping note that was barely legible. I scanned the black and white photos of Santa Monica, where thousands stood along the shore praying for her to be found. Another photo showed Sister Evelyn standing in the back of a caboose amidst a massive crowd gathered at Union Station. There were more courtroom photos of the trial. A few more of Sister Evelyn covered up in bed looking sick. My eyes were drawn to an article from the *LA Reporter.*

LA REPORTER - JUNE 4, 1925
Sister Evelyn and the Ghosts of the Flaming Cross
Reported by Edward Norvel

I followed Sister Evelyn as she stepped off the stage and hurried down a hall toward the alley behind the church. As soon as we were outside, a limousine was waiting. Our wrists were seized, and we were pushed into the backseat, where two hooded figures, with narrow slits for eyes, sat across from us. Sister Evelyn had given me the exclusive, yet had refrained from any details. I do not know how much time passed, nor did I fear for my life, for I was with a woman protected by God himself. A woman of such notoriety and strength, not even the ghosts dare harm her.

On this night, we traveled into the depths of downtown, blindfolded to conceal a secret location. In total darkness, we were led into an elevator that carried us to an assembly hall. Once the doors opened, our blindfolds were removed. Sister Evelyn stepped forward without an ounce of fear as a mass of voices recited, "United to protect our country, our flag, and the supremacy of the white race."

I stepped aside and watched hundreds of white-robed Klansmen turn their attention to the only woman in the room. A red robed ghost kneeled before Sister Evelyn and assured her of the Klan's support of her ministry by offering a bouquet of red roses.

"We acknowledge your godly mission in our blessed city. May these roses reflect the blood of all who respect the purity of your character, the ideals that unite us, and the army standing at the ready to protect what is most valuable to us all."

Sister Evelyn accepted the flowers and stepped onto center stage. With a steady voice, mixed with drops of sweetness and anger, she said, "I have heard many stories of young women betrayed by the men who swore to protect them. That is why I am dedicated to defend the weak. I am thankful to God that I have never been a transgressor. I wonder though, how many souls will stand the full light of day. How many will stand forgiven before the Savior? So, I will pray that your intentions are pure and ask that you do the same for me. Goodnight."

Another man seated behind a desk rapped on a table, and the red hooded ghost uttered a benediction, including a chilling promise to guard Sister Evelyn the rest of her days. An invisible company was ready to defend her and the message she preached. The lights lowered, and the ghosts prayed amidst a flaming cross. We were ushered from the assembly hall and returned to the alley behind the church long after midnight.

Two weeks later, Sister Evelyn stood behind her pulpit and gazed out on hundreds of white-hooded figures that lined the aisles of her church in Bel-Air. A packed sanctuary waited in ominous silence, some in utter disbelief. Again, the ghosts carried a flaming cross and placed it in the center aisle.

Sister Evelyn preached, "As I traveled the long roads from New York to Los Angeles, I spent many nights preaching and singing about the Savior. But there is one night that has remained vivid in my memory. A young Negro boy stood outside of a church entrance while the city's prominent leaders found their seats in the front row. I sensed the boy's heart soften as the sweet-voiced choir poured out their praises. Yet he never entered, because he was not invited in.

"From the stage, I glanced at the beautiful high-beamed ceiling and intricately stained glass. I watched as heads were buried in hymnbooks, unaware of the courage this young boy mustered to take a step inside. He slipped into a back pew, where an usher grabbed him by the shoulder and began to push him outside. I shouted, 'Stop! All are welcome here!'"

Sister Evelyn gazed out across the sanctuary and up into the balcony. Her words echoed off the ceiling and caused some to jump in their seat. She paused and allowed the room to silence once again.

"I will never forget that wide-eyed young boy as he walked down the center of the church and sat on the steps near my feet." Sister Evelyn waved her arms around her. "All are invited to worship the Lord. Those who are hurt, broken, and weary are welcomed to rest in our sanctuaries. You see, this is not my church, nor is it yours. Stained glass, shiny brass, and polished wood will never make our churches magnificent. Unashamed, unrelenting, unwavering love for others is all that matters. Only then, when we believe this to be true, will they stare into the compassionate face of the Master himself."

Sister Evelyn's eyes twinkled as she stepped around the front of the pulpit. A Negro man seated in the back stood to his feet, his clothes and boots worn from many days and nights on the road. He stepped out into the aisle and walked towards the stage with tears in his eyes. Sister Evelyn stepped off the stage directly in front of the burning cross. A furious intensity swept over the room as she preached with fire in her soul and a Negro by her side. Her eyes were alight towards the Klansmen who had professed their loyalty only weeks earlier.

"You have pledged yourselves to this great nation and pride yourselves on patriotism. Yet you have failed to understand the meaning of freedom— freedom is only found in Jesus Christ. You cannot worship a Jew, yet despise all living Jews. You cannot follow God, yet despise those he loves. There is only one Master who is both judge and jury. And until I see him face to face, I will continue to love those in need, no matter the color of their skin or the size of their bank accounts. Therefore, I have no need for an army of hooded men. For an army of angels is simply a prayer away."

One by one the men stood to their feet. Then by the dozens, the Klansmen lined the aisles and walked out the doors. If I had not witnessed it myself, I would not believe it to be true. On this night, a war between Sister Evelyn and the Ghosts of the Flaming Cross was set ablaze.

23

Neco Rimoldi walked a path that circled Echo Park, a landmark between Angelino Heights, Elysian Heights, and historic Filipinotown. With a forty-five-million-dollar renovation and the lotus beds in full bloom, the neighborhood was transformed from a gang-infested hood into loft apartments occupied by twenty-somethings who pushed newborns around the lake in their Bugaboo strollers beneath the smog-veiled LA skyline.

Rimoldi's attention remained directed across the lake at an elderly white man seated on a bench. Earlier that morning, Rimoldi picked up a message in Atwater Village to deliver the package to Echo Park. He was surprised to see the Ghost waiting for him.

Communication with the Ghost followed strict rules of engagement, most of which involved remaining unplugged from the grid. All communication was done through a maze of locations that had been used for decades. They had never met in person. He didn't know the Ghost's true identity, and he didn't want to know. Survival in this business was about asking as few questions as possible, and delivering results.

He seethed at being compromised by the crew who botched the clean up. Rimoldi prided himself on leaving no trace of his presence. He had no choice but to step in and neutralize the damage.

First, the LAPD officer, a simple pawn. Second, the detective he was hired to silence. He hadn't planned on the woman who fired back. But with one call, he knew her identity and an address. He had already paid her a visit. He only wished the Ghost had ordered him to silence her permanently.

The Ghost stood gingerly as Rimoldi approached. Dark eyes magnified behind inch-thick glasses. A boney frame arched forward steadied by a wooden cane. Both walked in silence. Rimoldi kept his eyes on their surroundings. The Ghost seemed oblivious to those who passed. Rimoldi waited until they were alone before slipping an envelope from his jacket and handing it over.

"Neco, you have served us well." The aged voice was barely above a whisper. "I assure you, we have dealt with those responsible for the unfortunate mishap last night. For your trouble, two million has been transferred according to your instructions."

"The contract was for a million."

"We decided another million was necessary to finish the task at hand. It seems Detective Lane is still alive."

"Where is he?"

"Montrose Hospital. Room 334."

"I will handle it."

"I know you will." The Ghost smiled slyly.

"What about the Fed?"

"We need her alive for now."

Rimoldi removed the thumb drive from his pocket. "I viewed the footage like you asked. There is a witness. Male. I need more time to find his identity."

"I have my sources. I will do that." The Ghost pointed the cane at the downtown skyline. "A war began in this city many years ago between an evangelist and the Ghosts of the Flaming Cross. She was a powerful adversary who was fearless against one of the many organizations we are sworn to protect. She believed all were created equal. Her actions fueled the religious fanatics. My predecessors failed to deal with her when she threatened to expose who truly ruled this city. They never should have allowed her to live. Perhaps we would already have what belongs to us."

"I'm not religious," Rimoldi said. "With all due respect, my loyalty has always been to the highest bidder. It just happens that you're my number one client."

"Angelo taught you well. But I assure you, faith causes people to be unpredictable. It sways the pendulum. We live in a world where morality is a myth, where religion is a luxury for the weak, and where only those who believe in retribution survive. Greed. Segregation. An unquenchable lust for power. Those are the commandments that allow us to operate in the shadows. That thirst manifests itself in wars, genocides, hijackings, assassinations, trafficking, and smuggling what society fights to ignore. Blind faith—a moral compass—has no place in the world we find ourselves in."

Rimoldi watched the Ghost open the envelope and remove a slim, portable hard drive. "There are times where persuasion and influence are as effective as a bullet to the heart. Warren was not always a man of faith. He kept his own skeletons locked away. That's why we recruited him. However, once he believed in this religious fervor, he chose not to accept our invitation. We exposed ourselves, and he has hunted us ever since. Until a week ago, we believed he had found nothing of value."

The two sat on a bench as a breeze rustled through the trees. A fountain in the center of the lake shot skyward. The Ghost's eyes narrowed as fingers tapped against the hard drive. Segregation. Liberty. Religion. Rimoldi quickly grew tired of the conversation. He knew the Ghost preyed on the weak, but he was not one of them. He was a mercenary whose allegiance was to no one but himself.

The Ghost turned to Rimoldi.

"Neco, whether you believe as I do or not, you are a soldier in this war. You have a gift to do what many are too weak to do for themselves, and you do it with extreme prejudice." The Ghost tapped the drive and paused as if running through a list of options. "Send a message that will not be forgotten."

24

Sister Evelyn, and the mysteries that swirled around her, captured more than my curiosity. She arrived with a megaphone in hand during an era when LA was known more for being Sodom than Mayberry. She was generations ahead of her time as she used influence, money, and public notoriety to feed the poor, care for those in need, speak out for civil rights, perform miraculous acts, preach to the masses, and ignite a revolution that couldn't be controlled by the religious zealots or the criminal underworld.

In many ways, if you believed the legend, she was as remarkable as she was untouchable.

To the religious bullhorns, she was a fraud and a hoax. To the Klan, she was a symbol of their twisted ideology who betrayed them after they publicly pledged their allegiance to her cause. To Cohen and the West Coast mob, she was a viable threat as she converted criminals faster than they were being recruited. To the gypsies, she was a healer who saved the life of their beloved King. And to the Angelenos, she was a beacon of light, a messenger of hope, and a carrier of salvation.

No doubt she was fearless, but in many ways she also seemed frail. Her displays of courage were often overshadowed by personal demons. Public fights with her husband, Bernard. Rubbing shoulders with the likes of Charlie Chaplin, Howard Hughes, and the late-night dinners with Arthur Elliott on the Sunset Pictures lot. Maybe her fight against the cynics drove her mad, but in the midst of the chaos, her love for people kept her sane.

What religious cause had ever been built without a few crimson stains? What charismatic leader had ever built a following without a few black eyes or backroom deals? After all, how could anyone reconcile these two worlds within themselves without there being collateral damage?

In my crash course of everything Sister Evelyn, these were only a few of my questions and observations. I believed there was something in what I'd found that might break the case open. I grew more convinced that Doc had pointed me to a hidden conspiracy that only the events of 1925 could explain. I just needed to pinpoint what that conspiracy actually was before I uncovered how it tied in with the events of the past forty-eight hours. I didn't have a clue how to connect the dots. Sifting through the piles I'd brought from the pool house, I refused to believe it was all in vain.

First, I had only scratched the surface on the secrets and controversy. Second, I liked Sister Evelyn's theology better than the televangelists who ran their multi-million-dollar enterprises with an iron fist, safely locked away in their beachfront mansions overlooking the Pacific. Third, Doc died protecting a secret he wanted me to find, and I wasn't going to stop until it was found.

Kate picked me up to go visit Detective Lane in the hospital to see how he was doing and find out what he could tell us about what he had uncovered. But by the time we pulled into the hospital parking lot, it was clear Kate wasn't in the mood to listen to the names I lobbed out into the air.

"Mary Hayes. Linda Morris. Both arrested for kidnapping plots. Another guy threatened to blow up the Bel-Air church. I found letters from people who claimed to know who grabbed her from the boardwalk. It's stuff I didn't find anywhere online."

"We need something credible," Kate replied, a bit on edge. "Preferably from this century."

"What about Frank?" I asked as we entered the lobby.

"Your father?"

"No." I held up my cell and pointed to an image of a typed letter. She glanced at the screen but kept walking. My ankle protested at the quick pace

95

she set. "Kate, he was paid a grand to kidnap her, then he lost the cash in a poker game in Detroit before being thrown out a window a few weeks later in New York."

"Jake, those are stories that have been passed down through the years. Any thread of truth has probably been embellished to boost her legend. We will never know if any of those people were credible. I don't see how any of them are related to the Warren homicide."

"Caffey Hastings."

"Jake, we don't have time for this."

"He was the Tombstone County Sheriff in 1925 who wrote a letter claiming to have seen a man driving a car with a woman in the backseat who was holding another woman on her lap only a few days after Sister Evelyn disappeared. He even offered to bring evidence for the trial."

"Did you corroborate his story?"

"Corroborate? He's dead." I wasn't even trying to hide my limp now.

"Exactly my point. They're all dead."

"What about the court documents from her trial?"

"Did you find any court records that connect to this investigation? Transcripts? Any evidence to back up any of these stories you're telling me? Anything that identifies who shot at us last night?" Kate stopped at the reception desk and flashed her badge. "Mitchell Lane's room, please."

The woman behind the desk tapped a few keys but never looked up. "Room 334."

I stayed on Kate's heels as we headed towards the elevator. I was frustrated that she wasn't listening or even showing any concern over my sprained ankle. I had rambled on since she picked me up at the house, but something had to be worth stealing from the crime scene. I didn't want to admit that I'd risked my life and signed away my marriage for nothing.

And there was also the mystery of who it was that called me. "What about the call?"

"Officer Anderson received one call from a burner before he dialed 911. There's no evidence that he called your cell."

"Kate, it sounded exactly like Detective Lane."

"Like I said already, voices can be manipulated digitally."

"So, we've got nothing."

"Forget the kidnapping, Jake. We need to stick to the facts."

"Doc called me for a reason, and I need to know why."

"Maybe he hired you to write his memoir and had no idea someone was after him. Maybe he was going to tell you some deep, dark secret that got him killed. We need to find the clues that get us closer to the truth, not take us back to the 1920s."

"When Doc talked, it was like he was reliving her life right before his eyes. He called it the genesis. He knew parts of the story that I didn't find anywhere else. Why tell me all that if it wasn't important?"

"Jake, you're not listening."

"Doc said she escaped by attacking her kidnapper, and then walked through the desert for hours on the verge of death. The versions online tell a different story. The detectives who worked the case said when they arrived at the hospital she looked unharmed, especially after spending thirty days locked in a shack in the desert. Someone lied for a reason."

"There's no proof what Doc said is true either."

"Or it was a cover up," I argued. "If she was dangerous to the politicians, the Klan, and to guys like Mickey Cohen then maybe she was telling the truth to protect herself."

"Pure speculation. The only way to solve this is to put the pieces of the puzzle together until the whole picture makes sense. None of what you're saying fits this case. You have to trust me on this. You chase the leads that are right in front of you based on the evidence."

"Fine." My shoulders slumped. "So, what evidence do we have?"

The elevator doors opened. "Not enough."

We stepped inside the elevator and were joined by a resident in scrubs who wheeled in a young girl on a gurney. I was reminded of the late nights spent in the ER with Samantha. Since she was born, I had tried to comfort her when the doctors failed to know the answers. Now it was up to Rachel to decide if I'd be there in the years ahead. For the thousandth time, I pushed the guilt aside and reached for a thread of optimism.

We rode up to the third floor where the doors opened. The resident pushed the gurney into the corridor and headed in the direction of room 334. I caught sight of the girl and then noticed something familiar about the resident.

My mind flashed to Doc's study as I ducked behind the chair and peeked around the edge of the armrest. I pictured the shadowy figure, only this time my memory was more vivid. I visualized a dragon's head; a chill shot through me.

"It's him," I whispered as we stepped off the elevator. I nodded towards the man pushing the gurney. "That's the guy from Doc's house."

"Are you sure?" Kate raised her eyebrows.

"I recognized the tattoo on his neck."

"I thought you didn't see him."

"Kate, I'm telling you that's him."

"Okay. Wait here."

25

Kate focused straight ahead as she closed in fast. Nurses and orderlies busied themselves with their normal routine oblivious to the danger among them. One look in his eyes, and she knew Jake was telling the truth, which meant the suspect in front of her was a trained killer. The fact that he was there left only one scenario.

Kate never broke stride as she watched the suspect roll the gurney against the wall directly outside of room 334, and then casually walk towards the exit at the end of the hall.

A doctor stepped out from one of the rooms. Before he said a word, Kate flashed her badge and motioned for him to clear the corridor. The doctor flagged down a nurse and several orderlies who immediately ushered patients wheeling IV poles into the nearest rooms. Another nurse ducked behind her station and dialed security.

Kate zoned in on the suspect. He killed Warren. She was sure he was there to kill again, but he'd passed Mitch's room. It didn't matter if he was armed, there was no way he was going to escape this time.

With her .45 pointed towards the floor, she flipped the safety off. The suspect was already halfway out the door. Calling for backup should've been her next move. That's what she'd been trained to do, but she was afraid of losing him in the wind. She approached with weapon raised and pushed the exit door open. Cautiously, she checked the stairwell below but was surprised to hear footsteps above. An uneasiness caused her to pause and glance over her shoulder. Jake stood in the center of the corridor. She motioned for him to stay back. Then she headed up two flights of stairs until the footsteps stopped.

Kate was about to check the sixth floor when she heard a door slam. She rushed up to the roof access. She breathed in deeply, steadied herself, and made her move.

The first blow knocked her off balance and sent her firearm flying. A second blow sucked the air from her lungs. The suspect grabbed her by the hair, pulled her to her feet, and then wrapped his arms around her body. He picked her up and slammed her against the metal door. She tried desperately to free herself from his iron grip. Another knee to the stomach, and she dropped on all fours. Her training quickly turned to survival. She gasped for air.

She wiped blood from her mouth and instinctively reached for her weapon. A boot swept across her chin and everything spun wildly. She landed face down on the concrete. Pain seared her bones. Another kick dug into her midsection. Her vision dimmed. Every breath burned her lungs. She tried to keep her wits about her, but it was all a blur.

"Give me the name of the witness." She felt his presence standing over her. "Now, Kate."

He knew who she was. "You broke into my house." She coughed up a mouthful of blood.

Kate felt his breath against her face. "You need to ask yourself, is he worth dying to protect?"

She got to her hands and knees, but his forearm jerked around her throat in an unbearable chokehold. His knee dug deep into her side. Her rib cracked, and she cried out.

Amidst the fog, she heard a faint thumping noise that grew increasingly louder until it drowned out all other sounds. The pressure around her throat loosened as a strong force pushed against her body. She dropped to the concrete and caught sight of the suspect running towards a helicopter that hovered a few feet above the roof.

Every muscle screaming, she reached for her weapon. Air filled her lungs, but each breath tore at her ribs. With a burst of strength, she grabbed her .45. From her knees, she aimed at the chopper and emptied her clip. Bullets pinged off the metal, but it wasn't enough to stop it from lifting higher and heading west.

Her head dropped back, and she stared at the blue sky. She gripped her side, not knowing for sure how many ribs were broken. Struggling to get to her feet, she staggered as she heard her name being called.

A deafening thunder and a violent jolt caused her to stumble toward the edge of the building. Seconds later, a blast ripped through the roof, sending large chunks of debris flying. Kate's arms and legs flailed, trying to grab anything to stop her momentum as the front of the building collapsed.

A second blast erupted. Concrete split like paper. Flames burst skyward from the floors below. Exposed rebar jutted out as black smoke engulfed the chaos. She hit the edge of the roof and went airborne for an instant before something grabbed her. It felt like her arm was ripped from its socket as she dangled helplessly above what was left of the building. She glanced down at the destruction while the ringing in her ears intensified.

Blood curdling screams and shouting cut through the noise. Another burst of flames flared skyward. A chunk of concrete dislodged, slammed into the floors below, and then exploded into pieces onto the parking lot. An alarm blared.

Kate craned her neck to see what stopped her fall. Jake lifted her inch by inch while she gritted her teeth and fought the pain until she was safely in his arms. She hugged him tight.

He'd saved her. Again.

26

A soft glow illuminated the dark cabin with custom leather seats, mahogany wood, and a full bar. After fighting gridlock traffic, Alan Leung boarded a private jet in Van Nuys, which departed as soon as he sat down. He gazed out the oval window as a sunset spread across an endless sky. Bright oranges mixed with golden yellows and deep shades of blue. The ocean below was a soothing sight as it disappeared beneath the clouds.

A message from President Palmer was scheduled to begin in a matter of minutes. A reporter jabbered on about what he might or might not say while someone in the background hurried to secure a dozen microphones clustered together in the center of the podium.

The Ghost emerged from the queen-sized bedroom without a disguise. Dressed in jeans and a T-shirt, she leaned back in her seat and poured a glass of Hundred Acres cab. Leung joined her as the *vino* marked the end of a day where the Brethren flexed their power. He rubbed his smooth head and watched the reports with satisfaction. The Ghost had created a spectacle, and a message was delivered. In war, there was always collateral damage, and Leung knew better than to question the Ghost on the details of the day's devastating blow.

On the screen, President Palmer walked down a hotel lobby with Mayor Osoria, Marcus Thompson, the LA Police Commissioner, and Joel Howard, Executive Director of the NSA. The fact that the NSA was present meant Washington had already determined this to be an act of terrorism. The room quieted as the clicking of photos stopped.

"I know this has been a difficult day for everyone," the President said with a steely glare. "While I will not be going into details regarding the investigation, I will say that so far there are 104 casualties. Nurses. Doctors. Patients. Moms. Dads. Law enforcement. Friends and neighbors. We will not be releasing any of the names as we are still in the process of notifying family members. Search and rescue is still on the scene doing a thorough check for any more survivors. The area surrounding the hospital will be off limits until further notice. That includes all aircraft other than law enforcement. Let me be clear, this was not only an attack on Los Angeles but on our nation. A mass murder—and an act of cowardice. We all share an unwavering anger towards those responsible, and we will direct our full resources to bring them to justice swiftly. I assure you, there will be no distinction between those who committed these acts and those who harbor them.

"In times like these, there is a terrible sadness felt across our nation. My prayers go out to the victims and their families. Those lives lost will never be forgotten, and our lives will never be the same. On this day, meant to celebrate all we have to be thankful for, I pray God will give us strength to bring evil to justice, to bring mercy to our nation in the midst of our grief, and to stand united in defending the freedom we share as Americans."

Leung turned off the TV. As leader of the free world, President Palmer stole the spotlight from his fellow Washington cronies and gave a master class in how the game of politics was played. *Well done, Mr. President.* Leung turned his attention to the Ghost as she plugged a hard drive into a USB port. An icon appeared on the desktop.

"Reach out to him tomorrow and offer your condolences." The Ghost ignored his stare. She methodically clicked down a list of folders. "Push him for the mining deal—and offer the debt negotiations as an olive branch once more."

"I'm curious. What was in the envelope I handed him?"

"Leverage."

The Ghost opened the first folder to find a series of video thumbnails.

Another click and a video played of a man walking up to the front door of a house. White. Late twenties, possibly early thirties. Six feet. His face was blocked once Warren stepped out from the doorway. She paused the video and stared at the profile for a long time.

Leung paid a steep price for the Brethren's protection, and over the last six months he had grown to respect the Ghost more than any business opponent he had ever faced. She was there to protect him and to ensure his road on the election was successful. She was also using him, and he was cautious about prying too deep into her agenda.

"Who is he?" Leung asked.

"A face from the past," she said quietly. "Someone who shouldn't be alive."

Leung poured another glass of wine as the Ghost continued down the video clips. He kept quiet as she opened another folder that contained sub-folders labeled with dates and locations. Bangkok. Lusaka. Manila. Phuket. Kowloon. Beijing. Toyko. Sao Paulo. Rio De Janeiro. Buenos Aires. London. Ireland. Berlin. New York. Los Angeles.

Leung questioned. "Is this why—"

"Alan, you will forget that you have seen any of this." The Ghost's fiery eyes pierced through Leung. "Understood?"

"Of course."

"I need Kone to fly to Lusaka."

"When we land, I will make the arrangements to refuel and bring in a new pilot."

In his world of global business, there were relationships that were kept off the grid, including a strategic one with the Triads who had made the introduction to the Brethren. He watched the Ghost methodically scroll through more folders and mentally categorized them. Triads. Russians. Afrikaans. Italians.

The amount of data was troubling for anyone in the underworld and especially for someone who was running for political office. Yes, he needed the Brethren's protection, but he could not risk being associated with the rest of their clientele. He felt the tension in the cabin rise when the Ghost stopped at a file labeled LAZARUS.

Fourteen hours later, the Gulfstream X banked sharply east as it descended over Victoria Harbor in Hong Kong, a place filled with a buzzing nightlife aboard cruise ships docked at Star Ferry. Tourists danced to the techno beat while sailors stumbled between nightclubs in the red-light district. American dollars exchanged for high-priced electronics at rock-bottom prices. There were even those who disappeared into dark alleys to be lost for a night in a web of brothels and massage parlors known to the locals as Wan Chai.

Leung gazed out the window at a neon-colored skyline surrounding a majestic symphony hall extending out into the bay. Sampans draped in bright white lights drifted in the still waters, a reminder of centuries past now forgotten by most of the seven million who lived within the borders of a city known to the rest of the world as the New York of Asia.

The Gulfstream neared a private landing strip at Kai Tak, once one of the most dangerous airports to land for a 747. Below, the plane passed high-rise apartments so closely one could see the clothes draped on bamboo poles sticking out of barred windows.

Five minutes later, the tires screeched against the tarmac, and they taxied toward a hangar at the far end of a secured area. The streets directly outside the fence were alive with double-decker buses swerving between red and silver taxies amidst the midnight madness of Kowloon.

Cabin lights switched on.

The Orient was a hot, humid, and sticky world. A place most Westerners hated at first, and perhaps that is why he loved the moment he stepped foot on its soil. Tonight, it seemed the distinct tropical climate embraced him in a unique way. A few seconds passed as he admired a stunning neon rainbow that glowed amidst the skyscrapers of Hong Kong Island. Each one signified proof of an exploding economy now under communist rule.

At the bottom of the steps, an immigration officer in a perfectly tailored uniform and shiny badge waited with an iPad in hand as they exited the aircraft. The Ghost stayed quiet as Leung handed over their passports.

"Welcome home, sir." The officer scanned the passports and pointed toward a black Mercedes with tinted windows. "Your car is waiting."

"*Mugoi*," Leung answered in Cantonese. Thanks.

The chauffeur grabbed their luggage and loaded it into the trunk while they slipped into the backseat.

With the chauffeur still outside, the Ghost turned to Leung. "The Triads most valued bounty is alive."

27

Two stories beneath an abandoned warehouse off east Fifth Street, in the heart of Skid Row, the black site was fully operational. A large room buzzed with activity as analysts and personnel from government agencies concentrated their efforts on finding a lead to the unidentified bomber. At one end of the room, a massive screen captured the hub of intelligence.

Most of the city was on lockdown, as the manhunt spread from the initial blast area. It was a decision Mayor Osoria opposed, but in a private phone call, President Palmer issued the order and there was no further discussion. All flights leaving and landing at LAX, Burbank, Van Nuys, and John Wayne were grounded as F-18s from Port Hueneme circled the city. Travelers were stranded indefinitely with all eyes glued to the latest news reports. Parents rushed to pick their children up from school as bumper-to-bumper traffic deadlocked the 110 to the 405 to the 101.

A dozen drones broadcasted live feeds across the city in search of the helicopter. A sketched rendering of the bomber was posted on the opposite side of the screen, as well as a blurred image of him entering the hospital. Both were placed next to faces that scrolled through facial recognition in search of a match across all government databases. Late forties, possibly early fifties. A partial dragon tattoo on the side of his neck. One screen played thumbnails of videos captured moments after the explosion from bystanders who posted to Vine, Twitter, Instagram, and Facebook. Intel flowed at a rapid pace, but it was like searching for a needle in a haystack without knowing if the needle was still there.

A glass door opened and in walked Brad Cunningham, Director of Ops for the Bureau's LA intelligence site. He sat on the edge of a titanium-framed conference table, set a folder on the glass, and then directed his attention to Kate. "I've read your briefing. I'm sure when the dust settles, there'll be a congressional hearing regarding today's events."

"POTUS will protect us, right?"

"Did you know he directed me to run interference while you secured the asset?" Cunningham nodded at the glass. "So, I need to know what makes Jake Harris so special?"

"Honestly, I don't know. I was only following orders."

"Kate, I can't help you if you don't tell me what's going on."

She leaned forward. "Any evidence of an IED?"

"Not yet, but we're fairly certain there were two blasts. One originated from the third floor, and the other was a county van parked at the entrance."

"It's my fault," Kate whispered from behind the fingers she clasped over her mouth. "I should've known one of the IEDs was underneath the gurney. It's the only way he could've slipped it past security. He didn't care who else died...which means he's not finished." Mitch never had a chance, with the bomb right outside his room. Any knowledge of what got his partner, Dexter, killed and his theories on how that tied into this case died with him.

"When innocent Americans are killed, it is an act of terrorism." Cunningham paced the room. "When they are killed on US soil, it is a declaration of war. Identifying our enemy is all that matters right now. We need to find him before he acts again."

"We need to move Jake's wife and daughter."

"I've already made the call—but, you need to tell me what you know."

"Brad, all I know is that POTUS ordered me to find him and keep him safe."

"A chopper is ready to take you to San Quentin. I'll keep an eye on him while you're gone."

"He goes with me."

"Kate, do you know who his father is?"

"A consultant for the government?"

Cunningham slid a folder across the desk, opened to the first page, and then stepped back. Kate leaned in and scanned the classified documents. At the top of the first page was a Presidential seal above a report outlining a covert operation – LAZARUS – run by a Level Ten operative for the Agency.

She asked, "Robert Langston?"

"Worked deep cover for twenty years—mostly in Asia. His legend was an American smuggler from Sudan. He infiltrated the Triads' smuggling operations based out of Hong Kong. In the mid-nineties, he was ordered to create a highly-classified, experimental operation that trained and inserted underage operatives in order to identify and neutralize key leaders within the Triad organization. He was also one of the few who knew of the Golden Triangle, a route used by the Triads throughout Asia and possibly other continents as well. You'll notice that not one word of this report has been redacted."

"You got this directly from POTUS?"

Cunningham nodded. "Which means this is far outside the boundaries of the Agency."

"Underage operatives?"

"Ranged from eight to fourteen."

"How is that possible?"

"Langston sold the operatives to the Triads and then tracked them. Details of the operation were kept hidden from Congress and the Senate. In fact, when the operation began in '97, Langston personally selected and trained the team."

Kate interrupted, "You mean children."

"By the time they were in the field, they were no longer innocent. Training consisted of extreme interrogations, sharpshooting skills, survival tactics, and hand-to-hand combat. It's all there. I suggest you read it."

"Langston had to report to someone."

"Straight to the Secretary of State, which at the time would've been POTUS himself."

"And the children? Who were they?"

"Langston is the only one who can answer that question. You'll find their legends in the report. No real identities."

"How did he recruit them?"

"That was never disclosed."

"Is the Program still operational?"

"Shut down and wiped from the history books after communication with the operatives was lost. You're looking at the only paper trail left. POTUS gave this to me for my eyes only. You can't tell a soul. It's a bloody stain on our government that would cause national and global outrage if it were to ever go public."

"Brad, our government sent children..."

"When the operation was scrubbed, Langston resigned and disappeared. No one knew he was still alive until a few days ago when Maldone told you Warren was going to be killed because he'd unlocked Pandora's box. Robert Langston's name was also on that list."

"Wait a minute. Warren was Langston?"

"No. But Warren knew Frank Harris."

"Harris and Langston are the same person." Kate paced the room. "That's why the President wanted me to protect Jake."

"His father served this country at the highest level, but the timing of his disappearance isn't a coincidence. Something bigger is at play. We've got nothing to go on, but my gut tells me Maldone knows more than he's telling us. You're the only one who can get the answers we need. I don't care how you do it. Get him to talk."

"I'll need leverage."

"We got a hit off the partial plate from the van. It belonged to one of Maldone's old businesses out of the Valley that we busted for trafficking after he was arrested. I know it's not much, but that's all we've got."

Kate flipped through the pages inside the folder as Cunningham watched. She tried to grasp the reality of children trained by the US government going into the underbelly of the Triads. She paused and stared blankly out the glass wall toward Jake who was sequestered in another room with two agents. She thought about hiding him for his safety, but there was no time. He was safer with her than with anyone else. There was a good chance he knew something about Robert Langston or the father he knew as Frank Harris.

For a moment, she was distracted by footage that played on the walled screen. The front of the hospital was gutted from the second floor to the roof. Red lights spiraled from dozens of fire trucks that cast an ominous glow. Paramedics lined the perimeter in hopes of finding more survivors. Search and Rescue climbed through the rubble and listened for any possible noise or voice. At the slightest sound, everyone stopped and waited eagerly in silence. It had been a slow and tedious process without many positive results.

Kate witnessed the carnage and was sure it would haunt her for a lifetime. Missing appendages. Screaming children with deep lacerations. Survivors who held victims as they cried for help. Many breathed their last breath whispering the names of loved ones. The number had grown to one hundred and eighty-six lost souls. Including Detective Mitch Lane. She hoped he never knew what hit him.

Cunningham checked his watch. "ETA fifteen minutes."

Kate turned her attention back to Cunningham. "He's not one of them, you know."

28

In the last twenty-four hours, I hadn't slept much. My ears still rang from the blast. After arriving at the black site, I showered and washed the dirt and debris from my body but not my mind. I changed into a fresh pair of jeans and T-shirt. The blast shook me to the core and unlocked even more flashes I couldn't clearly identify. Minutes passed in the glass room while those flashes looped in my mind.

Alone in a pitch-black room with my fingers wrapped around the grip of a weapon. A rush of adrenaline surged without fear or emotion—only peace. I sensed I wasn't alone, but I couldn't tell who else was there. The more I visualized it, the more it was real.

At the wash, I didn't hesitate to drive into the chaos. I followed Kate to the roof without a second thought. My instincts pushed me towards decisive action. That didn't mean I found some type of miraculous courage, but it was definitely out of character.

Kate handed me a windbreaker on the elevator ride from the command center. When the doors opened, I stepped out and walked across an empty warehouse. I stopped at the edge of the doorway and watched the rain pound against the pavement. As I stared at the empty parking lot my migraine pulsed. I needed sleep. And a drink.

"I made you a promise." Kate stepped out from the shadows. A glint from her eyes reflected a full moon. She had changed into jeans, a black top, boots, and a leather jacket. Her straight brown hair was no longer in a ponytail but draped across her back. "We've moved them to another location. If anything happens, I'll be the first to know."

Without taking my eyes off the rain, I asked, "Why am I here?"

"I'd be dead without you."

"I'm not part of this, Kate."

"We need to trust each other."

I turned to her. "Trust isn't an easy thing for me."

"It's the only way we'll get through this."

I crossed my arms. "What do you need to know?"

"Tell me about your father."

"Even though I lived under his roof and followed his rules, by the time I was sixteen I was already gone. Not much else to say really."

"What about your mother? Where is she?"

"I don't know." I paused for a moment. It had always been difficult to talk about a woman I'd never had a chance to love. I'd only spoken of her once in all the years Rachel and I were together. I said in barely a whisper, "I've never known."

"What do you remember about your childhood?"

I gave Kate a curious stare. "No memories. No photos. No relatives. Nothing. I think my earliest memory was the first day of high school. Before that, it's like I never existed. Why are you asking?"

"Your father never explained your memory loss?"

"It's what we argued about the most. He told me it was better left alone. You don't understand what it's like to not remember your past. I've tried to leave it behind—to forget about it—to create my own family and memories. Now that's gone too."

"I bounced around in foster care until I was eighteen." Kate stuffed her hands into her pockets. "Many of those years I've tried to forget too. Even though I've locked those memories away, there are times I see them clear as day. I guess some people block out the past because it's too painful. Jake, deep down we all want to know where we came from so we know who we're supposed to be in this world. Digging for memories can be a fork in the road." She turned her gaze out towards the rain.

"What aren't you telling me?"

"There's no easy way to say this, so I'm going to give it to you straight."

"What is it?"

"Your father worked undercover for the CIA. He trained special operatives in a highly-classified program. When the program was shut down, he disappeared from the Agency. You were sixteen when you both resurfaced in LA. During those missing years, you were both gone without a trace. No sign of where you were after the operation was shut down. Now he's gone again. We don't think that's a coincidence, considering his friendship with Warren. That's why we need to find him."

"I've called him a dozen times. Still no answer."

"Keep trying."

"You're saying he knows who killed Doc." The downpour intensified. While it didn't answer all my questions, it offered a glimpse into why my past had remained a secret. "Why didn't he tell me?"

"He's the only connection we have to what's happening," Kate said. "I'm convinced Detective Lane was targeted at the hospital because he was investigating the homicide. Everyone else was collateral damage. Your father may be the only one alive who can tell us what's going on. And if this is really over or just the beginning."

"Am I next?"

"There were security cameras on the property."

"I want to see it."

"I'm afraid the footage is missing."

"Now you're lying," I argued.

"It's a long story." Kate exhaled. "Jake, on the roof of the hospital the suspect nearly killed me to get your name." She paused. "I didn't tell him because I'm protecting you."

"Anything else I need to know?"

"That's it."

A white light approached in the sky before the thumping of its blades grew loud enough to drown out any chance of continuing the conversation.

Once the helicopter landed, we ducked and moved quickly onboard. We each grabbed a pair of headphones and buckled in. Within seconds, we were airborne headed north over the skyscrapers of downtown.

As we flew along the coast, I stared out at a full moon that sparkled off the dark waters below. Slowly the weight of what Kate had said sunk in. Frank wasn't a consultant for the government. He was an undercover operative for the CIA. I didn't know how to wrap my head around that one.

Ninety minutes later we landed outside the gates of San Quentin.

29

Four hundred and thirty-two acres of desirable waterfront real estate, large enough to have its own zip code, overlooked the north side of the San Francisco Bay.

With a 130 percent occupancy rate, San Quentin was maximum security where the guilty lingered within barbwire fences that surrounded the yard. Whites. Blacks. Mexicans. Asians. Survival rested on keeping with your own kind.

Uniformed guards watched over the population, including seven hundred inmates in the Condemned Unit. Head shots of each inmate were posted on a wall in each block. The ones incarcerated on death row, condemned to die for the sins they inflicted on the innocent. Their only form of grace was a lethal injection instead of the gas chamber.

In socks and rubber slippers, DCDR #722 shuffled down the corridors in an orange jumpsuit as the ankle chains dragged along the concrete. His seventy-three-year-old frail frame was strong at one time, but the cancer in his bones had spread aggressively in recent months. His sunken eyes, wildly thick hair, and scraggly beard covered deep grooves in his face. He was a far cry from the charges on his rap sheet, but he was still dangerous enough to require three guards instead of one. He followed the guards into a stark, white walled room where he was led into a steel cage large enough to turn and stand in one spot. He eyed the floor as the guards stepped off to one side.

Kate watched through the vertical glass as the caged door locked. Then she entered and motioned for the guards to leave. She stood only a few feet away from Angelo Maldone and never flinched.

"It's good to see you, Kate."

Maldone's raspy voice disgusted her.

"I need a name," she replied.

"That's my girl, always on the hunt. Tenacious. Dedicated. Persistent. Qualities I've always admired about you. I heard you took some time off since we've seen each other last. I must say, you're looking well rested and as beautiful as ever."

"Who's behind the bombing?"

"I warned you there would be trouble," Maldone hissed. "Now we have all paid the price. The loss of life is a terrible thing. Unavoidable in the end, I suppose."

"We have evidence that connects Warren and the bombing to you." Kate bluffed, unsure whether Maldone would bite. "Not to mention you're the one who told us he was in danger."

"The doc says I've got less than six months. I'm looking forward to the other side. Time is a cruel mistress. Please tell me you have something more than a burnt up van and a list of names I don't remember."

"We have a witness."

"Kate, there's so much I wish I could tell you, but I'm afraid you've already been left behind."

"I need to know who's next—and how to stop it from happening."

"We were born into the chaos, pawns in a game more complicated than either of us can comprehend. Whatever you think you have, you're not even close. Cain and Abel. Saul and David. Genesis through Revelation is filled with great battles between extraordinary adversaries. If you believe the Good Book to be true then you already know we are not heroes or villains in this war. We're simply the pages in between."

Kate pointed to the ink on the top of his hand. "Let's start there."

Maldone locked eyes with her. A smirk pursed his lips as his eyes narrowed. "My memory is cloudy these days. Must be the drugs. Being locked away in a cage tends to make me act my age. If only I were a few years younger, perhaps the two of us would go on this adventure together."

She pulled out her cell and pointed the screen toward Maldone, close enough for him to see a partial drawing of the dragon tattoo. Then she snapped a photo of his hand.

"You're not the only one with one of these."

"You win the prize." Maldone chuckled. He leaned in until his face pressed against the bars. "Kate, you are in so deep you don't even know you're drowning."

"Anderson received a call from a burner shortly before destroying evidence. I bet if I dig deep enough, I'll find that the two of you crossed paths. Right now, guards are turning your cell upside down."

"What a shame when one of LA's finest is taken from his family in the line of duty. Anderson was not one of mine—or maybe he was—none of that really matters now. You failed me, Kate, when I needed you most."

"I'm done playing games." She turned towards the door. "You're wasting my time."

"Then start asking the right questions," Maldone seethed.

She stopped. She was leading him where she wanted him to go. He had always been in control, but tonight it seemed he was on edge. She turned. "I'm here to cut a deal. What will it take for you to talk?"

"There was a time when I dreamed of spending my last days with Theresa, with my feet in the ocean, sipping fresh Brazilian coffee as a cool breeze brushed against my face beneath the clear blue skies."

"I can make that happen."

"Remember the trial? When you took the stand and promised to tell the whole truth? I can tell when you're lying. You haven't only disappointed me, Kate, you've failed Theresa."

"You'll go to the grave and burn for your sins."

"Believe me, I'm not the only one who will bear that cross."

She stepped in closer and lowered her voice. "I can get you out of here within twenty-four hours if you tell me what you know. Don't you want to see her again?"

"More than anything," Maldone whispered. "You think I'm safer out there than in here?"

"Once I walk out the door, the deal's off."

"All that is left for me to do is say a prayer, and all my sins will be forgiven. Isn't that how it works?"

"Someone on the inside told you about Warren," Kate suggested. "You made up the other names as part of your twisted game."

"You stupid girl." Maldone clenched his fists. "Always willing to say or do anything to get what you want no matter the cost. Tonight, something of value was taken from me. What you need to ask yourself, is what do you value that will be taken from you? You failed us both. Now it's your turn to face the dragon lurking in the mountains."

"You're a washed-up hit man with nothing left but cancer eating at your soul."

"Aren't you going to ask me about Robert Langston?"

For a moment, Kate gazed at the floor. She looked up with a steel jaw. "What about him?"

"I want five minutes with his boy in exchange for a name." Maldone grabbed the bars, his smirk tightened. "You won't find who you're looking for in any of your databases or on Interpol. And you won't find who he's working for or what they're after. We both know this isn't over. We need each other one last time, Kate."

"Five minutes."

"Neco Rimoldi, my protégé."

"I need more than that."

"I'm halfway in the ground." Maldone's smirk turned to a scowl. "Now send him in."

30

The helicopter hovered above the glowing red lights of the Roosevelt Hotel in the heart of Hollywood. On the rooftop, Kate barked orders as she handed me an earpiece and headed straight for the stairwell.

"Confirmed. Room 330."

I heard Cunningham's voice in my ear speaking to Kate. "Third floor hallway is empty. Confirmed one individual in the room. Standby."

We reached the third floor and were joined by six Navy Seal types dressed in full tactical gear.

"No one goes in until I give the order." Kate turned to me. "You're sure that's the number?"

"He said this is where we'd find Rimoldi." I wiped beads of sweat from my forehead. Maldone had better be right about this. "Room 330."

Cunningham's voice cut back in. "Maldone was found dead in his cell. Looks like he hung himself with a bed sheet. No cell phone was found. Proceed with caution."

Kate muted her mic, pulled me aside, and whispered. "Turn off your phone."

I did exactly as she asked. She unmuted her mic. "Okay, I'm ready."

"I'm going with you," I insisted.

"No way."

"Kate, he stays back," Cunningham ordered.

I lowered my voice. "I'm trusting you. Now you need to trust me."

"Fine," Kate answered. "No matter what happens, you stay behind me."

The elevators dinged as we approached. Kate reached for her .45 but kept it holstered while the door opened. A group of twenty-somethings laughed loudly as they stumbled out into the hall. They never noticed anything out of the ordinary. After several attempts, they found the right key to the right room and disappeared for a night none of them would remember in the morning.

"We've tapped into the hotel's security feed," Cunningham said. "If he moves we'll know."

"Copy." Kate motioned for me to move as she approached the door. Behind us, the tactical unit secured the hallway. "We're right outside the door."

I slipped the keycard into the slot, waited for a blinking green light, and then opened the door. Kate entered first. I followed a few steps behind. An ominous glow cast distorted palm-tree-shaped shadows against the sheer curtains. A few more seconds and my eyes adjusted well enough to see the outline of someone sitting on the edge of a bed facing the balcony.

"Federal Agent," Kate said sternly. "Don't move."

A woman sobbed. "Help me, please."

Kate checked the bathroom. "Are you alone?"

"Yes."

Kate glanced over her shoulder as I held the door open. "What's your name?"

"Maggie."

"I'm going to turn on the lights, but I don't want you to move."

"Okay." The woman's voice shook.

I stayed by the door as Kate flipped a switch and the lights blinked on. She holstered her weapon and watched the woman wipe tears from her cheeks. Early fifties. African American. On the table next to the bed was leftover room service.

"Stand down," Kate said into her mic. "It's not Rimoldi."

Cunningham's voice rang in my ears, "Who is it?"

"Warren's housekeeper. Brad, give me a few minutes."

"Copy."

Kate removed her in-ear and switched off the receiver. She motioned for me to do the same and to close the door. She sat on the edge of the bed across from Margaret Johnson.

"Maggie, my name is Kate. I'm a Federal agent. You spoke with Detective Lane yesterday morning, didn't you?"

"Yes, I was nearly out the door when he called. After I hung up, I drove here. I saw what happened at the hospital…"

"Were you supposed to meet someone here?"

"I followed Frank's instructions."

"Frank Harris?"

Tears rolled down Maggie's cheeks. She wiped her face with her sleeve and answered, "I worked for Doc and Frank."

"You told Detective Lane you were Mr. Warren's housekeeper."

"That's just what they told me to say if anyone asked. I did research for them."

"What kind of research?"

I was still reeling from hearing Frank's name. Maggie looked frail, nearly broken, not what I would've expected from a CIA operative. But she never said she was, did she? What kind of research? How much of what I had taken from Doc's was from the CIA and classified? How much of what I had burned was what we needed to put the pieces together? What had Doc and Frank done that caused so much chaos and pain?

Kate shared my stunned expression. She turned her attention back to Maggie. "I'm here to help. Now, has Frank Harris contacted you?"

"I called and texted, but there's been no response. I wasn't sure what else to do."

"What were you supposed to do when you checked in here?"

"I don't know. Honestly, I never thought this was possible. I'm the only one left who knows they exist."

"Who?"

She looked past Kate directly at me.

I stood there like a statue, unable to move from the thoughts swirling in my head.

Kate reached out and gently placed a hand on her leg. "Maggie, you need to tell me what you know."

"I'll need to see the files."

31

Maggie sipped a cup of hot tea with her eyes fixed on the photos and papers taped to the French doors at Frank's house. It was past midnight and we were running on fumes, but sleep was not in the cards. The perimeter of the compound was heavily guarded with sharpshooters perched on the roof and hiding in the bushes. I'd never seen anything like it, except during one visit to Pennsylvania Avenue in Washington DC.

"Maggie, do you know what all this means?" Kate sat across from her.

"Doc called it the genesis."

"That's exactly what he told me." I shot a quick look at Kate to say I told you so, even though I still didn't know what we were looking at.

I picked up one of the pages. The mystery seemed to start with Sister Evelyn's disappearance. "Who are James and Alice Adler?"

"Doc's grandparents." Maggie set her cup down and got to her feet. "When Doc was born in '49, his parents legally changed their name from Adler to Warren."

She paced back and forth for a minute before getting on her knees and shuffling through a pile I hadn't yet posted on the French doors. We waited patiently, unsure of what she was searching for, but it was clear she had seen the piles before. She looked up when she found it and handed me a black and white photo of a man dressed in a dark suit holding a Tommy gun. Draped on his side was a woman in a silk dress with a long slit up her leg. I stared at the photo for a few seconds and passed it along to Kate.

"James Adler was a low-level mobster in the late 1920s—nothing to write about in the history books. He was a bottom feeder for Mickey Cohen. He did what he was told and that kept food on the table. He delivered booze to one place, picked up cash from another. It was a different time back then. You did whatever you had to do to survive. The whole country was on the verge of the Depression. Corruption was everywhere. The Mob, the Klan, and City Hall fought over who controlled the city. Well, James wanted more than survival, he wanted to be somebody. So he looked for any opportunity to climb the ranks. When he was given his chance, he forced Alice to help him."

Maggie grabbed another black and white from the collage I'd taped to the glass. It was a photo of Santa Monica beach where thousands lined the shore.

"When Sister Evelyn disappeared, the city was in turmoil. Some believed she was drawn up into the clouds like Elijah. Others were convinced she was with Arthur Elliott in Santa Barbara. The preachers despised her flashy religion because she spoke with such conviction and charisma from the pulpit. They despised how she allowed pregnant teenagers to stay with her in the parsonage until they had given birth and were back on their feet.

"Bel-Air was a place filled with high-society socialites, and the sight of young girls flooding into Sister Evelyn's home was one that was not welcomed by the community. Her faith made her dangerous, not only to the religious but to others as well. Death threats were common. Several attempted kidnappings failed. She stood in the line of fire whenever she took to the airwaves and called out Cohen and his men. She needed to be silenced."

I tapped the photo. "Are you saying James and Alice are the ones who kidnapped her?"

"She was at the beach that day when James approached her on the boardwalk. He asked if she would pray for his sick wife. Sister Evelyn followed him to the car, and that's when he forced her inside. Alice was there waiting to tie her up and blindfold her. For several days, she was kept at their house just outside of downtown. James waited for orders. He thought Cohen was going to extort money from the church and send a message to back off. Then he would get the notch of respect he wanted. Neither of them realized they had hammered nails in their own coffins."

Maggie eyed the ransom letter and then the other typed letters written by supposed eyewitnesses. She ripped each one from the glass and tossed them onto the floor until the only one left was from Caffey Hastings.

"James was told to drive to the Arizona border and call for instructions. He did what they said, and when he called he was given directions to the shack. There were dozens of sightings, ransom notes, the Santa Barbara Cottage registration, but Caffey Hastings was the only person who saw them. No one believed his story."

I eyed the Caffey Hastings' letter. "Maggie, what happened at the shack?"

"Sister Evelyn was locked inside. James checked on her every other day and brought food and water. Alice refused to go. You see, when they were at the house Alice listened to Sister Evelyn share about her faith. That caused a rift between the two newlyweds. Alice wanted to let her go, but James convinced her it would be over soon."

I leaned forward and grabbed a slice of pepperoni pizza, mainly out of nervousness. I was exhausted, on the verge of collapsing, but I hadn't put on twenty pounds by eating salads. I needed more calories to stay awake. I offered the last piece. Both waived me off.

Kate put down the photos she had been scanning. "How did she escape?"

Maggie pointed to a photo on the glass. A square, clay structure sat back against a hill with a single, glassless window frame on the front. The top of the roof was flat and seemed to be built of wood, though it was hard to tell. Maggie's hand touched the photo gently.

"James and Alice argued the night before. When he arrived the next morning, he left his gun in the car, unsure of whether he had the stones to do it. He was distracted, and that's when Sister Evelyn seized her opportunity. She escaped into the desert. James was left with a gash in his skull and a bounty on his head."

"He picked Alice up from a motel in Tucson and headed east. He knew once Cohen heard he'd failed, they'd both be dead. When they reached Dallas, they started over and raised a family away from their past. Many years later after Alice had died, James was on his deathbed and confessed the whole story to Doc, who was leaving for law school at UCLA. Doc never spoke of it to his parents—or anyone else—until he told Frank and me."

I waited to see Kate's reaction. Doc had piqued my interest in the story, but hearing it from Maggie's lips left me speechless. She methodically scanned the photos for the next beat.

"When sister Evelyn returned to Union Station, there were thousands of people to greet her, including the DA, David Strong." Maggie pointed to the first headshot and continued. "In a matter of days, she was charged with corruption of public morals, obstruction of justice, and conspiracy to manufacture evidence. Her attorney, Finn Bleeker, begged her not to repeat her version of the kidnapping under oath. The prosecution's star witness was Madison Sawyer, who said she had seen Sister Evelyn with Elliott, even though the police found tracks more than eight miles from Agua Prieta where the farmer testified he had first seen her.

"Strong pursued Sister Evelyn with a vengeance. She stood her ground under questioning, and in the press, declared the trial to be her own crucifixion. When Madison Sawyer took the stand, the defense revealed that she was a former inmate of an insane asylum in Oregon. The judge declared her confession to be fraud. Strong had no choice but to drop all charges because his star witness was unreliable.

"Sister Evelyn was vindicated to the world. Some believed Howard Hughes played a role with a late night call to the judge, but in all my research, I've never seen anything to corroborate that theory. When it was over, Sister Evelyn was on the verge of a nervous breakdown. But she pushed forward in her mission and grew more dangerous than before. To someone like Mickey Cohen, the power of her faith was disruptive to the West Coast mob's operations and plans to build in Vegas. To many, this one event became her legacy. I think that perhaps more than anything, she longed to return to the days when she was a missionary in Hong Kong, with her first love, Nathan."

Maggie's body tensed as she returned to the same row of headshots, only this time, she emphatically pointed down the line. "David Strong, sentenced to San Quentin. Judge Carl Hyde, impeached. Finn Bleeker, found dead inside a car in a ditch. Thomas Welch, the go-between during the ransom demands, found dead of an apparent suicide. Arthur Elliott's wife suddenly left the country, never to be heard from again. Sister Evelyn died from an overdose. Elliott never made another film after her death and was considered a recluse until his own death."

She spun around and faced us, her eyes now fiery. "Doc and Frank hunted those who protect the underworld, an organization first created to silence Sister Evelyn, and one that has existed for nearly a century. This organization executed Doc's parents shortly after the announcement he would be the newly appointed DA. He found them in the kitchen with a note on the counter that read: "THE WAGES OF SIN IS DEATH.""

Maggie stepped away, visibly shaken, and slumped into a leather chair. Her words hung in the air. She glanced between us. "You think I'm crazy."

"What was in the safe?" Kate pressed forward.

Maggie had spun quite a tale, but she didn't look crazy. Conspiracy theorists would've been in a feeding frenzy with every word. The unknown, uncovered, and unproven were rooted in Sister Evelyn's story that linked directly to Doc's family lineage. I thought of what he had said from the beginning—the truth depended on who was telling the story. Could Maggie be trusted? If a secret society existed as protectors of darkness, was she our only link? Were they the ones behind Doc's murder?

"Identities. Locations. Lists of people they protected. Anything we found was backed up onto a hard drive to be documented and stored. It took us years to narrow down a list of names, including one we called the Ghost."

"The Ghost?" I asked.

"Frank believed this was a name passed down through the generations to the one who ruled over twelve assassins known as the Brethren. Six months ago, he intercepted intelligence that led him on a hunt throughout Asia. Doc and I compiled everything he found and tried to make sense of it all. It's been like fitting pieces of a puzzle together. You begin in one corner and then find yourself lost somewhere in the middle. A week ago, we met Frank at the Roosevelt. He had eyes on one of the twelve: Damas Kone."

"Where?" Kate sat up.

"He was caught on security cameras at Lusaka International Airport in Zambia."

"Maggie, does the name Neco Rimoldi mean anything to you?"

"I don't know that name."

"Have you ever been here before, in this house?"

"Never."

"Ever meet anyone associated with Frank, other than Doc?"

Maggie eyed me closely. "Not until tonight."

I stood and faced the mantle. "You know who I am?"

"The eyes are a dead giveaway."

Kate leaned forward. "When did you first meet Frank?"

"Nine or ten years ago." Maggie kept her eyes on me. "At first I didn't believe Doc's story, but I would do anything for the man. We were very close." Her eyes moistened as she fought to compose herself. "Doc introduced me to Frank at the Roosevelt. Room 330. That's the first time I heard the story about Doc's grandparents."

"Did you know Frank was ex-CIA?"

"I knew he worked for the government." Maggie pointed to the TOP SECRET files. "That's why he agreed to help Doc." She picked up the stack and thumbed through them slowly. She paused, grabbed one from the middle, and handed it to Kate. "This is the only one I was ever allowed to see."

Kate set it on the coffee table. I approached and stood over her shoulder. Inside, were photos of an alley where a body was crumpled on the pavement next to a dumpster. There were several more close ups of an Asian woman, long black hair, early thirties, her ivory skin decomposed.

"The photos are identical," Kate said.

Maggie pointed to one. "That's Frank there in the crowd."

I craned my neck for a closer look before Kate flipped the photo over. A few more pages revealed a toxicology report. She read it aloud: "Methamphetamines were found in the victim's system. Cause of death was ruled a single GSW to the back of the skull."

"Her name was Abigail," Maggie said softly. "Abigail Chang."

Kate flipped to another page. On the back was stapled a single photo. I stood frozen with fear as Maggie and Kate turned their attention towards me. I stepped back, my legs grew weak, as I awkwardly stood on center stage. A familiar feeling washed over me. There was something Maggie needed to say, and I was afraid her words would pierce me deeply.

32

Forty-eight hours after the bombing, Mayor Osoria lifted the citywide lockdown. Planes were airborne, school buses flashed red lights at the curb, Angelenos texted while slowly rolling over the Sepulveda Pass, and the purple and gold once again illuminated at Staples for that night's game.

Kate and Brad, along with a team of others, questioned Maggie for two days at the black site. Between sessions, Kate found herself glued to the TV as reporters stood amidst the candlelight memorials engulfed by hundreds of onlookers who gathered in Montrose.

At first, the aerial shots of the hospital were hard to digest. Soon they turned into graphic bumpers between many of the victims' stories that left a nation in mourning. A lump lodged in her throat as she listened to family members share about those they loved and lost.

Kate contemplated Mitch's funeral the following week. She cursed under her breath as politicians from one side echoed the President's condolences, while the other side was quick to voice outrage at the administration's lack of preparedness.

Protecting freedom has nothing to do with politics.

In a few months, the debris would be hauled away, stories would fade, and families would return to a new normal. President Palmer would go before the nation during primetime and reassure the American people that this was an isolated incident. He'd end his message with a rallying cry to rebuild stronger than before. Rebuilding was one way to move on—one way to divert responsibility—but it was never a way to forget.

Kate gripped the steering wheel of the Denali as she headed up the coast dressed in a freshly pressed pantsuit and white blouse, her hair pulled back in a ponytail. Her body was as bruised as her ego. Two cracked ribs and a dislocated shoulder that still ached from being popped back in its socket. She failed to stop what Maldone predicted, and that hadn't settled well. He had given her a name, but so far Neco Rimoldi was a dead end.

Morning traffic opened up once she passed Ventura.

When they finished questioning Maggie, no one knew what to believe, or how much of it was true. The woman wove quite a tale, one that Kate admitted to Brad was impossible to corroborate. A search in the FBI, CIA, and Homeland Security databases found no search results for Neco Rimoldi, or anything remotely connected to the Brethren. Brad denied any further knowledge of the operation Robert Langston/Frank Harris led off the books. She needed to read the file again to see if she'd missed anything. That would have to wait. She'd been called to a one-on-one.

Maldone took the coward's way out.

What bothered her more than that was she believed him. She didn't have a clue what was really happening. Rimoldi was in her house, which meant, he should've been there to tie up loose ends. The fact that she was still breathing led her to believe he was searching for something—something more than the video footage on the thumb drive. She feared that *something* was Jake. She should've been more careful. She should've moved quicker. Maybe she could've ended it right there in her backyard. Her anger boiled over when the team swept through her house to ensure the place was clean. None of it brought peace of mind. Her decision was made. The house was going on the market as soon as this was over.

Maggie's story was intriguing, a made for Hollywood blockbuster. In many ways, it wasn't believable, or factual, without the hard drive she claimed was in Warren's safe. A retired DA and his female companion stumble upon a global hit squad birthed out of a fight between an evangelist and a mobster a century ago, and then they partner up with an ex-CIA operative whose last assignment with the Agency was training child operatives. Saying it out loud sounded insane. If the Brethren existed, there would've been a blip of its existence on the intelligence radar, but there wasn't a single shred of evidence.

No one keeps a secret for a hundred years.

In every case, there are rabbit holes. Who was behind the death of Warren's parents and the note left at the crime scene? Did Maldone know Warren had compiled intelligence on the Brethren? Was Maldone connected to the Brethren? If so, why warn the Bureau? If it wasn't Maldone behind the hit and the bombing, then who was it that Rimoldi worked for? Who was Damas Kone? Where was Frank Harris/Robert Langston, or whoever the hell he really was? While these questions swirled, the most troubling one was how did Maldone know Jake was Frank's son?

Kate glanced at the cold case file and the photo of Abigail Chang with her arm around a young American boy. Jane Doe, who was found dead in an alley off Sunset, finally had a name. And the similarities between the boy and Jake were undeniable.

Maggie was right. The eyes are a dead giveaway.

Maybe Abigail was a trafficking victim, which would make Jake one too. That lined up with what she'd read in the file, and might explain how Maldone knew him. But that didn't answer why Warren was killed so many years later, or what connection Mitch said he'd found in the cold case. She stared at a younger Robert Langston/Frank Harris in the background and then at the TOP SECRET files in the passenger seat. She turned her attention back to the road as her cell chimed.

Brad's voice cut through the sound system. "You nearly there?"

"Pretty close."

"Risk assessment determined another attack to be unlikely, so we'll downgrade the threat at the press conference this afternoon."

"We're not dealing with another Kennedy conspiracy?" Kate felt a bit delirious and needed to lighten the mood.

"We're not planning on firing missiles into Cuba, if that's what you're asking. CIA is pushing to step in, so we'll hand over what we've got over the next forty-eight hours."

"What about Rimoldi?"

"Still nothing. If he's for real, it's possible he's already out of the country. We'll keep working through back channels and see what we can dig up."

"Any of our sources know about the Brethren?"

"If they do, they're not breathing a word."

"Maybe the President can shed some light."

"Remember, you've never seen that file."

"Have I ever shared any of our secrets?" Kate joked. After an awkward silence she asked, "What about Maggie?"

"She passed all the psych evals, so she's definitely not insane. I haven't ruled out delusional though. I've talked with the other agencies, and they've got zero that corroborates her story. If you ask me, I think she had a soft spot for Warren so she believed him. It wouldn't be the first time blind love caused someone to step out of reality."

"Anything on Frank Harris?"

"Nothing. He's our wild card."

"How do you explain the photo?"

"I can't. But that doesn't mean we're chasing a global assassin squad either."

"Did you offer Maggie protection?"

"In return for a signed confidentiality agreement regarding what she claims to know about the Brethren. We needed to keep her story from going public, and we needed to keep those files from going viral. So, she signed the agreement but refused witness protection."

"She'll take it to the grave. If she was going to leak it to the press it would've happened already. I still can't believe what's in those files. POTUS has some explaining to do." A few seconds of silence followed. "Brad?"

"I'm still here. Kate, you need to remember that he's the Commander in Chief."

"How could someone make that kind of a decision without oversight?"

"We both know that happens all the time. Look, I agree with you, I don't like what's in those files either. But our task is to contain the situation we're dealing with now and hunt down those responsible. I need to know that your head's straight."

"You know me better than anyone. I'm not stopping until this is over."

"Okay, then call me afterward so we can figure out our next move."

"Fine."

The line went dead. Kate caught a brief glimpse of the Pacific before exiting on South Salinas Street opposite the Adree Clark Bird Refuge. She cut down Old Coast Highway, rounded the Montecito Country Club, and continued up the hill.

About a mile out, she recognized the unmarked car that followed her and the Suburbans parked every hundred yards. By the time she approached the front gate, Secret Service was there waiting for her arrival. After a quick inspection of the vehicle and thumbprint confirmation, she entered the property and drove up a long, windy road toward the main house.

Kate checked the buttons on her blouse in the Denali's side mirror, and then fixed a few strands of hair that strayed to one side. She slipped a weathered saddlebag over her shoulder and tugged down on her coat. It was still awkward to be back, especially after the Maldone case. The hunt for Maldone brought her and Brad closer, but the aftermath complicated things.

When Maldone was captured, she stood proudly in the background amidst other law enforcement agencies as Brad made the announcement to the world. When the cameras and lights were gone, they hit the town and celebrated. It wasn't a date—or maybe it was—that part was still unclear. Besides, he was ten years her senior and rumored to be recently separated from his wife of fifteen years. Something neither of them had talked about.

Brad was a highly decorated agent who leveraged the family name to climb the ranks. He trained her at Quantico, mentored her in DC, and then assigned her to the biggest case of her young career. For Brad, running the LA Black Ops site was a steppingstone. Brad was an optimist who believed he had more to offer than hunting down the FBI's Top Ten Most Wanted.

She knew it was only a matter of time before he jumped into the political arena and left covert operations behind. All he needed was an opportunity.

A Secret Service agent met Kate halfway between the parked Denali and the front door of a single-story, Spanish-style house with its curved archways and textured walls. She followed the agent into a large living room where they crossed the terracotta tiles out to a brick patio overlooking a marine layer that hung thick over the Pacific.

"The President will be with you shortly," the agent said. Kate nodded and expected him to leave. Instead, he stood guard next to the glass doors.

Her mind was preoccupied with a night she wished to forget. A little too much wine. A dimly lit restaurant. Finally exhaling from years on the chase. She let down her guard, and like a parishioner locked inside a confessional, exposed her darkest secrets. She rambled on about the men she desperately tried to escape and the family she'd never known. Things grew fuzzy when they left the restaurant and climbed into a cab. The next morning she woke, naked under the covers, with no idea how she got there. Alone in the room, she tried calling Brad's cell but there was no answer. Another thing they'd avoided speaking about.

Kate kept her eyes on the agent and texted Jake: **CALL ME. IT'S IMPORTANT.**

The last few days, she had tried countless times to call him without an answer. She couldn't shake the sight of Jake standing in Frank's living room as the documents were boxed and hauled away. Brad denied her request to bring Jake back to the black site. That pissed her off. She owed Jake that much. Instead, he stood there like a lost child. He saved her life, and she left him behind.

President Palmer stepped across the threshold dressed in plaid shorts, a canary yellow polo, and a Goorin Bros flat cap taller and thinner than he seemed on TV. Welcoming her with a firm handshake, he caught her with those piercing eyes that turned shades of blue and a reassuring smile that won the first election. He was, without a doubt, the most powerful man in the free world.

It was easy to be disarmed by his charm. Within a matter of seconds, he made you feel like you'd been best friends for years. Combined with his message to lower taxes, offer mortgage relief, return jobs to US soil, and to negotiate an economic deal with China to ensure the US recovery he won in a landslide against a less charismatic opponent.

In his first term, the American people loved him. Now the climate had changed. Congress launched a public battle against him over immigration reform and slammed the gavel denying an overhaul of Social Security. The housing market plateaued, leaving millions of citizens underwater in mortgages they couldn't afford. A bailout of Detroit turned the Motor City into a ghost town. Millions survived on food stamps, Medicare, and other government subsidies from agencies that were millions over budget. The war against ISIS was fought with a strategy that shifted weekly. And another trillion had been added to the national debt.

With all of his charisma, President Palmer had turned from an optimistic candidate to an embattled politician desperate for a victory to secure his legacy. His run for reelection was a dogfight against a steady decline in approval ratings and an opponent willing to dig deep into the coffers.

President Palmer motioned for them to sit around a small table beneath a bright red umbrella. "Kate, thanks for driving up. You've had quite a week."

"It's an honor to be here, Mr. President."

"We've got a name?"

"Neco Rimoldi. Nothing on him in any of our databases or Interpol though."

"You're sure Maldone told the truth?"

"I'm not sure about that, sir. Candidly, it's our only lead."

"Is Ms Johnson's story credible?" Palmer waved his detail inside. "I mean, a conspiracy theory about an evangelist from the 1920s and a global hit squad. It sounds a bit far-fetched, don't you think?"

"I'm not sure what to think." Kate shifted in her chair. President Palmer's eyes remained locked on her. "Mr. President, why did you order me to protect Jake Harris?" With everything happening in the world, why was it so important to protect a man with no connection to the government, terrorist organization, or organized crime?

He leaned back and nodded slowly, as if deciding how to respond. "Kate, if men were angels, no government would be necessary." He paused for a moment. "James Madison understood the high-wire act of protecting our freedom. History decides whether my predecessors or I will spend eternity in heaven or hell. But I can assure you that right now evil is on our doorstep. The American people expect a response, and I believe Jake Harris is the one who will deliver it for us. So, what I'm about to tell you must be kept off the record."

"I understand, sir."

33

I groaned beneath the blanket before poking my head out from the covers. A ray of light streaked across the wood floor. I shielded my eyes and fumbled for my cell, which was buried under a pillow. Ten missed calls. One text. I listened to my voicemail. One thing I'd have to take care of, one way or another.

I tossed the cell on the sofa, disappointed that Rachel hadn't reached out to see if I was alive. She must've known by now that I was in over my head. Maybe Kate and the Feds had kept it from her.

I gripped the edge of a sofa with both hands and shook off the same dream I'd had the last few nights. I counted beer bottles lined up on the riveted airplane winged coffee table. I'd wandered the house, showered, and raided the Viking until the shelves were bare. I searched every room of the house, including the study. Nothing.

I waited for the news to announce an arrest. I spent even more hours glued to impromptu memorials. The stories of loved ones lost chilled me to the bone. I was there, but I couldn't tell a soul. I was part of the story, but now I was erased. Whatever Kate wanted to say, I didn't want to hear it. I was a fool to trust her. I didn't even know the woman.

The irritation in my ankle annoyed me as I itched my beard. I grimaced at the shooting pain and hobbled to the bathroom. It seemed heartless to dismiss the tragic events. It seemed impossible to pretend it never happened. Selfishly, I needed to figure out what I was going to do with the rest of my life. I couldn't stay cooped up here forever. It was pointless to think I could help find Doc's killer. And finding Frank wasn't in the plans. Part of me was relieved I'd been shut out.

But then there was that photo. Maggie had opened the door to my past. It was wishful thinking to believe I could forget about it.

Whatever Doc saw in me—whatever he meant to tell me—couldn't stop Neco Rimoldi from destroying innocent lives. Detective Lane was wrong, there was nothing I had to offer that would bring the answers the world needed. Whatever Kate wanted from me was irrelevant. I wasn't a warrior, and this wasn't my fight.

A hot shower eased my hangover but left me off balanced. I got dressed and grabbed the last beer from the fridge on my way to the garage. I needed a less conspicuous vehicle for this jaunt. I downed the beer and took a moment to make a choice. My truck was recognizable, and the others were too flashy. Deciding on which car to drive seemed to be far too difficult of a decision with the tempting horsepower that stared back at me.

Thirty minutes later, I parked the Range Rover across the street near a Shell station in Sunland. I watched the movers load my sofa, coffee table, nightstands, mattresses, microwave, and boxes into an unmarked white truck. Several cars behind sat a black SUV, which I assumed were the Feds. It was a long shot to think I'd get a glimpse of Rachel and Samantha. I missed them both more than I ever thought possible.

I knew Rachel was pissed, especially after having her life turned upside down. By now, the ink on the divorce papers was dry. Without Rachel's trust, it would be impossible to find common ground. I was Samantha's father, and that would never change. I convinced myself that none of this was my choice. I needed to know they were okay, and that they understood how much I still loved them. I feared that conversation might never happen.

Tap. Tap. Tap.

I jumped at the sight of a butch-cut, muscular-but-lean man who stood a few feet from the driver's side. He waited for me to roll the window down.

"Mr. Harris, you'll need to leave the area."

"I'm parked on a public street," I said defensively. "I'm not doing anything illegal."

"Following orders."

"I want to speak to Agent McNaughton."

"Mr. Harris, we're here at your wife's request."

"I want to talk to her." Blood heated my cheeks.

"She asked for you to leave."

I rolled the window up and cursed at the agent. I turned the ignition and wondered if that's why Kate called. I pulled away from the curb, blood boiling inside, and took one last look at the apartment. I wasn't ready to say goodbye. I circled onto the 210, the same freeway I'd barreled down a few nights earlier with Detective Lane bleeding to death in the backseat. I nearly missed the Lake Avenue exit as I cut across three lanes of traffic. Tires screeched and horns blared. At the red light, I avoided the glare from a woman in a Honda cursing me at the top of her lungs.

The office building was three blocks south. I pulled into the parking lot and found the first vacant spot. I entered the building, not knowing for sure if I was doing the right thing. I rode the elevator to the ninth floor. My stomach tightened as the elevator doors opened, and I headed down an empty hallway towards suite 908. For a moment, I paused outside the door and mustered up the nerve to knock. I heard footsteps approach. The door opened and a man dressed in a tailored Armani suit stood with a folder in one hand.

"Are you Mark Watson?"

34

"Freedom is rarely achieved without sacrifice." President Palmer lit a cigar. An earthy smell with a hint of wood wafted as a bluish tint hung in the air. Kate inhaled the strong odor and waited for the smoke to evaporate. She never cared much for cigars, but it was widely known that the President regularly lit up during cabinet meetings and on the golf course.

"Great leaders do what is necessary to ensure the liberties of their people, even if those decisions twist their moral compass. Hamas. Israel. Al Qaeda. Russia. Ukraine. Afghanistan. Iran. China. They fight for ideals, values, and convictions no matter how skewed they seem to the rest of the world. When you believe in something greater than yourself, you're forced to choose sides. Rhetoric is not enough to fight against our enemies. Protecting our freedom means we must fight against those who kill and destroy the very fabric of our independence. We must be willing to go into the depths of darkness to restore the light."

"Is that what the Program was about?"

"Brad trusted you enough to let you in. We both know that's why you're here." President Palmer smirked. "The Program was Frank's brainchild. Much of what he did was kept even from me. As Secretary of State, he was my responsibility. I kept it from those above and below. It is a decision I have regretted, especially in times like this. I know more than anyone how it would be seen as a black mark on our nation's history. I'm sure you understand the global implications if it were to ever be made public."

"You sent children into war, sir." Kate tried to harness her anger. "The mere existence of such an operation would be considered a crime against humanity. And impeachment for any president who covered the truth from the American people."

"Bombing of the USS Cole. Oklahoma City. Pan Am Flight 103. September 11. Our embassies attacked in Nairobi, Kenya, Tanzania, *and* Benghazi. Every president walks a fine line between morality and justice. We carry the burden handed down by our predecessors. While I didn't create the Program, I cannot deny how effective it was in shutting down the Triads and the Golden Triangle."

"How far must one be willing to go, sir?"

"To the ends of the earth." President Palmer took another drag from the Cuban and glanced towards the house. "Frank understood the evil that lurks beneath the surface. That's why I gave him the authority to put the Program into action—to infiltrate the Triad syndicate—and to hunt the Brethren."

"So, the Brethren are real?" Kate was surprised.

"To this day, they pose a great threat to our national security—and to the rest of the world."

"Do you know where Frank Harris is?"

"The day after Warren was killed, Frank informed me that he was headed to Zambia. He had found one of the Brethren's assassins—"

"Damas Kone."

President Palmer nodded slowly. "I won't ask how you know. Frank believed Kone could lead us to the Ghost."

"And who is the Ghost?"

"Kate, I wish I could tell you. But I can't."

"What about the others from the Program?"

"Frank recruited them off the grid. I only knew them by their legends."

"So you could have deniability."

"Frank went underground for months at a time. He operated on his own without any support or supervision, which meant I had no control. Perhaps deniability was a bonus."

"You haven't heard from him?"

"Not since he landed in Lusaka."

President Palmer perched the cigar on the edge of an ashtray. A hazy wall of smoke billowed between them. Kate slid the folders across the table and tried not to inhale more of the strong aroma. She wondered what his stance was on second-hand smoke. President Palmer rested his hand on top of the short stack.

"Sir, why did you ask me here?"

"Every generation who chooses liberty faces moments when the fault lines of their ideals threaten to crack open for the world to see. There were twelve operatives in the program. Eleven were trafficked into the smuggling operations in Asia. As you may have read in the classified documents, they were not merely slaves but highly trained weapons. Due to their actions, thousands of women and children were rescued from the worst of humanity. That is until it all went wrong. The Triads enlisted the Brethren and vowed retribution. There have been great losses over the past decade, not to mention nearly a century-long war fought in the shadows.

"I believe it was Eisenhower who first referred to them as the Brethren. Reagan was the one who labeled their leader the Ghost. All of it documented in a book for the president's eyes only. Years have passed, rumors have circled, and a shift has occurred after the Program was shut down. There was evidence that men such as Angelo Maldone were connected to the Brethren, but we were never able to find a way into their inner circle. Frank believed a new wave of assassins were trained and unleashed to protect the underworld. My second day in office I gave him full authority to take the fight to them."

"You believe they are behind Warren's death. And the bombing?"

"Without Frank here to answer, I cannot be sure. Whatever it was that Warren guarded in that safe is possibly the match that lit the fire. We must assume it is in the hands of those who can do great harm to us. And that also means they know about Lazarus."

"You mean the Program?"

"Lazarus wasn't the Program. It was a person."

"I didn't see that legend in the files."

"It was never documented."

"We found this in Doc Warren's pool house." Kate slid the color photo across the table. She watched as Palmer eyed it closely, and then flipped it over. "Do you know who that is, and the significance of those coordinates?"

LAZ07 - 22.3167N, 114.1833E.

"I thought Frank and myself were the only ones who knew about this. Abigail Chang was an operative who defected from the PRC. She was also Lazarus's handler. Those coordinates indicate their last known location before they disappeared. When Abigail resurfaced three years after the operatives disappeared, she relayed these coordinates to Frank. Until that point, he believed she had been captured and imprisoned in Stanley and Lazarus had been killed during the last mission."

"So they agreed to meet at the Roosevelt." Kate chimed in to keep him talking. "Room 330."

"When Frank arrived, there was only one person in the room: Lazarus. Frank made sure that Abigail remained a cold case to protect our national security. From what Ms Johnson has already said, it leads me to believe that Frank enlisted Warren's help regarding the Brethren, which would explain his involvement. Did she mention anything to you about Lazarus?"

"I assumed it was code for the Program and the twelve operatives." Kate was putting the pieces together quickly. "She never referred to Lazarus by name."

"Frank kept his end of the deal, but it's only a matter of time before the Brethren realize Lazarus survived." President Palmer leaned forward, his eyebrows arched until the lines in his forehead grew deep. "Kate, if they know he is alive, they will come for him."

"He doesn't remember his past." Kate smelled the stench on his breath. "Mr. President, he's not a weapon."

"I need you to bring him back to life, to finish what he was trained to do."

Laughter cut through the silence. Seconds later, the First Lady and her daughter sauntered through the yard carrying beach chairs and towels. President Palmer stuck the cigar hard into the ashtray and stood. He kissed his wife on the cheek and embraced his daughter in a bear hug.

"Ready for the beach?"

His daughter did a little dance. "Surfboards are loaded."

The First Lady shot a disapproving look when she noticed the cigar. Then she turned to Kate and smiled. "I hope we're not interrupting."

"Not at all," President Palmer answered. "Give me five minutes to change."

Kate stood and stepped away from the table. Secret Service reappeared and assumed their standard position. President Palmer took the folders and handed Kate a card with the presidential seal on one side.

"Kate, I trust you'll give me your decision by the end of the day."

"Yes, Mr. President."

35

"Linda Vista will be placed on the market. Everything in the house will be auctioned. You'll get to keep a vehicle of your choosing. Once all the assets are liquidated, the trust will be transferred to an offshore account in the Caymans."

"I don't understand. Is he dead?"

"I am simply following his request to place all assets in a trust."

I stood by the window on the ninth floor overlooking Colorado Boulevard in the direction of Old Town. "Is this legal?"

"I'm required to follow your father's instructions to the letter while remaining within the boundaries of the law." Mark Watson pushed his round glasses up the bridge of his nose. "However, I suggest you keep the details confidential."

"What's the catch?"

"Excuse me?"

"With Frank there's always strings attached."

Watson scanned the letter as if my question threw him for a loop. Maybe he missed it, or maybe he was hoping not to deliver the bad news.

"Well...yes...there are several conditions."

He read the paragraph aloud:

The conditions of the trust will remain valid as long as my attorney, Mark Watson, continues as a signer on the accounts. Any funds withdrawn will require both the signature of my son, Jacob Lee Harris, and my attorney, Mark Watson. If there is a breach in the conditions, the full amount of the funds will be transferred to my granddaughter, Samantha Harris, and will continue to be managed by my attorney, Mark Watson, until she reaches the age of thirty-five. At which time she will be granted full control.

"There it is." My words sounded harsh as they left my lips. I meant every word, but to someone who didn't know our history, it sounded selfish, especially since the secondary beneficiary was Samantha. I tried to smooth over my reaction. "Mr. Watson, do you know where he is?"

Watson handed me an envelope and key. "Your first check, and a key to the Malibu house. I've written the address on the back."

I glanced around the empty Harris, Inc. suite. What kind of business transacted in this room? Who was behind the millions that exchanged hands? Where was he? Was he still working for the CIA? I noticed Watson seemed ready to leave.

"Jake, you must know that your father is a good man. He always spoke highly of you whenever we were together. I'll call when everything is done."

We both left at the same time and rode the elevator down to the lobby. We said a brief goodbye and went our separate ways.

I drove the winding streets of Linda Vista in a daze. By the time I pulled into the driveway, a semi-truck was already backed up to the front of the main house. I walked around the side and noticed most of the furniture wrapped and ready to load. The movers were in a steady stream of activity. I stopped between the house and garage and it hit me. My past and present were being packed up and hauled away on the same day. Everyone seemed eager to put it all behind, except me.

A dual-level eight-wheeler, specially equipped to transport exotic cars, was on the other side of the roundabout driveway. Most likely, they'd be at an auction within a matter of weeks. I selected a vehicle. It was the one I'd eyed the first night. I admitted there was nothing like having the car of your dreams without spending a dime. I tossed the keys to the Range Rover on a tool cabinet and climbed into the Cobra. White racing stripes popped against the metallic gray with a shiny chrome roll bar and dual exhaust pipes. Wide rally tires. Black leather bucket seats. It wasn't a practical choice, but I didn't care.

The Cobra rumbled to life. Before shifting into gear, I pulled the envelope from my back pocket. Curiosity got the better of me. I tore it open and stared at the zeroes on the check. Twenty-five grand. It was foreign to me. To think that I'd receive this every month was hard to grasp. I reached for a seed of optimism at the thought that my finances had gone from zero to hero with one deposit.

Whipping through traffic down the 101, I wanted to tell someone—anyone. I didn't have the nerve to call Rachel. There was no way to reach Samantha. I literally had no one left. I switched my cell off and zoned out.

A twinge of excitement struck me at the thought of hiding away in Malibu in what had to be a beachfront paradise. I accepted the deal, even though it was hard to swallow from a man I'd stopped loving long ago. I knew it was a double standard, but after the week I'd survived, somehow I wanted to believe I deserved it.

Who cares if it's from Frank?

In the rearview mirror, a black Denali changed lanes a few cars behind. I pressed the accelerator and cut across two lanes, and the Denali followed. I kept in the far right lane and slowed behind an elderly man in an old VW bug. I hadn't noticed the Denali at the house, which made me wonder how long I'd been followed. I switched lanes again, passed the VW, and then swerved off at Kanan Dume. At the red light, the Denali pulled up directly behind me.

I stared intently in the side mirror. As soon as the light turned green, I shifted into gear and the Cobra rumbled down a single-lane route through the canyons towards the Pacific. I gripped the steering wheel and hugged the turns. Even though it was overcast and the air was brisk, it was a perfect California day. The Denali remained in my rearview far enough back to keep up.

I had avoided her long enough. I thought of the photo of Abigail Chang and the young man who stood beside her. I didn't want to believe it was possible, but the resemblance was unmistakable.

36

I checked the number on the side of a rundown modular shack. It was far from the extravagant beachfront paradise I imagined, but there was something familiar and comforting about it—a hideaway to sort things out. With Rimoldi on the loose, I planned on staying out of sight. Being steps away from the sand was a chance to exhale and begin again.

Maybe I'd spend my days writing. I didn't need to work. Millions more would soon be on the horizon in an offshore account. That brought a sense of reassurance that the tide had turned from my downward spiral. Still, there was a dose of shame. How could I feel happy when so many others were in pain? How could I so easily accept money from the one man I swore I'd never allow in my life again?

Maybe that's how all trust fund kids felt in the beginning. I was sure they adapted. I'd never have to sleep on anyone else's sofa again. Maybe I'd have a chance to get back into Rachel and Samantha's life. Money had a way of wiping out past sins. Still, I couldn't shake the fact that one piece of paper had done more for me than anyone else.

It seemed like the moment I opened Sister Evelyn's diary, everything in my life changed. I sat on the porch steps and thought of the story she'd written—and those blank pages. An unsolved case. An international hit squad. Rachel and Samantha under twenty-four/seven protection. There were more pages left to write. I guess it could be a bestseller if it weren't true.

The fact that Kate had found me in traffic meant that those blank pages were a nightmare that wasn't going away until someone finished the story. I was afraid that what she wanted from me threatened to take me where I didn't want to go.

The Denali rolled up to the curb and Kate casually climbed out. She rounded the front of the vehicle. "I was sure you'd leave me in the dust back there." She gave a half smile. "You haven't answered any of my calls."

"I had some business to take care of." I answered a bit on edge. "I'm sure you knew where I was the whole time. Probably got a tracker on all the vehicles."

"Actually, it's implanted in you." Kate tapped the hood of the SUV. "That's why I'm here."

"What're you talking about?" The look in her eyes made me realize the scattered pieces were coming together. This nightmare was becoming far too real.

"Your father reactivated it the day Doc Warren was killed."

"Reactivated?"

"You've had it since you were eight."

I thought of the two-inch scar right below my left shoulder blade. I always thought it was from something I'd done as a kid, just another life moment I couldn't remember.

"Maybe we should go inside," she suggested.

"I'd rather walk."

I brushed past Kate and headed towards a dirt path between the bushes. All the questions I wanted to ask escaped me. I fought the urge to run. She caught up once we reached the edge of a cliff that overlooked a stretch of Point Dume. Waves rolled up against the shore. Seals perched on the rocks. Several locals bundled in hoodies and sweats walked their dogs. The path narrowed along the side of the cliff and grew steeper towards the top. I found a bench and kept my eyes focused on the picturesque coastline. Suddenly, neither of us was in a hurry.

"Abigail was a covert operative who worked for your father. She's the one who brought you back."

"Brought me back from where?"

"You went missing with the others during a mission."

"Kate, are you listening to yourself?"

"I know this is hard to hear—or to believe. I didn't know until a few hours ago when I spoke with the President. I was ordered to lead the investigation into Warren's homicide so that I could get close to you—to protect you."

"It has to do with the TOP SECRET files?"

"The photo of you and Abigail was proof of life for your father."

"How long was I missing?"

"Three years."

"What about the others?"

"Abigail didn't bring them back."

"Who were they?"

"I don't know exactly. Not yet."

I exhaled deeply. "For years, I've had this dream. I'm in a room. It's pitch black. I'm forced to my knees, my head is pulled back, and water is poured down my throat. I'm struggling to free my arms and legs. I'm choking so hard I can't breathe. My heart is pounding a mile a minute, and then it stops. I don't know if I'm dead. There's no bright light, no burning flames, just absolute darkness. I feel someone touch my face and a surge of energy rushes through me. I open my eyes to see who's standing over me."

"Who is it?"

"Abigail."

"Jake, maybe that's not a dream."

"I need to know what Frank did to me."

"Your father picked twelve children, ages eight to thirteen, whose aliases are in the files. But there's never been a file on you. He called the operation the Program and reported directly to the President, who was Secretary of State at the time. We don't know their true identities or how your father recruited them. What we do know is that Abigail was assigned to be your handler."

"What was the Program about?"

"You were trained to infiltrate the Triad's trafficking ring within the Golden Triangle."

"Golden Triangle?"

"It was a smuggling route they used, known only to their top leaders."

"You're telling me we were sold into slavery?"

"Only eleven. Each implanted with a tracker."

A whale surfaced with a spurt of water from its blowhole, followed by the back fluke slapping against the water.

"Was I one of them?"

"You were trained for the extraction, which means you were the one who brought them back. Jake, you hunted smugglers inside the Golden Triangle. Two years of training, which would've made you either ten or eleven, and another two years fully operational. You were around thirteen when you disappeared along with the others."

"I'll need more than just your word."

"Then there's something you'll need to see."

37

Inside the beach house, I perched on the edge of my chair, not sure what Kate was going to show me. Or that I wanted to see it.

Night vision goggles snapped into focus and relayed a shadowy image layered in a green hue. At the top of the screen, a brightly lit sign glared across the lens with the words, Jumbo. From the speakers, a techno beat pulsed as a party aboard the four-level floating nightclub buzzed. People near the edge of the boat laughed in their drunken state. From the grainy footage, it seemed like a party where the women were in tight dresses and the men carried loose wallets. A hand appeared on screen and reached for a railing on the side of a vessel outlined in bright lights.

A familiar voice crackled. "Extraction in fifteen." It sounded like Frank.

"Copy." That was me.

Hearing those voices pushed me to the edge of my seat. The point of view turned backward, and there was Abigail aboard a smaller junk, tying a rope to the side of the vessel. Again the camera turned and moved stealthily up two flights of stairs. A silencer bounced in and out of frame. No words could explain what I was seeing. It was like watching myself starring in a video game, only it wasn't CGI. The music muffled inside a corridor as other sounds emerged. Both sides of the hallway were lined with doors. A chill shot through me as I heard the innocence of youth being stolen.

I placed a hand over my mouth as my stomach tightened. What I was watching was more than troubling, more than criminal, it was pure evil. Kate reached over and placed her hand on my thigh. Neither of us took our eyes off the screen.

A door pushed open, followed by two flashes. A few seconds passed before two Europeans and an Asian girl, no older than fifteen or sixteen, stepped out into the narrow corridor wearing only their underwear. Their eyes met the camera, and it was clear they recognized the shooter. Behind them on the bed, an Asian man lay in a pool of blood with two bullets to the chest. The video pushed in and hovered over the man. A hand reached out and snatched a medallion from around his neck.

"I've got Jazmine, Moriah, and Scarlett." My voice on the video was hushed but steady. "Moving to the next room."

"Eleven minutes."

Methodically, from door to door, no mercy was shown for those who crossed the line of morality. Each time the thump of a bullet hit its target, I felt those same shots in my chest. When the last room was cleared, boys and girls of varying nationalities and ages stood in the corridor. None of them were concerned with their nakedness, all of them were ready to move. I counted twelve targets dead, eleven survivors.

"Where is she?" Several girls pointed upwards. The point of view swung to the rest of the group. "Tin Hua Temple. I'll be right behind."

"Eight minutes." Frank's voice crackled. "You need to move."

"Copy."

My body clenched at the rhythmic breathing while the night vision captured the stairs and guards who patrolled. Like a shadow, the camera avoided each with skill. At the top of the last set of stairs, the view ducked below a window, and then slowly lifted enough to peer inside the room. More movement showed arms and legs climbing through the opening. Not a sound on the landing.

"Five minutes."

"Almost there."

A flashlight switched on and a dull glow pointed towards a marble floor covered in blood. The light then pointed to a chair set in the center of the room. A woman was tied, with her head arched backward, eyes swollen shut as if she'd been beaten. Fingers were stubbed at the knuckles. Her throat was slit ear to ear. Dried blood was caked down the side of her body. The once steady breathing quickened as a hand touched her lifeless face.

My voice on screen whispered shakily, "Mom?"

The sound of bullets riddling the walls caused me to jerk. Kate never budged.

"Ugh!"

The night vision dropped to the floor, motionless.

Frank's stern voice shouted, "Jacob!"

Then the video cut out.

I darted to the bathroom, threw myself over the toilet, and hurled. My chest tightened until it felt like my intestines might burst. If I hadn't seen it for myself, I never would've believed it was possible. When I entered the living room, Kate handed me a glass of water.

I clenched my jaw. "Who killed her?"

"We don't know," Kate admitted. "Her body was never found."

"I knew their names."

"Yes, those were the legends of some of the eleven. Shortly after, communication and the tracking signals cut off somewhere between the pier and the temple. Same was true with yours."

"I was shot?"

"All we know for sure is this was the last time you were seen, until Abigail brought you back."

I pointed at the blank screen. "How did my mom end up there?"

"I can't answer that."

"You can't? Or you won't?"

"I swear we don't know anything about your mother. There is no evidence she was part of the Program. I'm afraid only your father can answer that question."

"What happened to me—after this?"

"As far as the CIA, NSA, Homeland Security, or any other government agency is concerned, Jacob Langston never existed."

"Langston?"

"That's your real name."

My eyes grew moist. "He never should've—"

"Your father was the best of the best," Kate interrupted. "He believed if the Triad leaders were found and killed that would dismantle their extensive smuggling and trafficking operation. Sending in Special Forces was not an option, and there was no way Congress would sign off on any operation within Hong Kong, especially with the Brits and Chinese at odds regarding the handover in '97. The President assured me that thousands were saved because of what you and the others accomplished. Whether we agree with your father's motives or not, it was effective in shutting down the Golden Triangle. The Triads used this route throughout Asia, but it's possible it reached as far as the West Coast. Millions, if not billions, of dollars were at stake with the drugs and slaves who were trafficked."

"Who were those men who were killed?"

"The Triad Council—top leaders who represented key points in the route. When you killed them, their operations ceased, and we believe that is still true today. We have reliable intel that the Triads are far less powerful now than they were back then."

"How did Abigail get me back to LA?"

"If the route reached as far as the West Coast then it's possible she smuggled you aboard one of the shipping freighters. However she did it, once you were here, she contacted your father and agreed to meet at the Roosevelt. President Palmer told me that Abigail had information about what happened that night, but she wouldn't say over the phone. The following afternoon she was found dead in the alley behind the hotel."

"And Frank found me there."

"A few days ago this was given to the President—a message that someone else knows about the Program, someone who knows about your past."

Kate handed me an old color photo. I stared at it for a moment. A group of twelve children of various nationalities stood alongside a much younger Frank. I recognized Abigail from the photo Maggie showed us, as well as a few of the girls from the video: Jazmine, Moriah, and Scarlett. It was hard to believe, impossible really. There I was in a village somewhere in the world with a rifle slung over my shoulder next to a group of kids I didn't remember.

"Were there others—others I killed?"

"Forty-two confirmed."

"I lived. And they died." I paced the room and tried to process what I'd seen and what Kate was telling me. I turned. "My mom, Abigail, the eleven—they died because of my sins, because I'm Lazarus."

Kate didn't hide her surprise. "Where'd you hear that name?"

"That's what Maldone called me at the prison."

"Did he mention anything about the Program?"

"He spoke in riddles. Most of it I didn't understand, only room 330 at the Roosevelt. Kate, I don't know who that is on that video. Or who I'm supposed to be."

"I might be able to help with that." Kate retrieved a hard-sided, waterproof Pelican case small enough to fit in the palm of her hand. She opened the case and revealed five syringes sitting on the sculpted foam inside. "Each dosage will increase your memory. If you're willing, we can find those answers together. And find your mother's killer."

I glanced at the syringes and kept my wits about me. I needed time to think, but Kate was on a full court press. She needed something from me. Exactly what, I was unsure.

"What's the catch?"

"We need to locate your father. Until that happens, our priority is to find the identity of someone he referred to as the Ghost."

"Rimoldi?"

"We don't believe so."

"He killed hundreds of people."

"Thousands more are in danger."

"Who gave the President this photo?"

"I asked, but he wouldn't say."

My mind tried to grasp the whole puzzle. "Who else is going with us?"

"That's the thing. We're on our own."

"No way." I slumped into a chair. "That's suicide."

"I promised to protect Rachel and Samantha. Now I need you to do this in return."

"You're a Fed. Isn't there a team of highly trained super agents you can put together?"

"I turned in my resignation an hour ago. That was part of the deal too. Only the President knows what we are doing, which means there are no rules. Do you understand what I'm saying?"

"No rules." I nodded at the box of syringes. "You really think that'll turn me into Lazarus?"

"I'm counting on it."

The room pushed in on me. I wanted to punch a hole in the wall, to release the aggression that was building inside me. A piece of me had already made the decision. I needed to know more than ever now.

"So, you and me are going to save the world."

"Something like that." She smiled warmly.

I held out my arm. "Go slow. I hate needles."

Kate removed one syringe from the case. "That makes two of us."

38

Hours on the clock passed.

Kate left to make arrangements with plans to pick me up in the morning. I didn't know where we were going or how long we'd be gone. I waited two hours after she left before I sent the text. Then I moped around the house, which was a shack compared to the Linda Vista estate where a realtor sign was most likely already posted at the front gate.

I checked the bedroom closet, nightstand drawers, and the kitchen cabinets. All I found was inch-thick dust and dead roaches. I stood in front of a mini fridge and weighed my options. I fought the urge for a cold one. An addict never conquers an addiction alone, especially if the drug of choice is staring him in the face. I wasn't hungry, my throat was dry, and that's what I needed to ease the tension. I grabbed a beer and popped the top.

Did I want to remember my past? Did I want to remember the forty-two? Was I willing to risk my life to find Frank? And what about the others from the Program? Were they still alive?

A part of me hoped the serum did the trick. Another part wanted to turn the clock back and never walk up those steps to Doc's front door. I didn't know if I had the courage to see this through. Revenge. Retribution. Redemption. Those were foreign words to a guy who needed a fix from a bottle. Maybe the serum would change all that. Maybe one injection of the magic potion would unlock the nightmares. Maybe.

Frank turned me into a stone-cold killer, and then wiped Lazarus from my memory. He sacrificed children in way I couldn't begin to imagine. Kate seemed to believe it was heroic. One thing was for sure, I'd never tell Rachel about any of it. Flashes of the video hit, and I shivered at the sight of Mom's lifeless body. I knew it would haunt me well after I killed whoever it was that took her life so brutally.

Being cooped up indoors left me restless. I grabbed my cell and scrolled through my contacts. I paused on Rachel's name as my thumb hovered over the screen. I needed to write something. It was possibly, no, it was probably my last chance. What do you say to someone you love when they don't feel the same?

Leaving town for a few weeks. Want to see Sam. Please! Love you both.
Swoosh.

I sprawled out on the couch and dozed off until my phone beeped around six-thirty. I hoped it was a reply from Rachel. That thought was a bust. I locked the door, climbed in the Cobra, and drove over the canyon towards Glendale.

An hour later, I stepped off the escalator in the lobby of the Americana and was lost in the steady flow of people beneath a golden statue in the center of the plaza. A lighted fountain switched colors to the music's crescendo. My pace quickened as I passed the Cheesecake Factory before ducking inside Barnes & Noble.

I waited near the bestseller rack and casually glanced out the window to be sure I wasn't followed. I still had the tracker inside me, which meant it wouldn't be long before Kate knew I wasn't at the house. I rode the escalator to the top floor, ordered a latte, and slipped between aisles of books until I stepped out onto a balcony that overlooked the entire plaza.

Teenagers laughed at one table. An older Armenian man sipped coffee while reading a Connelly hardcover. I found an empty corner table and did exactly as the text instructed.

Once I saw her through the glass I was relieved. She headed towards me. I kept my eyes focused on who was behind her to be sure she was alone. Our eyes met as she slipped into the seat next to me.

"Maggie, I wasn't sure I'd see you again."

"They offered me witness protection, but I learned long ago to trust only those closest to you."

"I'll have to remember that."

"So, I take it you've seen the video."

I nodded.

Her dark features only heightened the whites in her eyes. "It was only a matter of time before the President played that card."

"Is that why Doc called me?"

"For a long time, he wanted Frank to tell you the truth, but your father refused. I think it was the only thing those two ever argued about." Maggie's eyes drifted. "They did everything in their power to protect you. You see, to the government you are a weapon, but to those of us in this war, we believe you are the one who will bring peace."

"I'm not a savior."

I handed over Sister Evelyn's diary. Maggie wasted no time in retrieving a pen from her handbag. She flicked one end and a purple glow illuminated the pages. She turned each page until she reached the ones that were blank. I was captivated once the ultraviolet light revealed handwriting on those pages.

"It's far from everything, but it's enough."

"Enough of what?"

"The hard drive from the safe was a backup of all the names, locations, and leads to the Brethren. This is the original—much too valuable to exist anywhere. Within these pages are secrets dating back to the days of Sister Evelyn. Secrets that must be protected from the Brethren."

"You're saying there are secrets in the diary that don't exist on the hard drive?"

"It was Doc's idea." Maggie looked up from the diary. "And it cost him his life."

"Maggie, I'm sorry for what happened. I should've been there to stop it."

"Nonsense. Jake, you were right where Doc wanted you to be."

"I still don't get how all of this started with Sister Evelyn."

"She fought the first battle in a war that has waged for nearly a century—a war that has taken many to the grave. Her faith made her powerful because she believed God was her Protector. There was a time when that was not the case, when she was broken. Her first husband, Nathan, was the love of her life. When she returned to the States after his death, she left a secret behind—the likes of which neither of us can fully fathom."

Maggie flipped a few more pages.

"After her death, the Brethren continued to protect the underworld from those who threatened to expose the darkest in society. A covenant was created and enforced by them, to ensure the balance between these criminal syndicates that today have infiltrated every continent. They exist to ensure that darkness not only survives, it thrives in the shadows. However, in recent days there has been a shift."

"What kind of shift?"

"It seems they are no longer satisfied with being the protectors."

"Maggie, you sound like more than a researcher."

"We each have our role to play, Jake."

I leaned my arms on the table. "Why did Maldone call me Lazarus?"

"He was a hit man for the mob before he was recruited by the Brethren. We believe at one time he was the one who trained the assassins—the Ghost. When he was found in LA and arrested, we realized that if that were the case, then the mantle had been passed to someone else. Frank believed Damas Kone could lead us to that person."

"Kate believes the Brethren know I'm alive."

"She is telling the truth. The photo from the President is confirmation."

"You're saying I can trust the President?"

"The truth lies in—"

"Who's telling the story," I said softly.

Maggie wiped a tear from her cheek. "Jake, you were spared for a purpose. What was stolen from the safe is valuable, but not as valuable as you."

"I find that hard to believe."

"If you choose to believe, perhaps you will find the answers you are seeking."

I leaned back in my chair. "Maggie, I'm not ready to be part of this."

"You are a born leader with a lineage of protecting others. It's in your blood."

"How can you be so sure?"

"Who do you think brought Sister Evelyn home from the desert?"

I rifled through the details of the story. "The shadow at the door."

"He was your grandfather, George Langston. Secret Service. President Coolidge assigned him to protect Sister Evelyn. He traveled to her crusades, shadowed her in every service, and watched from the back row during the Klan's secret meetings where she spoke. He followed up on every kidnapping and death threat. He admired her greatly, in spite of her shortfalls—or perhaps because of them. He blamed himself for failing to stop the kidnapping. When the verdict in the case against her was returned not guilty, he knew Cohen wouldn't stop until she was dead. He did what was necessary to put an end to the threat."

"He knew about the Brethren?"

"He was there in the very beginning, but he took those stories to the grave. He never even told your father." Maggie glanced around for a moment. "Frank found out about the Brethren when President Palmer was Secretary of State and showed him proof of what your grandfather had done. That conversation led to the creation of the Program—to save the innocent, and to protect what must remain hidden."

"How did he choose the others? And what is so valuable that it must remain hidden?"

"Those questions are not for me to answer."

I studied the diary in her hand. "Then tell me what I'm supposed to do."

"Destiny requires a decision. One that only you can make. If your destiny is to defeat the Brethren, you must be willing to sacrifice yourself to cut off the dragon's head."

"You're talking about the Ghost?"

"I'm afraid that is where your demons lie."

I swallowed hard. Her words pierced my soul. I was an addict, not a hero, and definitely not Lazarus. Fear lurked in the darkness because I was too afraid to fight in the light.

"What if I fail?"

"Then we will all fail, Jake."

39

In the pitch black, a helicopter hummed and vibrated from a strong crosswind. Kate, buckled in tight and wearing an aviator headset that muted the rotor noise, gripped the back of the pilot seat. From her vantage point, the instruments illuminated the cockpit and cast a dull glow across Brad, who said over his shoulder, "This wasn't exactly what I had in mind."

"No wine. No Caviar." Kate smiled. "Just a crime scene. That's all a girl needs."

The helicopter banked and redirected their attention outside at an endless night interrupted by a radius of spotlights directly below. For a moment, the pilot hovered over the scene before landing next to a Sikorsky CH-53 Super Stallion.

Kate climbed out as rotor wash kicked up dirt from the desert. She covered her face while the blades slowed and the whine of the engine cut out.

"You're not going to tell me?" he asked as they walked toward the site.

"Brad, I can't. He swore me to secrecy."

"I'm not accepting your resignation."

"You'll have to take that up with POTUS."

"You should've talked to me first," he said. "You're the best I've got."

"Flattery will get you everywhere," Kate teased. Her voice faded

166

beneath the hum of generators. She wanted to tell him everything, but she felt blindsided by it all. Still, she tried to keep it light with Brad.

She stopped and looked around. "You've done fine without me."

"That's not fair," he argued.

A tactical team guarded the perimeter beyond the floodlights that turned the desolate area into a forensic campground where agents dug beneath the bright lights. Kate counted twenty mounds of dirt so far before she noticed the dilapidated clay shack set back against the hill. Decades of extreme heat and bitter cold had taken a toll on the structure. Most of the roof was gone, but once she checked the image on her cell, that was all the confirmation she needed.

"We've got forty-eight hours," Brad said. "Then the Federales take over."

"We better load up what we can."

"Everything else gets left behind."

Kate's cell buzzed. She checked the screen, watched a red dot blink on the GPS, and stifled a groan. "Not now."

"Everything okay?"

"Yeah." Kate's jaw clenched as she glared at the screen. "Where's Nicki?"

A woman wearing latex gloves and brown oval glasses an inch think approached. Five feet. Early thirties. Piercing in her nose. "Kate, sorry to ruin your date."

Kate's cheeks burned as she shot Brad a quizzical look.

Nicki laughed. "C'mon, it's obvious you two belong together."

"What've you found?" Brad asked.

Nicki led them to the first mound. All three kneeled and stared into an empty hole about three feet deep. Nicki stepped over to the other side and showed them a set of decayed bones that were organized into a partial skeleton.

"So far all we've got is a femur, skull fragments, and a few ribs."

"Initial assessment?" Kate asked.

"I'd guess female, probably late twenties." Nicki pointed to the skull.

"GSW to the head. Probably been out here about ten to fifteen years. We'll know more once we've finished with the dig, and we're back at the lab."

Kate studied the other mounds. "Remains in all of them?"

"Seems like the closer we get to the shack the older they are. We've got twenty-four so far, but we're just getting started."

"How wide of an area?" Brad asked.

Nicki whipped out her touchpad and pointed to a rough diagram. "We're looking at about a hundred-yard radius. It's literally a minefield."

"There's no way we'll dig all of it up before tomorrow night." He planted his hands on his hips. "Nicki, do your best to recover as much as possible, but you've got to be gone by dusk."

"Got it." Nicki barked an order to two other agents who moved to another row. She pointed to the shack. "You're gonna want to see this."

Kate followed Nicki through the doorway. Inside a Kino light was on a stand high enough to give them a view of a naked body on the ground. Kate kneeled down to take a closer look. Brunette. Late twenties. Engraved crudely across her chest were the words: WAGES OF SIN.

"I didn't want to move her until you were both here." Nicki pointed to the bruises on the woman's neck. "No GSW on this one. I'd say cause of death is strangulation."

"DNA?" Brad asked.

"We'll preserve her body as best we can, and see what we find once we're back at the lab."

"Nicki, give us a minute." Kate waited until they were alone. "I know her. She was in the courtroom every day of Maldone's trial."

"One of his girls?"

"She was my CI." Kate pointed a flashlight at the woman's face then turned her attention to the corners of the room. She caught sight of something and moved in that direction. She carefully picked up a bloodied shirt with the tip of a pen. "Brad, I used her and tossed her to the wolves."

"Who is she?"

"Theresa Maldone."

Kate brushed by and stopped in the doorway. She motioned for Nicki, who was right outside pretending not to be listening in. She handed the shirt off. "How long do you think she's been here?"

"Less than a week or so. Now that's only a guess until I examine the body."

Dread filled Kate as she turned to Brad. "We gotta go."

40

I pulled off PCH at Moon Shadows after another day with more twists and turns than Baxter Hill. I found a spot at the bar and downed two quick shots of Scotch—a last hurrah. I stayed until closing, paid cash, and left the bartender a Benjamin. I stumbled to the Cobra in a fog. I don't remember how I drove back to the house. I kept hearing Maggie's words playing over and over.

Wages of sin...destiny...dragon's head...

The problem wasn't one drink. It wasn't even a few. There was something fractured, a piece of me that needed the alcohol. Maybe it was sin. Maybe it was the fact that my life had been turned upside down the past few years. I couldn't blame it on Rachel or Samantha. I couldn't blame it on Frank, even though he was responsible for permanently destroying my childhood. There was no clear explanation, even after listening to Maggie talk about the Brethren, a war, and me being the supposed chosen one.

I thought about my grandfather, a man I had never known, and his role in history. I had to admit, that part was pretty cool.

Am I ready to be Lazarus?

After a sleepless night, I tugged at the covers and buried my head underneath a pillow. The pain intensified until I couldn't take it anymore. I stumbled into the bathroom, hovered over the porcelain throne, and heaved as the room spun. Flashes struck hard again. Darkness. Drowning. Gunshots. I gasped as vomit burned my throat. I lifted my head for a second and gasped for air. Then I ducked back over the bowl until I was sure there was nothing left inside my stomach.

Handfuls of water splashed against my face. The reflection in the mirror was a far cry from who Maggie, Kate, or the President believed me to be.

Messy hair. Stubbly beard. Dark circles under my eyes. I was a mess.

After I had dropped Maggie at Union Station, an overwhelming sense of loneliness washed over me. At least that was my excuse for drinking until I couldn't see straight.

With everything that had occurred, the truth was I was an unemployed thirty-one-year-old man with a bulge over his belt and liquor in his veins. It was a reminder of how far I'd fallen. I was also a wealthy man who'd never have a chance to enjoy it. Money had been given with a burden, a debt that I now owed. To keep it, I needed to become someone I never imagined— an assassin. It was the underlying message I took from Frank's actions. Sure, he provided a way to care for Rachel and Samantha, but it meant returning to the person I'd seen on the video. Resurrecting Lazarus.

I slipped on a pair of jeans and a shirt, wondering how an injection could turn my broken, messed up, life into something meaningful. No one knew if it would even work. Were there side effects? I didn't even ask. I peeked between the blinds at the Jeep parked at the curb with Kate behind the wheel. I grabbed my backpack and slung everything I owned over my shoulder.

When I locked the door, I noticed the Cobra parked awkwardly with the front tires up on the curb. I took a moment and backed the American classic up before pulling it straight into the driveway and covering it as if nothing was out of the ordinary.

Kate smirked as she handed me a coffee. "Good morning, sunshine."

"Morning," I mumbled.

For a while, we drove PCH towards the 10 Freeway. It was still early enough that the sun hadn't fully risen, that time of day where you're only half awake. I sensed something was on her mind. I sipped my coffee, which offered a slight jolt, and kept quiet.

Silence was the best cure for any hangover.

She glanced over. "Late night?"

"Hardly slept. You?"

"Same."

"Any news?"

"We don't know where Rimoldi is. He's in the wind."

"Or he's following us," I joked. Kate checked the rearview. I raised my cup of java. "Here's to surviving another day."

Kate grimaced as I sipped loudly. "Looks like you needed that."

"I puked my guts out this morning—twice. Must be the shot."

"I'm sure Moon Shadows didn't help either."

My cheeks burned as I snatched my sunglasses and covered my eyes. I rubbed my shoulder as if it suddenly agitated me. "When do I get this out?"

"After last night, I think it's better I know where you are at all times." She paused. "Jake, we can't do this if you're—"

"Got it." I gazed at the ocean, and then said with a heavy dose of sarcasm. "We're on a top secret mission that'll probably get us killed. I just thought…"

"That's not funny."

"You're right. The fact that everyone thinks I'm going to magically turn into this killing machine—now that's funny."

After an awkward silence she said, "We need to make one stop on the way."

We passed the 405 interchange, which would've taken us to LAX.

"Do we get new identities? Back story? Change our appearance?"

"You've been watching too much Bourne and Bauer."

"Seems kind of obvious that's all." I drummed my fingers on the arm rest. "Don't you think they'll see us coming?"

"Jake, let me worry about that."

"Fine. You're the professional."

"You're impossible." She glared. "I hope you're not going to be like this the whole time."

"You haven't told me what the plan is. All I know is that we need to find Frank. We need to find the Ghost—whoever the hell that is. I don't even know where we're going."

The SUV veered left onto the 110 towards downtown and exited on West Olympic. Kate drove a few more blocks, turned right, and pulled over at the intersection of South Figueroa and Chick Hearn Court. The street between Staples Center and the Nokia Theater was blocked to through traffic due to LA Live, but there were black SUVs parked on both sides of the barricade.

I waited as Kate rounded the front of the Jeep and spoke with the same agent who'd chased me off in Sunland. I rolled the window down and glared at him as Kate approached.

"You've got five minutes."

"For what?"

"You'll see."

From across the street, an agent near a statue of Magic Johnson watched as we strolled down Chick Hearn Court. Two more guarded the entrance to Smashburgers. All of them dressed in khakis, polos, and in-ear coms. No bystanders. Tension filled the air as we entered. The lead agent spoke low into a mic clipped to his shirt.

Kate stepped aside, which gave me a direct line of sight into an empty dining area. I wiped my sweaty palms against my jeans and braced myself the moment I saw them appear from the back kitchen. Rachel held Samantha's hand and guided her towards me. I nearly broke down in tears. A lump lodged in my throat.

I glanced at Rachel, who looked tired and worried. Neither of us said a word. She stepped beside Kate and the lead agent, leaving Samantha standing directly in front of me. Her peaceful expression highlighted her curly brown hair and bright pink shades. I kneeled so I was on her level. It had been months since I'd seen her last. She was growing up too fast, more beautiful than ever.

"Hi Sam," I said softly.

She reached out and touched my face. Her smile brightened the room. I closed my eyes at her gentle touch. It warmed my heart to hear her voice.

"Daddy, you have porcupine whiskers."

I chuckled and hugged her tight. "I've missed you so much."

She whispered in my ear. "Are you coming home?"

"I wish, sweetie." I held back tears. "But I can't. Not just yet."

"Mommy said we're moving to a new home, but we can't tell anyone. If you don't go with us, how will you find us?"

"Don't worry, I'll always know where to find you." I glanced at the others. "Sam, do you remember your first day at school when those boys made fun of you?"

"Yeah, Rosie told them off," she whispered. "She's my best friend."

"That's what friends do, right?"

"Uh-huh."

"Well, Daddy needs to help some friends who are being bullied." I grit my teeth and said softly, "But I won't go unless you say it's okay."

"If they're your friends, you have to go." She placed the palm of her hand on my chest. "Then you'll come home, promise?"

"I promise."

I turned towards Rachel, but she avoided eye contact. I reached into my pocket, removed the envelope, and pressed it into Samantha's hands.

"Give this to Mom." I kissed her on the forehead. "Take care of her until I get back, okay?"

"Okay." Samantha leaned in close and whispered. "I love you, Daddy."

"I love you too, Sam." My eyes welled up with tears. I stood and took her by the hand. We stepped over to Rachel, a family broken over time. Kate and the lead agent kept themselves invisible. I let go of Samantha's hand and said to Rachel, "Thank you."

41

A week after the bombing, security at LAX remained tight. With Neco Rimoldi's identity kept from the public, the nation was on edge with a suspect still at large. Cable news worked around the clock to keep the tension high and the viewers glued to stay atop the ratings. Reports of more extremist attacks were squashed in a White House briefing, which stated the threat level had dropped to Level Two. Around the clock, LAPD Canine and SWAT continued heightened security as they patrolled Tom Bradley International Terminal.

A melting pot of travelers endured long lines and countless flight delays. Groups curled up on tiled floors surrounded by stacks of luggage. Screaming toddlers pushed the patience of anyone within earshot.

I joined the back of a line that stretched clear down a long hallway until I lost sight of the security checkpoint ahead. Kate waited beside me. She had given me space since leaving downtown.

Leaving Rachel and Samantha was hard to swallow, even if it was to find the truth. I was a danger to them. I could see it in everyone's eyes, except for Samantha of course. She was the peace I needed. Maybe I'd end up looking over my shoulder the rest of my life. The further I was away from them the better. Leaving was an impossible choice, but it was the right decision. If I said that a thousand times, I wasn't sure I'd ever believe it.

Travelers, bunched together in tight quarters, released a strong aroma of perfume, body odor, and dirty diapers. We inched forward until we were face to face with a TSA officer who scanned our tickets and passports. After a long gaze, I was motioned through to another line where I placed my backpack on a moving belt and stood in the center of a full-body scanner. Green.

I waited for Kate on the other side of security. I noticed that she didn't flash a badge or show any sign she'd brought a firearm. She caught up to me, and we headed down the terminal towards Gate 123. To anyone watching, we were two travelers embarking on an adventure to the Orient.

"Samantha's a beautiful girl."

"Takes after her mom."

"How long has she been…"

"Blind?"

"Sorry." Kate blushed. "Bad habit."

"She lost her sight when she was six. Doctor's could never explain why."

"Well, I can tell she loves you very much."

"How'd you do it?" I asked pointedly.

"Last night, the safe house was compromised."

"What do you mean?" I stopped abruptly, causing travelers to swerve around me.

"Someone broke into an upstairs window." Kate held my gaze.

"Rimoldi?"

"Agents swept through the neighborhood, but we don't know if it was him."

"You promised me, Kate." We started walking again.

"Rachel was pretty shook up. And pissed. She wanted answers. I told her your father worked for the government and was missing. And it was a matter of national security that you help us find him. I figured it was your decision whether or not to tell the rest."

"Sam said they were moving."

"It's better neither of us knows where—at least for now."

In that moment, all I wanted to do was find Rimoldi, Kone, and the Ghost. I wish I could say I'd never kill a man, but that would be a lie. The rage that fueled my veins threatened to push me over the edge back to a past I had not fully accepted.

We ducked into a booth at Scoreboard LA and ordered coffee. Local news broadcasted aerial shots of a black hearse heading down a freeway, a crowd gathering outside a church, black-and-whites flashing their red and blue lights, and officers saluting on an overpass as the procession passed below. The crawl at the bottom of the screen read: PRESIDENT PALMER TO SPEAK AT MEMORIAL FOR DETECTIVE MITCHELL LANE.

"Did he have any family?" I asked.

"A daughter and two ex-wives. I'm not sure if they were close. To the rest of the world, he's an American hero killed in the line of duty." Kate eyed me closely. "Jake, last night I wasn't at the safe house because I was in Agua Prieta."

"You found the shack?" I felt my eyes widen in disbelief.

"Exactly how Maggie described. It was a graveyard with remains of dozens of bodies. It'll take months to sort through it all, and most likely years before we know how they ended up there. Jake, I'm sorry. I should've been there for them."

"Did you find her?"

"Who?"

"Theresa."

Now it was Kate's turn to be shocked. "How'd you know?"

"Maldone said it was your fault she was dead."

"Jake, why didn't you tell me?"

"He said the Brethren knew I was alive, and they wouldn't stop until everyone I loved was dead too." I paused, deciding whether to tell the rest. "I was the only one he allowed to live. And I owed him a promise. I thought he was crazy."

"What'd you promise him, Jake?"

"That I'd kill them all."

42

Wipers squeaked across the windshield at a steady rhythm. Blown speakers crackled a mix of Mandarin ballads and American pop. After a fourteen-hour flight, stomach-churning meals, and the onset of jet lag, the music was another form of psychological torture.

From the backseat of a red and silver taxi, I got my first glimpse of Kowloon. High-rise apartments jutted skyward. Every intersection swarmed with hundreds of pedestrians who crossed in less than sixty seconds. Even though it was late, the city was very much alive.

The driver maneuvered skillfully through the streets as someone who'd been raised beneath the suspended neon signs. It was a stark contrast to the overhead trees that formed a natural tunnel back in Pasadena.

Since landing in this concrete jungle, I searched for anything to spark my memory. Seven million people called this place home. To me, it was another world. Maybe the serum wouldn't work. Ever. I'd had time to think on the flight and realized why we were traveling under our real names. Bait. Kate wanted them to find us, maybe more than she wanted to protect me. I needed to trust her, but I wasn't sure.

A flash of lightening pierced the clouds, followed by rumbling thunder amid a torrential downpour that cloaked the city. The weight of my decision pressed down on my shoulders. I didn't belong in this foreign place. Fear. Hatred. Revenge. I weighed each one on the jaunt over the Pacific. I needed each one if I had any chance of resurrecting Lazarus.

The taxi cut down a narrow street as a double-decker whizzed by, inches apart.

One block east of Nathan Road we pulled over to the curb.

Kate checked the coordinates on her cell, nodded then haggled over the fare with the driver. The language barrier resulted in a barrage of curses neither of us understood. Frustrated, the driver snatched the cash and waved us out. We climbed from the taxi, crossed a sidewalk amidst a steady stream of trash flowing down the street, and ducked inside Hoi On Building in Tai Kok Tsui.

I wrestled with telling Kate about Maggie. If she knew I was at Moon Shadows, then she knew I'd been to the Americana and Union Station. I ran my fingers through a mop of hair and wiped the drops of rain from my face. I was drenched and drained from the humidity. My back ached, my ankle was tender, and I desperately needed an ice cold. . . shower.

We stood in the cramped and gloomy lobby beneath a dim fluorescent that blinked erratically. Rows of rusted mailboxes lined the walls across from the stairwell.

"You feeling okay?" Kate asked.

"I haven't sweat this much since I did two-a-days."

"You know what I mean."

"Nothing out of the ordinary."

"You'd tell me, right?"

"You'll be the first to know." I stepped over and eyed the characters scribbled above each mailbox. I pictured the page Maggie had shown me from the diary and searched the rows from memory. I visualized the characters vividly, as if engraved permanently in my mind. My pulse quickened as a surge of energy swept over my lethargy.

I'd found a match.

希望之家

I dug into my backpack and retrieved a pen. I roughly copied the characters onto my palm. I ignored Kate's curious stare and counted the rows then the number in each row.

"Thirtieth floor," I said. "Lucky number seven."

"How do you know?"

"Kate, we're in the right place." I headed for the stairs. "Come on."

I led the way for the first ten floors until my calves cramped. Dungy corridors, with green metal doors and faded numbers crudely painted in white, lined each floor. On the ground were bronze Buddhas next to sticks of incense that slowly burned.

Kate passed me on the twelfth floor, and I fell further behind the rest of the way. By the time I reached the last step, I was drenched in sweat and breathing hard. Kate looked as if she could go another thirty. I expected the floor to look like the others, but instead we took another stairwell to an iron gate that guarded a single entrance.

Kate turned to me. "Are you going to tell me?"

"Remember, I'm the chosen—"

"Please, don't say it."

I pressed the buzzer. A minute passed before the door opened and an elderly woman stood wide-eyed behind the barred gate. Her whisper echoed off the walls.

"Lā sā lù."

A bolt scraped against the metal until it slid into place. The woman let us in then locked both deadbolts and left us standing in the entryway while she disappeared down one of two corridors separated by a common wall. I poked my head inside a room and flipped a switch. The space was filled with desks and a chalkboard. Painted on the wall where the same characters inked on my palm. I was about to point this out to Kate when the woman returned with a teenager who looked like he'd been asleep moments earlier. He rubbed his eyes and interpreted in perfect English what the woman said in her gravelly voice.

"She remembers you when you were a young boy," the teenager said, a bit awestruck. "She never thought she would see you again." I nodded, disconcerted, and tried not to look flattered. "There is someone waiting. Please follow me."

We stepped forward in unison, but the woman grabbed Kate firmly by the arm. "Zhǐyǒu lā sā lù."

Kate pulled back. The teenager stepped between them, but the woman's eyes never left me. It was the same look I'd seen in Maggie at the Roosevelt.

"We have a room for you," the teenager said to Kate. "You must be very tired."

"I'm fine," Kate shot back. "What'd she say?"

"Lazarus only."

"No way," Kate protested.

I put my hand on her arm. "Kate, I'll be fine."

Kate dialed her cell, and said pointedly, "Leave it on so I can hear you."

I slid my thumb across the screen of my cell. Kate slung my backpack over her shoulder and followed the elderly woman while I headed down the opposite corridor behind the teenager. The corridor was lit well enough to see the rooms as we passed. Each one had rows of empty bunk beds, with blankets neatly folded on each one. We entered an empty room where a metal ladder was cemented into the tiled floor.

I whispered, "Check. One. Two. One. Two."

Kate's voice answered, "Very funny."

"Headed to the roof."

"Jake, if it doesn't feel right…"

"A little late for that don't you think?"

"Remember, you're the chosen one."

"Neither of us should ever say that again."

"Just trying to boost your confidence."

"Well, it's not working."

"Okay, seriously, stay focused."

I held my cell in one hand and gripped the first rung with the other. When I reached the top, I glanced down expecting to see the teenager behind me. He was gone. My body shivered. I felt lightheaded. I braced myself against the wall as my senses focused into tunnel vision. It wasn't the humidity. It wasn't jet lag. As quickly as it hit me, my nerves dissolved until I felt numb, calm, peaceful, and fully aware. Determined, yet cautious. In the doorway, I steadied myself. With every beat in my chest, I harnessed a tsunami of emotions.

I stepped out onto the roof where a chain-link fence with barbwire surrounded the area. At one end were lunch tables beneath a metal roof. In the center was a metal swing and slide. To my right, a homemade basketball hoop hung about eight feet high. There was no time for an imaginary walk down memory lane or a quick game of dunk hoops.

What moved?

In my dreams it would've been my mom, the one person I longed to know, and the one I failed to save. I tensed at the alternative. I wasn't ready to face Frank. I flinched when a woman appeared directly in front of me.

We stood only inches apart. Only then did I realize the rain had stopped and the moon had peeked out, giving a glint to her golden eyes. Her features were striking beneath the moonlight. Bright red hair cast with a twinge of orange. Both arms sleeved with tattoos.

"Do you know who I am?"

Without thinking I said, "You're Scarlett."

"That's right."

"I thought you were dead."

She smiled softly. "I am very much alive."

"I saw a photo of all of us when we were kids, with Frank. Is he here?"

"I thought he would be with you." Her voice carried a curious tone.

"I haven't seen him in over a week." I glanced around the roof. "What is this place?"

She grabbed my hand and opened my palm. "Those characters mean Hope House."

"The woman downstairs recognized me, so I've been here before?"

"When we were both young, like in the picture you mentioned. Many others have lived here since. But it has become too dangerous for anyone to stay here now."

"I can't believe you're standing right in front of me."

"I am afraid there is not much time to answer questions."

"I need to know about that night."

"We were held by the Triads for nearly four months," Scarlett replied. "We were moved numerous times throughout the Golden Triangle and waited for you to come until that night when Abigail was with you. We followed your orders, but when we boarded the boat she turned back. I followed. When we reached you, you were barely alive. We never made it to the extraction point with the others. Instead, we brought you here. You were dead, Jacob. Not a single breath left in your body."

I was still shocked that she was someone who was there. Someone who knew where I'd been, and what I'd done.

She pointed to the tables. "We laid you right over there and prayed. I will never forget that moment when your heart beat again. It has kept hope alive for many of us during the darkest times."

"I'm sorry for what was done to you. I feel . . . responsible."

"Sacrifice is a gift one gives willingly when it is for the right reasons."

"I failed to save her," I said faintly.

"I know the loss of your mother is difficult. You rescued many others."

"After Abigail brought us here, where did we go?"

"She kept us underground until the Triad bounty was too high. She could no longer protect us. We needed to be separated."

"We were kids, Scarlett."

"I have never forgotten those days. We fought and battled together."

"Was your memory wiped too?"

"The drugs were not perfect. Not all has been forgotten. I'm afraid time has shown no mercy for our brothers and sisters. Those we loved have been lost in this war. Sadness has lingered for many years. Perhaps it has never left."

I exhaled fully. "Are there any other survivors from the Program?"

"Ghosts mostly. Dead to some, legends to others. Jacob, you have returned in our darkest hour."

"I'm not who you think I am."

"You have survived a war between two worlds."

"That was another life."

"In the past, the Brethren have killed for the highest bidder without mercy for the weak. Now, a new legion of assassins are under the Ghost's control—those who will remember you. No longer are they merely protectors of the underworld. The tide has shifted to something far more dangerous. You are the one to lead us—the Guardians—into battle."

"Slow down."

Scarlett glanced at the street below, across at the rooftop shanties, and then gazed at me with eyes that pierced straight through me.

"Your father was mistaken. You must leave this place, and never return."

43

"WAIT!" Kate walked briskly towards us. Scarlett stood her ground, not as surprised as I was by the interruption. "I need to speak with Jake for a minute." She didn't break stride. "Don't go anywhere."

She grabbed my shirt and pulled me far enough away to be out of earshot. The look in her eyes triggered a memory. It was the last time I was in the Sunland apartment. I had grown to love Rachel's fiery spirit, but that night it was clear we'd grown apart. Frustration faded to silence. Hurt words turned to deafening resentment. On that night, there was no yelling, cursing, arguing, or any attempt to save what was lost. I walked out the door and knew there would never be anyone who filled my heart so full, yet pierced my soul so deep.

She wasn't Rache. She wasn't someone I loved. I was just a pawn she needed in a game where one wrong move meant I was dead.

"She can help us find your father," Kate said in a hushed voice.

"A war between two worlds? Who are the Guardians? I don't know what she's talking about. "

"Right now, she's all we've got."

"You know, if the shots don't work we're screwed," I argued. "I'll let you down, Kate. That's what I do."

"You wanted the truth? Well here it is." Kate loosened her grip. Her eyes softened. "I won't let you fail. And it doesn't sound like she will either."

"I don't know how to become someone else?"

"Start by digging deep in that soul of yours and resurrect who you need to be."

"When you put it that way, it sounds impossible."

A sequence of events flashed rapidly. Me walking up the path to Doc's house drunk with excitement. I believed it was the day that would turn my life around. Instead, it turned everything upside down.

Another flash. Doc's lifeless body. In that moment, life shattered into a million pieces

I felt the steering wheel as Kate stared at me in the rearview mirror.

Boom! My ears ringing with an explosion that ripped through me. Kate's fingers digging into my arms as she dangled above the rubble.

The trajectory of life skyrocketed to a universe where failure, addiction, and loss were replaced with the legend of Lazarus—the boy who battled evil and was resurrected to life. In the pit of my stomach, I wanted to escape and drown my sorrows. Dealing with this reality was too much for one man to bear. Without the addiction flowing through my veins, I was paralyzed to change.

A few days of sobriety wasn't enough to conquer those demons. I was on a rooftop in Kowloon, in a place where I was immortalized for acts of courage, bravery, and sacrifice. Those words were foreign to me. I was cornered with Kate on one side and Scarlett on the other. I was being forced into a fight that had killed me once already.

An ounce of belief might reawaken what remained dormant. A seed of faith, like Sister Evelyn preached, enabled her to cause the lame to walk and the blind to see. History defined her by her failures, yet her strength was undeniable. Blind faith, that's what I needed.

I thought of Samantha and the way she could see the world like no one else. She always believed the best in me, even when my best wasn't close to being good enough. She made me believe the impossible was possible because she was convinced that one day she would see again.

"Is this your version of tough love?"

"You wish." Kate smirked. "Look, all I'm asking is that you keep trusting me."

I wiped my sweaty palms and said loudly, "Fine. I'll do it."

"Very well." Scarlett's eyes bounced between us. "We must keep his memory loss between us for now. We cannot let the others know or else there will be questions."

"Absolutely," Kate agreed.

"You were top of your class at Quantico," Scarlett said to Kate. "Frank said your skills will be useful. I hoped he would be here with you tonight. We lost contact two days ago."

"What do you know about Damas Kone?"

"He is one of the Brethren's assassins who protect the Triads, and he returned from Lusaka last night." Scarlett showed us surveillance photos on her cell. Two men near a black Bugatti and a Gulfstream X parked inside a private hanger. One African. One Asian. "Kone is on the left."

"Who's the other guy?" I asked.

"Some believe he is the Ghost." Scarlett turned to me. "Jacob, if they know you are alive—that you are here—the others will follow."

Kate eyed the photos closely. "Send those to me. I'll see what I can find out."

"Where are they now?" I asked.

"Kone checked into the penthouse suite at the Peninsula. We have him under surveillance. We will leave in the morning. I suggest you get some sleep."

"I'll need a weapon," Kate said.

"That can be arranged."

44

Water from a fountain shot skyward. A fleet of Rolls Royces lined an oval entrance to the Peninsula, a five-star hotel that overlooked Victoria Harbor in Tsim Sha Tsui. Doormen dressed in black suits and white gloves opened giant glass doors for each guest. Across from the hotel, green and white ferries passed in the harbor. A clock tower overlooked Star Ferry as well as Kowloon's central bus depot. Palm trees lined the harbor and shaded a fountain that stretched the length of the promenade.

I kept a few strides behind and took in the surroundings. A sampan with a bright red sail floated in the center of the harbor. Further down, an eight-story cruise ship docked at the pier and dwarfed Ocean Terminal. I caught up to Kate, who hid behind dark shades and blended in with the tourists who strolled by and posed next to a Bruce Lee statue.

Scarlett crossed the promenade and joined a man sitting near a fountain with his cap pulled down low and headphones wrapped around his ears. Both stared at a tablet. I guessed he was our lookout who had kept eyes on Kone all night.

"Do you trust her?" I asked Kate.

"We don't know anything about her, but she's already steps ahead of us."

"You're right. I mean why else would Maggie send us to her?"

"I thought we were following the coordinates," Kate replied.

"Maggie's how you knew we were in the right place?"

"I was going to tell you. What'd you find out from your guy?"

"Don't worry, I didn't tell Brad where or what we're doing, even though he pushed for answers." Kate eyed Scarlett closely. "A week ago the ambassador to Zambia contacted the CIA regarding a classified document. Only the President had the authorization to unseal the file, which he did the day Warren was killed."

"Did it have to do with the Program?"

"It was an investigation into an American citizen who died in the Philippines. His name was John Armstrong, and he was a close friend of the President. There was a list of a dozen political and religious leaders who were assassinated over the last decade. A common link to each one connected back to Kone, and possibly the Brethren. Brad ran Kone through the system and got a hit on Interpol's Most Wanted, which confirmed that his last known location was here."

"So this is personal to the President."

"Which explains why capturing Kone was a top priority."

"But Kone's here, and Frank's MIA."

"Scarlett said she lost contact. It's possible he's still on Kone's trail."

We glanced towards Scarlett as she approached. "Kone checked into room P7. He's in the Verandah eating breakfast."

"You think he'd be hiding," I said. "Especially if he's on Interpol's Most Wanted list?"

"He is untouchable as long as he protects the Triads."

"What about the Ghost?" Kate asked.

"We do not know if he is the Ghost," Scarlett replied cautiously. "His name is Alan Leung, a highly-connected businessman with a war chest of relationships deep enough for him to be invaluable to either side. He is also a candidate in the election to be the next CEO of Hong Kong."

"Why didn't you tell us that last night?" Kate asked.

The promenade grew more crowded. I scanned the area for the man who Scarlett spoke with, but he was gone. I waited for Scarlett to respond to Kate. Both turned their attention over my shoulder. I glanced back to see

Alan Leung walk down the steps of the Peninsula as a valet climbed from a Bugatti and handed him the keys.

"We need to split up." Scarlett texted and a second later Kate's cell buzzed. "We'll meet there at three o'clock."

Scarlett cut through the crowd as the Bugatti pulled out onto Salisbury Road. A white Toyota van stopped at the curb long enough for her to jump in, and then pulled a U-turn a few cars behind the Bugatti.

"We need eyes on Kone." Whether I was ready or not, we were on the hunt. I'd missed something in the conversation, but I couldn't put my finger on it. We dodged traffic and entered the hotel.

Inside, a high-beamed ceiling soared over a lobby bustling with business and pleasure. Asians. Indians. Americans. Brits. Africans. It was a virtual melting pot of the human race. A grand staircase led up to four glass elevators. Waiters and bellhops, dressed to perfection, moved unseen amongst the antique furniture dating back to the early 1920s. I tripped crossing the marble floor.

Kate grabbed my arm and whispered, "Breathe."

A maître de ushered us to a table in the Verandah where a large buffet separated two dining areas. Across from where we were seated, Kone drank coffee and eyed his cell. He never looked in our direction. Kate kept him in her sights.

"Why didn't she tell us about Alan Leung?"

"Maybe because she wasn't sure he's the Ghost," I suggested. "What is it?"

"He's leaving." Kate grabbed my hand. "Ready?"

Kone crossed the main lobby less than ten feet away. I tried to blend in, but I felt like a bullseye was painted on my forehead. He headed for the elevators. My knees nearly buckled when he turned back for a second. I kept walking, even though my heart skipped a beat more than once. I shadowed a bellhop then followed Kone towards the high-priced retail stores tucked away from the lobby. I stopped at Cartier and stared at rows of expensive watches. I spotted Kone's reflection in the glass. He picked up the pace. I wondered if he'd seen me. Kate was nearby so I continued out the back exit.

Kone was definitely moving quickly. I hurried along, narrowly dodging a taxi as it cut through traffic. I reminded myself that Kate was the one to keep me alive. I ducked down a side alley and was struck with a sense that I'd escaped death in this city once before. Soon I'd know if lightening struck twice. Only Scarlett wasn't here to pray for a miracle if this turned south.

I entered a crowded street market where vendors busied themselves loading in goods for the afternoon locals and midnight tourists. Rows of colorfully decorated stalls stacked with knockoff-branded clothing, watches, sunglasses, VCDs, and luggage. A strong stench filled my nostrils from fresh seafood on ice.

As I walked by the handcrafted bamboo birdcages stacked alongside boxes of moon cakes, I avoided getting too close to the dead pigs, chickens, and cuts of beef that hung in the store entryways. I lost Kone for a second when my eyes caught a vendor with a stack of bamboo boxes, similar to the one I'd pried open in Doc's pool house.

Kone slipped in and out of the crowd with ease. I glanced back to make sure Kate was still on the chase. She had barely reached the start of the market. The three of us picked up the pace.

Kone stopped abruptly in the center of the market, turned, and faced me. His dark eyes locked in.

A chill shot through me. I froze.

Like the night at the wash, something pushed me to be the aggressor. With Kone less than fifty feet away, I darted through the crowd. He reacted and sprinted towards the far end of the market. I stopped where I'd seen him last then caught sight of him boarding a double-decker bus.

In an instant, I went from being bait to being the hunter. I waved frantically at the driver, who slowed long enough for me to jump aboard. I never thought about the fare.

The driver yelled in Cantonese as I pushed through the passengers standing in the aisle. Kone glanced back, realized the bus wasn't moving, and exited. My chest burned with every breath. Kone cut across traffic and disappeared down a flight of stairs. I was in no shape to keep up, and I had no idea what I'd do if I caught him.

I dialed my cell. "Train station behind the hotel!"

"One block away."

"Hurry up!"

I cursed under my breath as my lungs burned. I scrambled down the stairs, knocking into several people, before I found myself in a large underground metro system. Ticket machines lined the walls. Turnstiles clicked as hundreds of passengers slipped their magnetic cards through the slots. Kone was nowhere. The plan was to spook him. Now I'd lost him.

I spun around as a voice startled me.

"Why are you following me?"

We were only a few feet away. It was the first time I'd seen him up close. We were about the same age. Slender. Dark skin. He didn't look like a killer. Then again, I didn't look like one either. I braced myself and hoped Kate would get there quick. I tried to keep my eyes focused on him, the same exercise I did with Frank.

From the opposite end of the station, Kate headed in our direction. She bumped Kone, apologized, and kept on walking. Kone turned his back and headed towards the turnstiles. The trap was set.

Kate had kept me alive.

45

We brushed through the turnstiles at Star Ferry and were instantly engulfed in a sea of people. It seemed no matter where you were in this city, the waves of humanity never ceased. A drawbridge slammed against the concrete. Within a matter of seconds, hundreds more disembarked. No sign of Kone since the MTR station.

A dozen more faces passed as we boarded. We slipped into a row of wooden seats at the bow of the ferry. It pushed away from the pier and drifted at a snail's pace across the harbor.

"That was intense." I leaned my head back. "I can't believe it worked."

"You did good." Kate checked her cell. A dot on a GPS map blinked. "We'll be able to track him as long as he keeps his cell on."

"I didn't think you brought any gadgets."

"A have a few tricks up my sleeve."

"What happens now?"

"We've set the trap, now we see where it leads."

"Is this how you caught Maldone?"

"I joined the same pilates studio as Theresa. Three times a week for six months. We became friends, grabbed drinks on the West Side, and I waited until she opened up to me. She told me her grandfather was a fugitive, but she hadn't seen him in years. I knew she was lying." Kate watched the ferries passing in the harbor. "She never gave him up. Twenty-four/seven surveillance and a tracker on her cell gave us the break we needed. Patience.

Persistence. It all paid off when we followed her to his apartment in Venice Beach."

"She never knew you were an FBI agent?"

"That was kept from her until the trial." Kate looked out over the water. "We offered her protection, but by then she didn't trust me. I don't blame her. If she'd listened, maybe she'd still be alive."

I turned towards her. "Kate, how do you do this?"

"You become someone else until it's over."

"That really works?"

"Not always." Kate stared directly at me. "Jake, what we do in life defines us. Our choices. Our failures. Our successes. I should've told Theresa the truth, but I risked Maldone slipping through my fingers. She was in tears in the courtroom, as the jury listened to the names of the victims. She never knew the monster her grandfather had become. If he was the Ghost, and trained others in the Brethren, no one had a clue. I betrayed her trust because of the crimes he committed. It was the only way to get justice. Sometimes you have to be willing to do whatever is necessary for the end game."

"Maldone should've died in the gas chamber."

"Seeing her body at the shack, well…"

"Why did he keep me alive?"

"Maldone was extremely calculated. If he spared you that night years ago, then there is a good reason. And if what President Palmer says is right, you're a weapon that threatens the existence of the Brethren. Now their only course of action is retribution. Maybe Maldone realized you were his best chance at revenge."

A puzzled look crossed my face as a drawbridge slammed and snatched us from the conversation. A weapon? An unsettling feeling spiked through my senses. Maybe there was more to the Program than I was being told. I intended to find out once I had Scarlett alone. She viewed me as a hero, and our past together might give me the answers. It was strange to think that I had blamed Frank all along, while I should've been blaming myself. Mom's death was on my bloodied hands.

To reawaken Lazarus—to become a weapon—I needed to unlock the darkness in my soul where only vengeance and revenge endured. Of course, I had no idea how I was supposed to do that.

We navigated our way through the crowd along Man Yiu Street towards Edinburgh Place. A few more blocks and we reached the Peak Tram Historical Gallery on Garden Road. We sauntered through the gallery and waited in line next to a bright red tram with gold lettering parked at the bottom of a steep mountain.

I wiped sweat from my neck and shook off a dizzying sensation. I'd chased Kone through an open market, onto a bus, and into a train station. Absolutely out of my mind. My body was fueled with adrenaline. Now I suffered the emotional crash after the chase. Searing humidity seeped into my bones and sucked the last ounce of energy from my veins. I struggled to keep my balance, struck with the thought that those I loved might die before the end.

"Jake, are you okay?"

"Yeah. I'm fine."

We boarded at exactly three o'clock.

The tram climbed the tracks steadily at a forty-five-degree angle. A drastic ascent, mixed with skyscrapers and apartments jutting from the mountainside, gave a mesmerizing illusion that the world was a bit off kilter. A migraine jolted me back in my seat, so intense that I barely noticed when the tram stopped and passengers disembarked into the hillside. By the time we neared the Peak, we were the only ones left. I leaned forward as my body shook. I felt my organs shutting down.

The tram stopped again. This time, the driver shuffled down the aisle and stepped off. I struggled to keep myself from rolling out of the seat. Kate tensed when a man stepped aboard and stood in the doorway. Jet-black hair. Dark-rimmed glasses. Tall and slender.

"I am with the Guardians," he said in a British accent. He shook our hands vigorously. "My name is Timothy. It is an honor to meet you both."

In a daze, I followed Kate and Timothy off the tram. I stood on the side of the mountain as a warm breeze washed over me. The steep grade stretched my calves and agitated my ankle. Something wasn't right. I stepped forward as another rush flooded through me. I heard Scarlett's voice as my legs buckled, my vision blurred, and I collapsed to the concrete. I tried to speak—my words were muffled. I heard more voices but didn't understand the words. As everything faded, I felt a prick on the back of my neck.

46

"Do you believe common ground is possible?"

Alan Leung stood opposite a CNN reporter as the camera panned across a wide shot of the two of them in a boardroom high above Central.

"I am running for Chief Executive Officer, not because I need more to do, but because I believe we are in a unique position to bring these two powerhouses together. For too long, our leaders have undervalued the significance of our partnership with the United States and the PRC. They are the most important relationships of the century."

"President Palmer has questioned the PRC's monetary policies. Do you agree?"

"That is a debate that has existed for decades." Leung laughed. "Both believe they are the biggest shark in the room. I have been successful because I understand that negotiation is about giving each side something they want. I promise you, I will foster these relationships and increase Hong Kong's influence globally."

"Do you agree with the US Congress who wishes to impose tariffs on Chinese imports?"

"We have the Policy Act of 1992 to protect us from any US sanctions. What they decide to do in regards to the PRC is out of our control. However, the PRC is the largest foreign holder of US debt and could use that to leverage their position. The US needs to stop borrowing money to solve their economic problems. Suggesting a tariff on Chinese imports to assist in their recovery will not strengthen a relationship that is deteriorating. From the moment I am in office, I will work to bridge the divide that we must admit exists between them."

"How will you bridge the gap?"

"Once I am the CEO of Hong Kong, I will bring them to the table and mediate the road ahead, knowing that both sides need what we have built within our borders. Failure of the US economy will affect the growth of the PRC in global business, which means our involvement in negotiating bilateral agreements to promote trade and investment will help to stabilize both sides."

"In recent months, the relationship between the US and the PRC has grown increasingly strained. The Americans have accused the PRC of cyber-hacking and have publicly questioned their human rights practices." The reporter glanced at her notes. "President Palmer was quoted as saying, 'The Chinese government has a long history of repression and coercion.' In response, the PRC has accused the US of spying on its own citizens, gun violence, and rising homelessness."

"Hong Kong is autonomous," Leung said matter of factly. "We have separate customs territory. No changes to our borders. No changes in the PRC controlling our exports since the handover in '97. We are one of the world's most appealing tax havens for conducting commerce. We are the gateway for the world and the strongest ally to the PRC. For the West to build a strong strategic partnership with the Mainland they need us on their side."

"You were quoted in *The Standard* as saying Hong Kong is an asset to the US and a danger to the PRC."

"Admittedly, I struggle with the meddling from the PRC in regards to business and social issues. However, I am also a realist. I believe our future rests on becoming an economic power that does not solely rely on the PRC or the US. We do not want to end up in a financial collapse like Greece. We must embrace our democracy responsibly."

"How would you have voted on the bill that stipulated Beijing's approval for any candidate that wishes to run for the Chief Executive office?"

"Do I believe anyone should be able to run for office? No, I do not. We have a difficult enough time with the candidates who are selected by politicians and special interest groups who have selfish agendas."

"How were you selected?"

"As you know, I am a very private person who has been lucky enough to build a successful company. While it is true that I was initially approached by the PRC, it was not until I spoke with local businessmen and government officials that I considered running for office. I took their request seriously. When I looked at the potential of our future as Hong Kongers, I believed I could make a difference on a broader scale."

"You said you are a very private person," the reporter stated. "Not much is known about your family, only that you were raised in an orphanage."

"Yes, I was raised at the Hope House in Tai Kok Tsui," Leung replied. "I do not know anything about my parents. However, I was given a chance, and I have taken advantage of the opportunities that have presented themselves."

"Let us talk for a moment about your strongest opponent. Polls suggest that Xu Li Ma has garnered the younger voters. She believes there should be free elections where the people decide who will run for this position without a governmental selection committee."

"She has also filled their minds with false truths," Leung shot back. "In recent weeks, we have seen this next generation rebel against our government. It is a dangerous precedent to set for our future. Peace and love without economic stability will not take us to the Promised Land. I am about doing what is best to ensure our freedom in the years ahead. If that means arresting thousands of twenty-year-olds for breaking the law then that is what I am prepared to do. Xu Li Ma's own father was the Secretary for Justice before he was assassinated. I would think she would know better."

"Some believe he was connected to the Triads?"

"There is no proof that was the case, however, Xu Li Ma's suggestion to reopen the Golden Triangle leaves that in question. And the extent of her knowledge of this route is a question that should be asked. Imagine, if she were to win the election, she could unleash a web of drug smugglers and sex traffickers. Is that a risk Hong Kongers are willing to take?"

"She has publicly accused Mulfira Mining, a company you are heavily invested in, of illegal mining operations on a global scale."

"I've been a businessman long before I decided to run in the election. I have invested in dozens of global corporations, including Mulfira. But her accusations are baseless. Show me one piece of evidence that what she has said is true. I invest in corporations who operate within the laws of their respective countries. Look at my track record and you will not find one lawsuit connected to any of the companies where I am a shareholder. Xu Li Ma knows she cannot win unless she discredits me. Maybe that is a tactic she learned from her family."

"How confident are you that you will win?"

"I believe I am the right person for the job. I will work to resolve the conflicts between the US and the PRC. I will continue to bring Fortune 100 businesses into our city. And I will ensure that this Pearl of the Orient will shine brightly for years to come."

47

Alan Leung pressed his palm against an engraved dragon etched into a solid jade door that quietly slid opened. Inside, a bright light shone down on a circular room with smooth walls. He stood in the center as a red beam scanned his face. The round wall opened into a large living area leading out to a stone balcony beneath a curved tiled roof. In the distance, Happy Valley Jockey Club and downtown Central glowed in the night.

The Ghost waited on the balcony. Her petite frame caused many to misjudge her sadistic tendencies. Her snake eyes turned towards Leung as the aroma of money emanated from her skin. She was more dangerous than anyone he had ever known. And she was perhaps his greatest flaw.

"I always believed Lazarus was a legend," Leung said. "I heard about him for many years at the orphanage."

The Ghost stepped close to the edge of the balcony and gazed in the direction of Victoria Harbor. She was a serpent playing with her prey. She turned her gaze to him. "Alan, remain focused on the election."

Leung's eyes never left hers, as if drawn in by her lustful stare. He was vulnerable around her, but it wasn't love. Neither believed in it. She was his protector. Once he was in control of the city, he'd need her more than ever before.

"Vengeance can be a distraction," Leung said. "I need to know you will wait."

"He is of no concern to you."

"If the legend is true, then he killed without a second breath. If he has returned, and that same spirit is within him, he will be far more dangerous. I cannot risk losing everything I have built for a war that is not my own."

"Remember the terms of our agreement."

"You know where my allegiance lies."

"Beneath the sheets with most women, but not with me." The Ghost flirted. Her sly smile was gone in an instant. "The Brethren control the balance of power to bring order to the chaos. We are the ones who ensure the greed and vengeance of others will not lead to war amongst themselves. However, the bounty on Lazarus must be fulfilled once I am done with him. He carries something of great value to me." The Ghost kissed Leung gently on the cheek. Her perfume filled his nostrils. She whispered in his ear, "The time is near for the Brethren to evolve once again. It begins when we choke the last ounce of freedom from his soul."

48

Poised to move with purpose, I gripped a semi-automatic and listened to the sobs. I caught my balance as everything swayed. I blinked to get my bearings. I wasn't on the floating restaurant, but I was on a boat. A mixture of gasoline and exhaust filled the cabin. Reality and dreams, mixed in a fog of memories, hung thick as the vessel dipped with each wave that slapped against the hull.

I doubled over as pain ripped through my bones. The migraine remained rooted in the back of my skull like an exposed nerve. Did I hit my head when I passed out? Was it a spike in my memory? Or was it a lack of liquid courage? My body was wrecked. I figured it must be from the withdrawals. No addict finds sobriety without a little self-retribution.

I'm an addict.

Months of late night binges, empty bottles, and losing all I loved finally brought those words to my lips. It wasn't the best timing, seeing as everyone needed me to be Lazarus. How was I supposed to fight my demons when they needed me to fight theirs?

My heart ached for Rachel and Samantha. I missed their laughter, their touch, and their presence. Even though Rachel had ended it, I still needed to be with them. I wished I'd told them how special they were to me when I had the chance.

Drinking was the one thing I controlled. I needed it. I wanted it. Even when everything was stripped away, I thirsted for it. Addiction brought me to Doc's door. Now my road to sobriety was a narrow path to a forgotten world, a place where being someone else was the only way to survive.

An engine clanked and rumbled to a steady rhythm.

I braced myself against the wall and gingerly hobbled as my muscles shredded from my bones. I was broken in more ways than one. A wave of regret smacked me in the face. Brokenhearted. Scared. Thirsty. Was I losing my mind? I reached the top step and stared out on a night far from the bright neon lights.

I stopped cold as Scarlett's voice hung in the dense fog. "His bloody heart stopped!"

"I had no choice," Kate answered.

"You do not know what you have done."

"I saved him. He would've died back there."

"You nearly killed him."

"He knows the risk."

"He is not ready, and neither are we."

"There's too much at stake."

"He doesn't know a bloody thing," Scarlett argued. "Have you told him what you're injecting into him, why you've brought him here, or who we are protecting him from?"

"The Brethren have killed countless innocent lives over the decades. I will do what is necessary to stop them. That's why I'm here. I will see this through with or without your help."

"How can he possibly know the sacrifice that is expected of him?" Scarlett countered. "I will not be part of this unless I am convinced otherwise. The President must realize we are not waging war against one, but against them all."

"And I am sure that Frank told you why Jake is the one."

"You have not fought a darkness such as this," Scarlett said. "Survivors never return the same to those they love. This war will not end simply because you have brought Jacob here."

"Freedom hangs in the balance. You believe that too, or else you wouldn't be helping us. You know what he is capable of, and I need your help to bring that out of him."

The silence was deafening. I dared not move.

"Then I must take him to where it began," Scarlett said. "After twenty years, he deserves to know. Only then will we be sure he is the one."

"We have less than a week," Kate replied flatly.

A chill shot through me. I was a pawn that needed to be kept in the game. It sounded like Kate was willing to lay me on the altar, like she'd done with Theresa Maldone. Well, at least Scarlett defended me. I think. Her words left me with even more questions.

Who were they protecting me from?

I winced in pain as something brushed my shoulder. Timothy stood in the dark, looked past me. "They've been arguing since we left." His voice was hushed.

"Wha—what?"

"You dropped like a rock, Mate. We had to carry you most of the way. You've been passed out below. I came to check on you, but you weren't where I left you."

"How long?"

"About two hours."

"Why'd I…"

Timothy's eyes darted between the women. "You're friend, uh…"

He hesitated. Even though my body screamed on the inside, I waited. I needed to vomit, or curl up in a corner and groan in misery. "What'd she do?"

"I'm not supposed to…" Timothy shot another look towards them. "She jabbed you with a bloody needle."

"What?"

"When you dropped to the ground, she stuck a needle in you."

I slumped to the floor. All the energy flushed out of me. Timothy caught me on the way down. His firm grip stopped me from rolling down the steps. A wave of exhaustion—or was it disappointment—crashed into me. "How many times?"

"Once at The Peak and once when we brought you aboard. Scarlett tried to stop her, but well, you see how that's going."

I shook my head. "Where are we going?"

"Tai O."

I lowered my head until it was between my legs. The nausea grew stronger as sweat seeped down my back and stuck to my shirt. I trusted Kate, but she crossed the line. Two injections in a matter of hours was the perfect recipe to cause the pain in my body. It was unforgivable. I wanted to confront her, yet I was too sick for the boiling anger to surface into rage.

"Help me up. I need some air."

"Right. Good idea."

I draped one arm over his shoulder as he helped me out onto the stern. Kate and Scarlett stopped talking when they noticed me. Timothy set me down near the edge. I leaned against the teak planking, rested my head on a rubber tire that was split in half over the side of the junk, and tried to slow my rapid heartbeat.

Kate called out, "Jake, are you feeling better?"

Her words grew muffled and disappeared amidst a ringing in my ears. I squeezed my eyes closed and tried not to puke on myself. When I struggled to open my eyes, everything was blurred as the ringing only intensified. I blinked a dozen more times but nothing improved. I cramped and pressed both palms against my skull in a pointless attempt to squeeze the pain from my pores.

I sensed someone kneel beside me. Kate's voice was barely a whisper, "Tell me what's going on."

I mumbled, "I trusted you, Kate."

I allowed all my weight to lean against the tire. As long as I didn't move, the pain didn't worsen. Kate didn't speak again, at least not any words I remembered. I breathed in the muggy air and prayed for the noise to fade. After a while, the pain grew bearable before it passed. I listened to the waves as the world returned to normal.

I realized I was alone on deck as the junk drifted amidst a bluish hue cast over the evening, and maneuvered down a narrow canal between shanties perched on tall stilts sunk beneath the water. A fog lifted enough to see smaller boats with outboard motors tied to makeshift docks beneath the soft glow of a seaside village.

The engine idled, and we coasted towards a two-story dwelling with an open balcony. Clothes hung from bamboo poles. Shadows leaned over the edge as if eyeing me from above. Timothy appeared, grabbed a thick rope, and jumped off the junk to the bottom floor. He tied the rope around two stilts that supported the structure.

I inhaled the peaceful night in Tai O.

It was the one place I remembered.

49

I followed an enticing aroma to the second floor and dropped my backpack at the top of the stairs. I felt rigid, yet starved at the same time. I ignored Kate. She betrayed our short-lived pact of trust. As soon as Scarlett went out to the balcony, Kate pulled me aside.

"Why'd you do it?" I asked.

"I can explain."

"I want the doses, tonight."

"I had no choice, Jake."

"You don't even know what you injected into me." I shook my head in disbelief. "Tell me, are you really here to find Frank or to use me like you did Theresa?"

Scarlett returned with two new faces that stood next to Timothy. She started the introductions with a slender, shaggy-haired blond sporting a goat beard.

"William Fargher, ex-pat, and our resident computer hack." William nodded.

Next to him stood a bald Asian with tattoos down both arms and around his neck. "Bao Wong. Born and raised in Mong Kok. Knows the red light districts better than anyone.

"And, of course, you have already met Timothy. He gathers all intelligence. E-mails. Texts. Social media. He'll tell you he's a better hacker than Will, but I'd say they are dead even."

William, Bao, and Timothy were no older than early twenties. Scarlett pointed towards the opposite side of the room. A folding table was covered with monitors, laptops, and piles of photos and maps. Everything in the room seemed portable, including the kitchen. No other furniture. Only sleeping bags rolled up in a corner, and backpacks lined up next to where I had dropped mine.

"Boys, this is Kate McNaughton. FBI."

"Whoa." William rocked back on his heels. "I didn't know we'd have their help."

"Technically, I'm not longer with the Bureau."

"Oh," Bao mumbled. "So, it's just us then."

My cheeks warmed as all eyes turned to me. I stepped forward, awkwardly avoiding their stares, and shook hands. "William, Bao, Timothy, it's nice to meet you guys."

Kate didn't mask her skepticism. She asked Scarlett, "You are all the Guardians? Is there anyone else?"

Scarlett ignored the question and asked William, "Have you got Kone's signal?" He nodded. "Keep eyes on him. The rest of us will pack up everything tonight so we can head out before sunrise."

"We also have the live feed from Leung's house in Happy Valley," Timothy added. "He hasn't left since you followed him there."

"Stay on the house," Scarlett said. "Let's see if anyone else pays him a visit."

Bao moved towards a wok that sizzled over an open gas flame set beside a small rice cooker. He dug out a scoop of steaming rice and piled a heaping spoonful of barbeque pork over the top. Timothy and William followed.

I found a seat at a folding table near their portable command center. The lingering effects of the day left me exhausted, but the sweet aroma was too much to resist. Scarlett set a bowl in front of me, and I shoveled a mouthful to avoid conversation.

"A moment please," Kate said to Scarlett.

I stayed hunched over and kept shoveling.

.J. WILLIAMS

Once I knew they were outside, I glanced up at the others.

William spoke first. "I thought you'd be bigger."

Bao chuckled, "Thinner."

"More mysterious," Timothy added.

"Just another *gweilo*." Bao laughed. William and Timothy joined in.

"I know that word." I surprised myself. "You called me a foreign devil."

The table fell silent as the three exchanged embarrassed looks. I stabbed at a piece of pork with the chopsticks before bursting out laughing. It was strange to hear myself around a table of strangers. As if it had been so long since I'd felt the warmth of a smile. Besides, it was better than being caught in the middle of a catfight.

50

Neco Rimoldi rendezvoused with a smuggler who guided him through a maze of tunnels from San Diego to Tijuana guarded by the Cartel. Pursuing the witness and the Fed were no longer a priority. In his world, death was a commodity, and the price for his expertise had risen since the bombing. His skills were requested elsewhere, most likely a higher-priced target. By the time he reached Mexico City, a private jet waited, courtesy of the Ghost.

For the past three days, he stayed holed up in sleazy motels around Phuket. He never stayed in the same room more than one night, switched aliases daily, paid cash, and was meticulous about leaving no footprint behind. For an old pro, it was second nature.

By now the FBI, CIA, NSA, and Interpol were chasing a shadow. It was only a matter of time before blame for the bombing was placed on some lone-wolf terrorist organization in the Middle East.

For nearly thirty years, he looked death in the face and pulled the trigger without a second thought. Some fought courageously, while others died in fear. Theresa Maldone was terrified in her final moments, but at least she fought to the end. He expected Warren to fight, to run, or to beg for his life. He would've respected him more. He loathed the prayer. He killed a coward. A man who believed it was better to die on his knees than swing with his fists. His bones would rot in the ground like those in Agua Prieta.

Rimoldi closed the blinds and passed the hours scouring security footage from Warren's house. Going back a month, the only visitor was the housekeeper who stopped by twice a week. He looped the video from that morning in an attempt to snatch a screen shot of the witness. As a safeguard, he'd copied the footage before handing it over to the Ghost. The exercise of viewing it over and over again was futile. Warren blocked the doorway perfectly and the backyard footage cut out exactly at 8:06 AM.

At the wash, he peered through a scope as the car skidded into his line of fire. Then there was the hospital rooftop. He only caught a glimpse of the man, but if they were one in the same, then the witness showed no regard for saving himself. That bothered Rimoldi more than putting a bullet in a brain. Boarding the helicopter he had broken the golden rule: Never leave loose ends alive.

His mentor taught him that valuable lesson. It was, of course, Maldone's mantra. For years, he abided by those words, and they had kept him alive. He imagined the old man's rage when he realized his prized apprentice killed his flesh and blood at the request of the Ghost. Leaving her to rot in Agua Prieta was a way to pay homage to all the bodies that were buried there because of Maldone's own hands. Dust to dust, ashes to ashes. Death was an act of mercy on the weak. It was never personal, merely a means to an end.

At eight o'clock, Rimoldi swept the room and left. A short Tuk-Tuk to the airport and he was wheels up, destined for Hong Kong. He landed at Kai Tak and drove the route to Aberdeen shortly after midnight. Outside the warehouse, the moonlit sky shone through a row of broken windows. Tension lurked beneath his skin.

He entered to find a man slumped over in a chair. Both wrists and ankles zip-tied. Someone had already inflicted a severe dose of pain.

A deep African voice said, "Neco, good of you to come."

Rimoldi relaxed. "I thought this might be you."

"It has been a long time since Mindanao."

"I still say that was a lucky shot."

"Skill, my friend," Kone replied. "I am surprised the Ghost requested you to be here. It is a young man's game these days."

"I haven't lost my edge." Rimoldi nodded towards the man. "Who's he?"

Kone stepped over to a table equipped with tools of the trade. He picked up a syringe and pressed the needle into the man's forearm. Rimoldi assumed the cocktail was a mixture weak enough to allow pain, yet strong enough to keep his heart beating. Even though Kone was his junior, Rimoldi considered the African an equal, evidenced by his reputation and tactics.

"I hear you climbed a few spots on Interpol," Rimoldi said. "You're untouchable."

"The same cannot be said for you. I hear you left quite a mess in Los Angeles."

"We both know who ordered that. The question is, why are we both here?"

The man lifted his head enough to see his captor. A bright light reflected off his dilated pupils. His face was caked in a mixture of fresh and dried blood. He gnashed his teeth as saliva dripped down his chin.

"Where is Lazarus?" Kone demanded from the man. When there was no response, Kone struck him hard in the face. A gash cut across the man's cheekbone and blood oozed down his neck. Kone casually picked up a scalpel and pointed it at him. "You will answer. Or I will cut you like a pig."

"Damas, you're not going to kill me," the man groaned, "so let me speak to her."

In Mindanao, Rimoldi was the spotter when the African fired a single shot from three blocks away. The bullet nailed the target and the two slipped into the shadows. Tonight, this man called Kone by name, and Rimoldi knew in their business that was trouble.

Kone stabbed the man in the leg, yanked his head back, and pointed the scalpel a centimeter from his pupil. The man cried in agony.

It was clear to Rimoldi that he was there to keep this man alive at least until the interrogation was over. He was the more seasoned pro. He had only known Kone to be controlled, but it was clear the African was strangely on edge.

"Tell my friend what he needs to know," Rimoldi suggested, in an attempt to slow Kone down from what he might do next. "I assure you, he will not hesitate to kill you."

Kone was wide eyed as he grabbed a second syringe.

"Damas," Rimoldi held up his hand. "Who is he?"

Kone brushed by Rimoldi and stuck the needle in the prisoner's arm.

"Langston."

51

Chopsticks were not my forte.

I stabbed at a second bowl of pork and rice while William and Timothy busied themselves behind laptops split-screened on a single monitor. All their gear fit onto a single folding table, and paled in comparison to the underground juggernaut back in LA. I leaned against the wall and watched the red dot on the monitor for an hour before it hit me.

Why hadn't she called in the cavalry? President Palmer could order a full arsenal to capture and interrogate one of Interpol's Most Wanted.

No rules. No restrictions. I guessed that meant no savior squad either.

I wrapped myself in this place, not as it was now, but as I imagined it had once been. It was more than four walls. It was home. I mulled this over and wondered if this was the beginning of the memories—my genesis. I was struck with a premonition of standing in this room united for war with others who shared life, love, and loyalty.

Scarlett knew who I'd been. Maybe that's the exact reason Maggie sent us to her. I couldn't imagine the pain inflicted on her during the Program. I was embarrassed to ask her about it. Begging her forgiveness for what she endured didn't seem enough. Why didn't Abigail bring her with us? How had she survived? How deep was she in this war? Were there others who were part of the Guardians? If not, how were the six of us going to defeat the Brethren?

No one asked that last question out loud, but I knew we were all thinking it.

William monitored a live feed from a GoPro mounted in a tree across from Alan Leung's residence. A window popped open on screen: Bank of China. He typed at a rapid pace. Seconds later, the screen blinked before changing to a series of numbers and letters. I wasn't sure how many firewalls he'd burst through, or how many international laws he'd broken. He entered a series of codes and the business tycoon's financial transactions whipped by.

"Grab as much history as you can." Scarlett's fiery hair and colorfully tatted sleeves seemed darker in the dim light. I stared at them for a moment, trying to identify the images and symbols.

William worked with speed and precision. I wondered if his expertise was strictly surveillance, intelligence, and code breaking. The ability to hack into the world's most guarded financial institutions was invaluable. Who knew what else this group of misfits was capable of doing behind the digital curtain?

"How'd you find all that?" I asked.

"Black web," William answered.

"That's for real?"

Timothy turned. "Oh yeah. It's where we spend most of our time."

William accessed the server for Mulfira Mining, a European company with shares owned by Alan Leung. He scrolled through a list of contacts, legal documents, and mining locations. Then he downloaded everything through some type of filtering program.

"The longer we are in here, the greater the risk," William said to Scarlett. "We already have more than enough to keep us busy."

"We're not sure what we're searching for, so take as much as you can." Scarlett turned to me. "Why don't you get some sleep?"

"I'm not tired." The truth was I was afraid to close my eyes. When your heart stops beating from a mystery serum with unknown side effects, the result is a permanent case of insomnia. I glanced at the others and couldn't shake the feeling they were a bit disappointed that Lazarus had yet to make an appearance. It would be so much easier if I returned to my former glory to bring justice to the world and be the hero who led his army into battle. If sin was the mark of the Brethren's power, virtue was the only way to defeat them. That meant the odds were stacked against me. I wasn't sure any amount of virtue could outweigh my sins.

"Leung's worth a bloody fortune." William entered another algorithm. "No obvious offshore accounts, but that doesn't mean anything."

"A half billion so far," Timothy added. "He could be hiding his money in bitcoins."

"We will never get past their firewalls."

"What about his connection to Kone?" Kate asked.

Timothy suggested, "We can cross-reference flight manifests."

"Brilliant," Scarlett replied.

William pulled the surveillance photos and logged into the Kai Tak records. He danced across the keys and searched the flight logs and found a Gulfstream X belonging to Leung Holdings, Inc. with a match on the tail identification.

"Departed, November 15. Destination: Lusaka." He scrolled down. "Refueled, and departed for Los Angeles via London."

Kate leaned in closer. "What day did it leave LA?"

"November 24. Landed at Kai Tak, refueled, and departed again for Mozambique early on the twenty-sixth."

"We took those photos on the twenty-ninth," Scarlett said, "Must have been when they returned."

"Passenger manifests from the LA flight?" Kate asked.

William clicked a few more times. "No records."

"Which airport did it depart from?"

"Van Nuys."

"Same day as the bombing," Kate said under her breath. "Which also puts Leung or Kone in LA around the same time Warren was killed."

"Latest flight was today. Roundtrip to Phuket." William printed out a list of the flight's destinations. "No names on this manifest either."

"Leung has someone on the inside," Scarlett said, "who's allowing him to travel without proper documentation."

"That will have to wait," Timothy interrupted. "Kone is moving."

He enlarged the main lobby cameras at the Peninsula. Kone stepped out from an elevator, walked across the screen, and disappeared out the front entrance. Timothy's fingers blazed across the keys at a frenetic pace. Smaller thumbnails appeared. Street cameras followed Kone's movements until he disappeared into an MTR station. For the next twenty minutes, the red dot moved, stopped, and moved again.

Timothy called out each station. "Central. Garden Road. Bowen Hill. Tin Wan."

Then the dot moved at a slower pace.

"He's off the train," Kate said.

"Location?" Scarlett asked.

Timothy swiped through the layers of windows and punched in the coordinates. A map magnified until it filled the screen. "Aberdeen."

"How far is that from here?" Kate asked.

"Half hour," Scarlett replied.

52

President Palmer wrapped a briefing aboard Air Force One with his Chief of Staff and several White House staffers. The events of the last forty-eight hours in Zambia left its people in a state of shock as they mourned their greatest leader and celebrated the death of their fiercest enemy. Details were sketchy. Palmer wondered if Frank's silence meant he was still on the hunt. Or if he was dead.

Without Frank, there was no other option than to send Agent McNaughton and Jake Harris to Hong Kong. It was a Hail Mary to believe that they could stop what might happen in the days ahead. Palmer checked his private cell. No calls. No texts. He turned his attention to Malcolm Whitman, ambassador to China, who waited patiently on the satellite feed. Palmer shifted gears and took Whitman off mute.

"Malcolm, where do we stand?"

"Two frontrunners, sir."

"One of them Alan Leung?"

"Yes, sir." Whitman shifted in his seat. "Mr. President, Xu Li Ma is up ten points."

"Did we leak the intel Leung gave us to the Mainland?"

"I provided them with the information, but it was not a surprise to them."

"They're okay with electing the heir of a known Triad leader?"

"For now, they are refusing to acknowledge her family history is an issue."

"I guess sins of the fathers don't translate to the sins of their children."

"She has garnered the younger demographic, which I believe caught everyone here off guard. Leung is definitely the safer choice, for them and for us. I doubt we will be able to persuade the PRC to go public with the damage Xi Li Ma's father inflicted on their own people, especially right before the election. Up until now, there has only been speculation about his connection to the Triads."

"Have you heard anything related to the Golden Triangle?"

"Leung was right when he said that Xu Li Ma has alluded to it in previous speeches. However, we're not sure exactly what her intentions might be at this point."

"She could be planning to resurrect that part of the family business."

"That's a possibility, sir. She wouldn't be the first elected official with roots to the Triads, and I'm sure she won't be the last. Convincing the Chinese to release to the press what we've shown them will only put us in the hot seat. For one, we'll have to divulge how we came about the intelligence."

"So, you're saying we need Leung to win this election."

"I believe he can strengthen our relations with the PRC. An alliance that could help keep the debt negotiations with the Mainland from going sideways. Perhaps divulging Xu Li Ma's connection to the Triads was a gesture of good faith on Leung's part. I know you don't agree with his stance on shale mining, but I think we need to consider the alternative if Xu Li Ma is elected."

"Lesser of two evils. Malcolm, how close are we talking?"

"She could win, Mr. President. People want change from the old regime, especially the twenty-and thirty-somethings. She's charismatic, and that garners votes. If she's elected, then the Mainland will be forced to flex their foothold on controlling democracy if they are to keep Hong Kongers from rioting in the streets. I'm sure you've already seen the demonstrations. I've never seen the city so tense, sir."

"We can't rely on the luck of the draw on this one."

"I'm doing everything in my power."

"Keep the pressure on the Chinese—and call in a few hours with an update."

"Yes, sir."

The video screen switched to CNN. Reports were still fluid on the situation in Lusaka, Zambia. The events of the past few hours bumped the running commentary of the administration's failure to capture the suspected terrorist cell responsible for the Montrose bombing. Family stories had been cycled through, and the clean up was off-limits to the press. The media latched on to the next global catastrophe and milked it from every conceivable point of view.

Palmer reached into a desk drawer and retrieved a Cuban. He leaned back in his leather chair and rested his head against the presidential seal stitched into the headrest.

The world had grown increasingly more complicated since he took the oath in his first term. Winning the election was child's play compared to the decisions that faced him now. ISIS replaced Al Qaeda and Iran as enemy number one. While the housing market had begun to bounce back, it was overshadowed by a volatile economy that left Wall Street baffled by huge declines blamed on China and Japan's stock market woes. His crowning achievement of healthcare reform was on the verge of being dismantled by a House majority who despised him. The financial recovery plan was rooted in another trillion-dollar loan from China.

Whoever was elected to be the next CEO of Hong Kong would be the voice that defined a great deal of the US recovery. Not to mention, the photo Leung had given to him left him with only one decision.

As Commander in Chief, all of this fell squarely on his shoulders. That's what the most powerful man in the free world signed up for when he threw his hat into the ring. Palmer weighed his options. He was convinced Leung was backed by the Brethren and protected by the Ghost. Who else would've known about Lazarus?

On the other hand, if Xu Li Ma was elected as the CEO of Hong

Kong, the freedom of the world was at stake with her ties to the Triads. Palmer knew from Frank that the Brethren had protected the Triads for nearly a century. Even if she denied it publicly, it was still in her DNA, and it was feasible to think she was also protected by them. There was no clear winner in this battle. Either Alan Leung or Xu Li Ma could destroy his legacy and the economic future of the nation. It was time to roll the dice.

Palmer reached into a drawer underneath the desk and retrieved an aged leather book. This book of secrets began in the days of Washington and continued through the eras of Eisenhower and Bush. It was the only written detailed record of the Brethren, as well as a secret hidden within the Golden Triangle. Eisenhower referred to it as a "weapon of biblical proportions."

A knock at the door grabbed Palmer's attention. His secretary poked her head in. "Special Agent Cunningham needs to see you."

He puffed on his stogie. "Send him in."

Cunningham entered. "Mr. President, we've got a problem."

53

President Palmer stood stone faced as a grainy video played on the screen and a voice spoke off camera. "What is your name?"

His heart sank the moment he saw Frank tied to a chair. His best asset lifted his bloodied face and grunted, "Langston...Robert Langston. I'm an American citizen."

A shadow stepped into frame and punched Frank squarely in the face, then stood over him. Cunningham paused the video and pointed at the tattoo.

"Matches the sketch from Jake Harris. It's not a positive ID on Neco Rimoldi, but it's definitely a distinguishing mark."

"And the voice?"

"We're running it through our database. So far, no hits."

The video played, and the African voice continued. "You are the creator of the Program."

"I don't know..." Frank mumbled.

The shadow with the tattoo stepped into the frame with his back to the camera. He swung with such force that Frank's head snapped back violently. Frank spit out a mouthful of blood. The gash across his eyebrow widened.

"Where is Lazarus?"

Frank answered faintly, "I don't know who that is."

Another strike, and Frank's body slumped forward.

D.J. WILLIAMS

Palmer was about to speak but froze when a face filled the screen.

"Mr. President, the bombing in Los Angeles is only the beginning. You will deliver Lazarus to the Brethren within forty-eight hours. If you choose to go against us, we will reveal to the world much more than the photo that was given to you. You will be seen as the deceiver that you are. We will contact you in one hour with instructions."

It took Palmer a moment after the screen went blank to take it in. Whether it was the Triads or the Brethren, they played an ace with a king. Now the deck was emptied, and all the chips were on the table.

"Damas Kone."

"Mr. President?"

"A week ago, Frank traveled to Lusaka after a TOP SECRET file was declassified in an attempt to stop what has happened in Lusaka. Frank had a lead to capture Kone."

"Well, he's not in Africa anymore."

"You're sure?"

"Kate contacted me and needed intel on Kone. She didn't tell me any other details. We've been monitoring her using the tracker in Jake Harris." Cunningham pulled up a live satellite feed. "They're in Hong Kong, which is where this video was uploaded less than an hour ago. Mr. President, we can have boots on the ground within the hour. In the meantime, we should tell Kate about the video and order her to stand down."

"You said when she gets on a scent she won't let up. Kone is the only lead we have left. I say we play this out until we hear from them again."

"She needs to be warned."

"We risk losing Kone *and* Rimoldi—if that's really him."

"She can't go after them alone. It's suicide."

"Until we know how much they know about the Program, we proceed with caution. Kate has Lazarus with her, so there is still time."

"With all due respect, Jake Harris is a civilian. And a liability."

"Frank seems to believe otherwise."

"And look where that's landed him."

"Brad, I don't need to remind you who you're talking to," Palmer

224

retorted. "I can assure you, Lazarus is a wolf in sheep's clothing. He is a highly-trained weapon far greater than you can fathom. He is our demon in the dungeon who must be freed."

"You realize that Kone, Rimoldi, and whoever else is behind this will kill Frank, and then release what they know about the Program. Sir, whoever you believe Jake Harris to be, it will not be enough to protect them. And it will not be enough to bury the details about the Program. You will be exposed. If I am to protect you, then I need to know the end game."

"I convinced Kate to accept this mission. I will take full responsibility." President Palmer sat on the edge of the desk deep in thought. The strong aroma from his stogie permeated the room. He jotted down a number on his Presidential letterhead and handed it over. "She'll answer at this number. Brad, if you want to help her, then Lazarus must choose narrow road."

54

I carried both AR-15s carefully below deck as the boat rocked and rolled. I held the rifle and thought of the days when I played hoops in the hood and barrios. I never thought I'd trade a .45 for a more high-powered arsenal.

With her back turned, Kate lifted her shirt and unwrapped her bandaged midsection. I stared at the deep purple, yellow, and bluish bruise that covered her right side, courtesy of Rimoldi and the hospital explosion. She glanced over her shoulder. Our eyes met. A rush of heat filled my cheeks.

"Are you going to stand there—" she smirked— "or help a girl out?"

Sheepishly, I grabbed a fresh bandage and reached around her waist. She grimaced when I pulled the material tight. I lifted the Kevlar over her head, down her body, and apologized each time she flinched.

"Cardiac arrest," Kate admitted. "That was the risk."

"You should've told me."

"You're right." She retrieved the Pelican case and handed it to me. "It should've been your decision from the beginning."

I slipped the case into my pocket, satisfied I had finally won an argument. "Which one of you brought me back?"

"Let's just say it was a team effort."

Kate checked the AR-15's safety and clip. Her cell buzzed. She pulled me into a nook large enough for a single bunk. A voice crackled through the speakerphone.

"Kate?"

"How'd you get this number?"

"That's not important. There's been a situation."

"Where's POTUS?"

"Unavailable. What's the status on Kone?"

"What do you mean?"

"We've been tracking you since you called. I know you're on his trail."

"Brad, put POTUS on the line right now."

"Listen, we are preparing a statement to the press that will name Jake as the top suspect in the Montrose bombing and Warren homicide."

"Why would you do that?"

"He will be labeled an estranged son of an ex-CIA operative, recently divorced, homeless, unemployed, and mentally unstable. Video from the hospital will be released to the press that shows Jake entering and running down the corridor minutes before the explosion. His statement given to the Glendale PD will also be released along with the toxicology report. A nationwide manhunt will be issued by the Bureau and Homeland with a one-million-dollar reward for his capture."

"Why are you throwing him to the wolves?"

"To protect him."

"You mean discredit me before I have a chance to defend myself," I blurted. "I'm a dead man."

The line went silent for a few seconds.

"Kate, go to the Embassy. You'll both be safe there."

"Brad, what's going on? Spill it or we're gone."

"Look, an hour ago, a video of Frank Harris was uploaded to one of our servers. It was proof of life. Kone, and we believe Rimoldi, were both identified in the footage. Kone demanded that we turn Jake over to the Brethren. We are awaiting further instructions."

"You can't be serious," Kate replied. "What's their leverage?"

"Besides Langston, they threatened to go public with the Program. We believe if we go first with Jake as our top suspect then it will make him less valuable to them."

"You don't know that."

"And what does that mean for Frank?" I asked.

"Jake, your father is highly trained. We will negotiate with them for his release."

I whispered to Kate, "We can't just leave him there."

She glanced at me. "We've got Kone's location. Give me a chance to assess the situation. Twenty minutes tops."

"That's all you've got before POTUS addresses the nation."

"Copy that," Kate replied.

The line went dead.

Nothing had made sense since I stood over Doc's body. What I thought was real was all a lie. Kate was ordered to protect me, yet President Palmer was about to lay me on the altar. While I didn't love Frank, the thought of him being tortured because of me caused a righteous anger. To think, the one person I'd hated for most of my life was now the one person I needed to save. I grabbed the Kevlar vest and AR-15.

"What're you doing?" Kate asked.

"You said it yourself." I stepped into her space. "I need to be pushed."

"Not like this."

"You heard what he said. There's not going to be another shot. It's now or never."

Kate nodded at the AR-15. "You know how to use it?"

"Safety. Point. Shoot."

"Don't think. React."

We joined Scarlett and Timothy above deck. The night grew eerily quiet as we drifted towards the pier. I wished I could turn back the clock, to do things differently with Rachel and Samantha. I pursued my dreams, and they paid the price. It didn't seem fair to them. I allowed the past to consume my future, instead of being grateful for the present. Voices in my head screamed to turn back. But on this night, it wasn't up to me whether I lived or died.

"Jake needs to disappear," Kate said to Scarlett.

Scarlett pulled a blade. No time for vanity. I pulled off my shirt and her fingers crossed over my right shoulder. She pressed against my skin until she found it. The anticipation of the blade cutting into my flesh caused beads of sweat to form on my forehead. With gritted teeth, I refused to utter a sound.

"Hold still," Scarlett said. "Nearly there."

My shoulder burned. Even after she stopped digging, it continued to throb. I turned to see her holding a bloody microchip in the palm of her hand. She crushed it beneath her boot, and then crudely butterflied the wound. By the time I strapped the Kevlar to my body, I felt the old life choked from me.

Scarlett grabbed my arm and gazed deep into my soul. "There's no going back—ever."

55

The Jumbo Restaurant, with its colorful lights, illuminated the concrete jungle of Aberdeen. I was immersed in a nightmare where I died as a child and a legend was born. But I wasn't here to resurrect a hero. I was here to atone for my sins.

Addiction was a trigger. My love for the game was fueled by it. My dreams were destroyed by it. It was my feeble attempt to keep the demons at bay, even if I hadn't been able to identify those demons before now. I pushed Rachel and Samantha away because I couldn't live without it.

I thought of the photos scattered throughout Doc's home. He was an addict of a different kind. Instead of losing himself to a bottle, or a brothel, he lost himself in saving the innocent. He believed it was enough. But even he said he'd been a fool who left things undone. Maybe that's why he offered me a gift—a chance at redemption.

I flanked Kate as we ducked between trucks and crates overflowing with dead fish. We squeezed between a locked gate and chain-linked fence before darting across an empty street towards an industrial building. A stench of sewage wafted in the air.

My adrenaline spiked with a quick series of flashes. Mom's lifeless body, shots fired, someone standing over me as the world turned dark. There was no time to determine fact from fiction. In that moment, I questioned whether I had it in me to pull the trigger.

Kate climbed a drainage pipe to the second floor then motioned for me to follow. I kept my head on a swivel, slung the AR-15 over my shoulder, and climbed. My forearms burned, but I forced myself to the window where she pulled me inside.

I glanced around the room. Tattered and stained mattresses were tossed on the floor. Square packages, neatly wrapped with duct tape, were stacked shoulder-width apart. And there was a pungent odor of urine.

I flipped the safety, surprised at how natural the rifle felt in my hands. It was as natural as the first time a basketball rolled off my fingers. I rested my index finger against the smooth metal an inch from the trigger. Kate cracked the door. I stayed on her shoulder as we moved with purpose. Doors on both sides were padlocked. We ignored them and headed downstairs.

Breathe, Jake.

I waited while Kate checked her cell. She nodded, which meant Kone was still here—possibly Rimoldi and Frank too.

In the shadows, I stared out on the warehouse floor that stretched the length of the building. A lamp burned in the center of the space. We both noticed the body at the same time. Kate raised her fist, but she was too late. I pointed the AR-15 ahead with tunnel vision towards the light.

A voice rang in my ears, different from that day at Starbucks. It wasn't the tone. No, that was a perfect match to Detective Lane. It was a slip of the tongue. *Rachel and Sam are in danger. Do exactly as I say.* Sam. Only Frank would have called her that. Those words were undeniable.

I stopped cold when I reached the chair. Even with his head slumped forward I knew it was him. A lump lodged in my throat. My eyes were moist, but I didn't shed a tear. I touched his hand and whispered, "Dad."

Kate kneeled beside me. Her eyes scanned the room.

For a moment, the axis of life stopped. Then the world spun again.

"Jake, we can't stay here."

My voice quivered, "I won't leave him. Not like this."

She pulled a blade from her pocket and cut the ties. "Can you carry him?"

A voice interrupted. "Put down your weapons."

Kate spun with her AR-15 pointed towards the echo. Kone, and then Rimoldi, stepped into the light with guns raised. I caught a glint of surprise from them both.

"I will not ask again." Kone's tone hardened.

Kate held her ground. I kept my eyes on Rimoldi.

"Careful," Kone warned. "Neco is ready to settle the score."

"Dead or alive," Rimoldi added. "Either way, I still get paid."

"Earlier today, I did not see it," Kone admitted. He stepped closer and eyed me with a steely glare. "It has been far too long, my friend."

"We're not friends," I blurted.

"We are family, Jacob."

Two red lasers cut through the dark and appeared squarely on Kone and Rimoldi.

Her voice startled all of us. "No more blood will be shed tonight."

"Scarlett," Kone said coolly.

Scarlett stepped into the light with a gun in each hand.

Kone turned to me. "Has she told you the truth about that night, about the Program?"

I gripped the AR-15 and slowed my heartbeat, even though my instincts were on overdrive. I glanced at Kate who looked ready to pounce. Scarlett was wrong. Someone was going to die tonight.

A split second was all Kate needed. She fired at Rimoldi with a single shot. He stumbled backward. I threw myself towards him.

Kone returned fire.

As I tackled Rimoldi, I got the wind knocked out of me. The AR-15 slipped from my grasp. I landed on top of him and began punching with every ounce of strength. When he stopped moving, I rolled off him and grabbed my chest.

Scarlett fired at Kone who ducked behind a crate, then headed for the stairs. Bullets ricocheted off the walls as she crossed the room and slid on her knees towards me. She grabbed my vest, where a slug was lodged in the Kevlar, then squeezed my arm as she pulled me to my feet.

"I'm fine," I grunted. "Go."

With that, Scarlett was on Kate's heels. More gunfire erupted. My chest burned as I reached down and grabbed the AR-15 and slung it over my shoulder. Then I picked up Rimoldi's gun and stood over him until he regained consciousness. Clutching his shoulder, a crimson stain spread across his shirt. I pointed the barrel at his head.

"You're a coward just like the old man," he raged.

I stared down at him with hatred in my eyes and ice in my veins. Protecting the innocent was never going to be enough. My penance was sealed. The only way out was to punish the darkness until it returned the light into my soul.

The wages of sin...is death.

I started to squeeze the trigger.

"Jake..."

56

One second the flash of a gun, the next Kone was gone. Kate searched the alley before darting back inside. She reached the second floor as footsteps rapidly approached from behind. She heard her name and lowered her weapon. Scarlett appeared and stopped next to her, both aware that Kone might still be in the warehouse.

"I lost him," Kate said. "Jake?"

"Took one to the vest. We need to clear these rooms."

"We don't have time."

"Kone is gone, Kate. But he will return."

In a matter of seconds, Scarlett picked the lock on the nearest door. At first glance, the room looked similar to the one a few doors down. More drugs. Urine smell. Kate pointed the Maglite toward the corners. She stopped once she landed on four children huddled together wearing dirty and worn clothes with sunken eyes and boney cheeks.

"Wǒ shì yīgè shǒuhù zhě," Scarlett said. I am a Guardian.

One of the boys stood and grabbed Scarlett's hand. Another gripped Kate's pant leg, and sobbed softly.

"It's okay," Kate whispered, unsure of whether the boy understood. "Don't be afraid."

Scarlett said, "There will be more."

"We need to make it quick."

Methodically, they cleared each room. Kate knew what Scarlett was doing, but that didn't mean she wasn't concerned about leaving Jake downstairs with Rimoldi wounded.

Scarlett dialed her cell. "Sixteen total." She paused. "Five minutes."

"You lied to us," Kate said.

"There will be time to argue later." Scarlett gathered the children and formed a single line. She led them downstairs and out a side door.

From the start, Kate was a true patriot who believed loyalty was paramount. President Palmer had baited her into a web far outside the lines, and that made every step forward complicated. One thing she knew for sure, she aimed high because she needed answers. She needed Rimoldi alive to stop Jake from going down in history as another homegrown terrorist.

She found Jake standing over Rimoldi, who had a second gunshot wound to the chest. She checked for a pulse then looked up at Jake for an explanation. When he didn't speak, she snapped a photo of Rimoldi and texted.

She lost herself for a second, stunned. Her cell rang. "I've lost Kone. Rimoldi's dead. I had no other choice."

"Kate, the President is on the line," Brad replied.

President Palmer's steadied voice added, "What about Frank?"

Kate turned to see Frank Harris face down on the floor beside Jake.

"He didn't make it, sir."

"Son of a— We've lost our signal on Lazarus."

"You ordered me to protect him. That's exactly what I'm doing. The photo of Rimoldi should be enough to spin another story and buy us some time."

"Target remains active."

"You have a speech to give, sir."

Kate hung up and turned off her cell. Then she walked over to the table, picked up the syringes, and tucked them into a side pocket. She turned to Jake, who still held the AR-15 in his hands. She didn't know exactly how it happened, and she wasn't about to ask. There was only one thing left to do.

Burn it down.

57

President Palmer stared out the window at the empty streets as the Beast rolled down Honolulu Avenue and parked where the memorial began.

"Any word?"

"I haven't been able to reach her," Cunningham replied. "There are reports of a structural fire in Aberdeen. Local authorities have the whole place blocked off."

"Kate is a fiery one," Palmer said. "It's not every day I get hung up on."

"That's why you chose her, sir."

Palmer and Cunningham strolled down the sidewalk lined with lilies, carnations, roses, and chrysanthemums. Photos of families were taped to makeshift cardboard stands with handwritten notes posted beside each one. For a moment, they took in the solemn sight.

"We have her to thank," Palmer said. "Today, our nation will unite over the justice that has been handed down. I suppose that has to be good enough."

"What do you mean, sir?"

"Without Frank, there is no Lazarus. Without Lazarus, we cannot wage war against the Brethren. They know too much about the Program already. And it wasn't only from Frank's confession. We cannot fight against an enemy we cannot see. Once the target has been neutralized, bring

Kate and Lazarus home. Let's leave the sins of our past buried for the time being. Instead of poking the dragon, we need time for our nation to heal."

"What if the Brethren post another video?"

"Then we do what our predecessors have done," Palmer admitted. "We'll label them as an extremist group who kidnapped an American— drugged, tortured, and forced him to lie under threat of being killed. Now that we have proof of Rimoldi's death, that helps level the playing field."

They strolled back to the Beast and climbed inside. Two motorcycle officers escorted them up the hill with Secret Service following close behind.

Palmer eyed Brad closely. "You're confident she'll eliminate the target?"

"Kate's never let me down."

Police officers, firemen, and construction workers stood alongside Mayor Osoria and Commissioner Thompson amongst the steel cranes, bulldozers, and cement trucks.

A camera followed President Palmer as he shook hands and patted backs while the Secret Service flanked him on all sides. Less than an hour earlier, a press release from the White House sent news crews scrambling. But they were kept blocks away from the site. This historic moment would be captured through only one lens.

President Palmer paused when he reached the Mayor and Commissioner. He leaned in close. "We got him." Then he was handed a megaphone and addressed the blue-collar crowd. "Less than an hour ago, the man responsible for the tragic events of November 24th was killed."

A handful of workers whooped and hollered.

"However, we lost one of our own during the mission—one of our best—who served this country with honor for nearly thirty years. Without him, justice would not have come so quickly. Due to the classified nature of the operation—and for the safety of those involved in the mission—the name of the operative will not be released publicly."

"In times like this, as we stand united, I am reminded of the liberties we protect. And of the generations who have fought to keep our nation strong. What links us together is not the color of our skin, religion, politics, or wealth, but the fact that we are Americans, and the light of freedom that shines in our souls will always burn brighter than the evil we cannot see. Tonight we will say a prayer for those we have lost so our nation will become stronger. God bless America."

President Palmer made his way toward the Beast and gave a few high fives along the way. The crowd shouted, "USA! USA! USA!"

58

"What happened back there?"

Scarlett sidestepped Kate and barked orders to William and Timothy, who were busy loading gear from the river house. The children rescued from Aberdeen remained below deck where Bao kept a close eye on them.

"Kone isn't only one of the assassins from the Brethren," Scarlett replied. "He's one of the eleven from the Program."

Kate grabbed Scarlett's arm and spun her around. "What about Leung?"

"I do not know." Scarlett jerked her arm free. The two stood nose to nose. "If Kone is coming here, we will be outnumbered."

Kate shot a fiery glance in my direction. I kept my eyes on the river. I was numb as I stared out into the night. Before Kate set the warehouse ablaze, we carried Frank to the boat. I don't know how I had the strength to do it, but I did. I couldn't leave him, not after his last act. He pulled the trigger when I couldn't. Timothy helped me wrap his body in a blanket. I stayed right by him, unsure of whether the emotions that flooded me were grief or rage. While I may not have honored him in life, in death there was no other choice.

"Jake, we need to go to the Embassy," Kate said. "Right now."

"I'm staying here," I answered. "They need to pay for what they've done."

Kate pointed at Scarlett. "She can't be trusted."

"I'm paying the price for the wrongs I've done, not you! This is the only way."

"We need to go," Scarlett interrupted. "With or without you, Kate."

"I still have orders," Kate replied. "A target."

Scarlett asked, "Alan Leung?"

Kate shook her head and boarded the boat as William untied the ropes. Timothy started the engine and eased away from the dock. We drifted down river headed south. Before long, Tai O was lost in the abyss.

Scarlett whispered to me, "I know the perfect resting place."

"When I heard him say my name—" a lump lodged in my throat— "I thought I'd saved him."

Kate pulled the syringes from her pocket and handed them to Scarlett.

"I need to know what they injected into him."

"Perhaps now is not the time," Scarlett replied.

"It's okay," I added. "We can't do this together if we keep secrets."

"After each operation, we were given doses of a drug. There were two formulas used to extract and erase our memories. If Kone needed answers, I suspect a large dosage of the extraction serum would force Frank to tell him what they needed to know."

"Is that the drug Kate injected into me?"

"At first I thought it was, however, your memories have not returned. This makes me believe you were given a hybrid to heighten a unique gene the twelve of us share. It is called the warrior gene, a gene that enhances one's ability to control aggression."

Scarlett scribbled a formula on her hand.

PMT/Entrez: 4128 + ENSG00000189221 + P21397 = MOA.

"I remember seeing that in the diary I gave Maggie."

"Diary?" Kate asked, surprised.

"It belonged to Sister Evelyn. I brought it to Maggie the night before we left, when she gave me the orphanage name."

"What else was in the diary?"

"Most of the pages were blank, but she used a light to read what was invisible. Some pages were torn out. Maggie said it wasn't everything, but it was enough."

"Frank carried that diary with him often," Scarlett said. "He showed me the handwritten formula on one of the pages too. He called the serum Monoamine Oxidase A."

Kate asked, "How does the drug work?"

"When you find yourself in a stressful situation, your adrenaline rises. When that adrenaline peaks, you will experience one of two things: fight or fear. We were given this drug when we were recruited to see which one of us was to be trained for the extractions. When our adrenaline peaked, we each felt different levels of fear when stress and aggression were at maximum capacity. Controlling our fear enabled us to fight and survive. Jacob exhibited the ability to react in these situations with a very low dose of the drug. When the warrior gene was enhanced in him, it strengthened his ability to fight *without* fear, and as you watched in the video, he never hesitated. However, there is a mutation in the warrior gene when mixed with the other drugs that causes cardiac arrest, blindness, memory loss, and other debilitating side effects."

Memory loss. Check.

Cardiac arrest. Check.

Blindness. That one stuck with me.

I thought of Samantha, and a blend of brokenness, guilt, and rage swirled.

"The mixture injected into Jake caused his heart to stop." Kate asked Scarlett, "How do you remember all this?"

"My memories begin that night on the Jumbo. Before that, I do not know where I had been or what I had done. Over the years, Frank filled in the holes. He told me about the dosages. When he brought us back after the extractions, we were given a heavy dose to remember what we'd seen, and then another dose to erase its existence. Jacob was never given either of those formulas, only the MOA. One simple reason was that he needed to remember the past so that he would recognize us when we were found."

I asked, "What happens if you give me a maximum dosage of the

MOA?"

"It is very dangerous," Scarlett warned. "Frank believed it would return you to who you had once been. What was taken from you has simply been locked away. A full dosage might bring back your training, but it also might alter your memories."

"Since we have the memory extraction drug," Kate said, "we can protect those memories, right?"

"That is a risk," Scarlett admitted.

I had listened to the conversation long enough. I pulled my cell from my pocket, flipped through the photos of Rachel and Samantha then removed the syringe case from my side pocket.

"Promise me," I said to them both, "you will bring me back."

Kate and Scarlett nodded. We went below deck where the children watched in silence. I pulled off the Kevlar and leaned back against the bunk. I exhaled fully and tried to relax. Both of my parents were dead, and I might very well stand beside them soon. Scarlett removed the first needle. I closed my eyes and felt a prick. A second needle and my breathing slowed. By the fourth, my muscles relaxed. And by the fifth, my mind went blank.

You're only reborn once.

59

The Eurocopter skimmed the Min River as it banked between the vast mountains of Sichuan. Alan Leung was behind the controls with the Ghost in the co-pilot seat. He flew low over an abandoned village before spotting a landing pad at the mining facility. Bright yellow pipes stood out from the surrounding farmland, pumping thousands of gallons of water from a nearby reservoir to an eight-story drill built to dig into the earth nine thousand feet vertically and ten thousand feet horizontally.

An employee in a red jumpsuit and matching hardhat escorted them across the property, dodging semis and excavating vehicles, toward a nondescript building. The employee ushered them into a conference room where Brian Fitzgerald, CEO of Mulfira Mining Corporation, was in a heated debate with Edmund Tsang, Chairman of the PRC State Council.

"Sorry I'm late," Leung said loud enough to halt the argument. "What have I missed?"

"Alan, good of you to join us." Fitzgerald motioned for them to find a seat. "Who is your guest?"

"Security," Leung waved his hand dismissively. "Please continue."

"I was just reassuring your colleague of the extensive safety measures we have taken."

"And yet there has already been an incident," Tsang said. "Alan, did you see the village upon your arrival?" Without waiting for a reply, Tsang projected the devastation on a screen at one end of the conference room.

Silence hung over them as the images scrolled by of the disaster zone. An aerial shot showed the point of origin and marked the destruction radius. Farmland was left in ash. Skeletal remains littered the streets. Children cried as Mulfira Mining trucks loaded survivors.

"Edmund, I understand your concern," Leung answered, calmly. "We have already relocated the villagers."

"What about the casualties? I have heard we are at nearly five hundred so far."

"All of the families will be taken care of with food, shelter, and basic necessities. We will help them rebuild their farms somewhere else. However, we cannot stop production."

"Is the water contaminated?"

"We believe the explosion was an isolated incident," Fitzgerald said. "Our experts have assured us that there will be no lasting effects."

"The operation is in its infancy. There are bound to be growing pains," Leung added. "Six months from now, no one will remember this, especially if it never leaves this room."

"There have been four earthquakes since the explosion," Tsang replied. "How do you suggest we keep that contained?"

"None registered higher than a 3.5. In the United States, that barely reaches local news coverage. We cannot risk the alliance because of this, agreed?"

"And if this is only the beginning?"

"Trust me, Edmund. If we shut down now, we will lose support and financial backing."

"When I agreed to your request to be included as a candidate in the Hong Kong election, it was under the impression that shale mining would be profitable and safe. The PRC will not stand behind this if your claims are false. We know the world is watching, and any event that is catastrophic will weaken our hold on the West."

"It took a decade to corner the market on rare earth metals," Leung said. "Who does the PRC have to thank for that?"

"You do not know how far the earthquakes will reach, you cannot guarantee the water is sanitary, and you do not know how many more will die before this venture is profitable."

"I understand what is at stake."

"Then you will understand the message I have been instructed to give to you. If there is another explosion, the PRC will cease all involvement in this operation and will void the exclusive agreement with Mulfira."

"That would be a mistake of epic proportions," Leung said. "Brian, why don't you tell Edmund the latest news?"

"We have President Palmer's ear on shale mining."

"You have his ear?" Tsang laughed. "What does that mean?"

"It means, once I am elected into office, I will be the one to negotiate a deal. I promise you, it will be extremely lucrative to the PRC for years to come."

"President Palmer has been against fracking since he was elected. What has changed?"

"As part of our negotiations, we will discuss the existing debt agreement. A balloon payment is due to the PRC for five hundred billion. If the PRC offers an addendum to the agreement that gives the United States a longer term with a revised payment schedule then the President will agree to join the alliance."

"He has agreed to those terms?" Tsang asked.

"I met with him personally." Leung lied. "I am telling you there is a deal to be made, but I am the only one to do it."

"Will you be in that same position if you lose the election?"

Leung's grin faded. He grit his teeth and fought the urge to dive across the table and punch the Chairman in the face. He had been in these kinds of meetings countless times and he knew that diplomacy was the best way to get what he wanted. If Edmund only knew the killer he had sitting next to him, perhaps he might choose his words more carefully.

"Do not discount what I am offering you." Leung leaned back in his chair. "I have not achieved success by failing. The PRC has been given great opportunity because of me, and I will do much more once I am CEO of Hong Kong."

"Alan, soon we will see if your confidence is simply arrogance in disguise."

"Gentlemen, may I suggest we reconvene," Fitzgerald interrupted. "Allow me the next thirty days to work on the challenges in front of us. Once we have a full update on our progress, we will discuss next steps."

Without another word, Edmund Tsang closed his laptop and left the room. When they were alone, Leung glanced over to Fitzgerald. "What about the secondary site?"

"Alan, we've found nothing that has registered out of the ordinary. Perhaps you can tell me what it is we are searching for?"

"Believe me, when you find it, you will know."

60

"Jacob, are you awake?"

I blinked several times and stared at the bottom of the bunk above. Fragmented memories flooded so strong, it was impossible to capture them all, like a bolt of lightning. My body was sluggish as I turned and gazed at a familiar face.

"How long have I been out?"

"Two days." Scarlett touched my forehead. "We were worried."

"I'm thirsty." She handed me a bottle of water, which I drank in two swigs. "Where is everyone?"

"Take it slow. First, tell me what is the last thing you remember?"

"Standing over two bodies inside a warehouse, and you sticking a needle in me."

"I'm going to say a few names. I need you to tell me if you know who they are."

I sat up on the edge of the bunk and stretched my aching body. "Shoot."

"Kate McNaughton."

"FBI. She brought me here, to track Kone."

"Damas Kone."

"That's right." My heartbeat quickened. "In the Program, his legend was Jackson."

A frown pursed her lips as she walked with me down memory lane.

247

Her jaw tensed. "Do you know why we were trained in the Program?"

"To hunt the Triad leaders who trafficked women and children." As soon as I said those words, I knew there was more. "We were searching for a hidden path in the Golden Triangle."

"We called it the Silk Road." Scarlett nodded and searched my face. "A few more names."

"Okay."

"Neco Rimoldi."

"He killed Doc Warren and bombed the hospital."

"Rimoldi was one of the bodies in the warehouse. Do you recognize the other?"

"Robert Langston. He trained us in the Program." A memory flashed of Langston tied up at the warehouse. Scarlett's eyes narrowed. I lowered my head. "He killed Rimoldi."

"You tried to save him."

I leaned over and vomited on the floor.

She handed me a towel to wipe my mouth then grabbed my hand. "You will feel better once you eat."

"There's more I remember. That night on the Jumbo."

"What about that night?"

"I woke up at the Hope House with you sitting there—like you are now—that same look in your eyes."

Scarlett pressed on. "Where did Abigail take us?"

"I can't— It's a blur."

"It is possible not everything you remember is as it seems. Tell me what comes to mind."

I tossed the towel on the bed. "I wasn't alone in that room."

"Jacob, do you know Rachel and Samantha?"

I searched for faces to match the names, rubbed my eyes, and itched my stubbly beard. "Who are they?"

Scarlett's golden eyes softened, and I wondered what I'd missed. "One more test." Scarlett removed a .45 from her hip and handed it over. "Take it apart."

I gripped the gun, and my hands moved on instinct.

Remove the magazine, pull the slide, check ammo, allow the slide to spring forward, pull the trigger. Pull the slide an eighth inch, fire to release the hammer, pull the slide down, push the slide forward, remove from receiver.

Five seconds flat.

I set the parts on the bed, surprised at how easily I dismantled the weapon.

"Muscle memory is good."

"Do you want me to put it back together?"

"Later." She handed me fresh clothes. "It is time to say goodbye."

61

A rolling mist enveloped the mountains as we followed a dirt path on a gradual incline. The clothes Scarlett gave me were comfortable, especially with the humidity. Even though they looked more like pajamas, they allowed my body to breathe.

Twenty minutes into the trek, we broke through the marine layer. I looked out over the top of the grayish fog as it slowly drifted across the island. At first, I didn't notice the tall concrete pillars that lined both sides of the path. I was too busy processing the random names and flashes that continued to fill my brain. Scarlett was right, there were definitely gaps. Life felt like a highlight reel, impossible to know when events happened or which pieces were missing. Strangely enough, the migraine that haunted me was gone. I was as clear minded as I'd ever been.

"After we left Kowloon, Abigail brought us here." Scarlett glanced back as I stared at the Chinese characters etched into the stone. "She said when we die, we will be remembered more for the character that defined us than the name that was given us. These characters represent each one's virtue. When we believed the others were dead, we set the first ten pillars ourselves."

"Scarlett, how many from the Program survived?"

"Kone is the only one we have confirmed." She ran her fingers over the characters. "I am afraid the virtues we attributed no longer exist within those who might still be under the Brethren's control."

I counted each one. "Thirty-seven."

"Those first pillars began a tradition to honor all who have sacrificed as Guardians. I have ensured that no one is forgotten."

I wondered which virtue would be etched into number thirty-eight. What escaped me was whether we were close. I knew he trained me, and that I followed his orders. Apart from that, there were no memories of a father and son. No memories of us together except for the missions that were slowly becoming clearer. My lack of remorse, hurt, or grief left me with a conclusion that our relationship was nothing more than what existed within the Program. Still, I felt numb from his death.

"Where are we exactly?"

"This is where we were trained, an island five miles south of Repulse Bay. It has become a place where we protect and care for those who are rescued."

"How many are here?"

"During the Program, it was hundreds. Since then, we have tracked the trafficking within Hong Kong mostly, so sometimes it is only a few at a time. We bring them here to help put their lives back together in a community. Once we know they are ready, we move them to the Hope House in Tai Kok Tsui. From there, they find their way back into the world."

"But the Hope House was empty."

"Six months ago, rumors you were alive surfaced. It has not been safe to send anyone since."

"How do you survive here?"

"Frank installed generators eight years ago. We use them sparingly, especially when we are at full capacity. We also have the ability to link to a satellite to connect to the outside on the black web."

I followed her gaze towards a row of cinderblock cabins atop the mountain, with more scattered along the hillside. Lanterns glowed at each one, and I imagined each light represented a person saved. As we passed, women and children fell in behind. By the time we descended the other side of the mountain and sunk our feet into the sand, there were hundreds of lanterns illuminating the trail behind us.

William, Timothy, and Bao waited near the water wearing the same clothes as me. I whispered to Scarlett. "Where's Kate?"

"She left yesterday."

I turned my attention to the glassy water as the sun disappeared on the horizon. Magic hour. That time of day before night engulfed this side of the planet. I thought of the mobile home in Malibu—how it must've reminded Frank of this place—and the faces too numerous to count.

"William, Tim, and Bao built it." Scarlett turned to me as we approached the handmade teak casket. "I hope it is okay."

I looked at the three of them. "It's beautiful. Thank you."

Paper lanterns glowed off the faces of the women and children who gathered on the beach. As Scarlett spoke in Cantonese, I understood every word.

"Day and night he fought for each one of us and for the thousands yet to be saved. While our grief leaves us broken, our spirit must remain strong. As we ponder and pray in the stillness, we hear an earnest voice call, a voice of the one who loves and holds us in his gaze. It is for him we sacrifice on this earth for what will be in eternity."

Scarlett looked up to the heavens and prayed.

"Lord, when you return, may those who have gone before us meet you from the depths of your creation, and may they bring with them the souls they have saved."

I kept my head bowed, not in prayer, but out of respect.

Scarlett's benediction was echoed with a hushed, "Ahmen."

William, Timothy, and Bao approached the casket. I joined them and we each carried a corner into the ocean until it floated on its own. William and Tim climbed into two canoes and slowly paddled with the casket between them. Bao and I returned to Scarlett's side, our clothes drenched, yet I hardly noticed. Women and children sang a somber requiem as they stepped forward and released their beacons out to sea.

62

Light glowed from a sea of cell phones spread across five blocks of Harcourt Road in the financial district. Bright yellow umbrellas marked each block of a perfectly organized, highly-funded, and calculated demonstration that trended on Twitter, Facebook, and flooded Instagram with moving and vibrant images of a new generation of Hong Kongers. Portable screens, with miles of electrical, were strategically placed along the route, broadcasting live to the Internet.

Sound bytes from supporters energized the crowd. Snapshots of homemade signs marked a growing revolution. DEMOCRACY IS A HUMAN RIGHT. ONE COUNTRY—TWO SYSTEMS. FREEDOM IS A BEGINNING.

Overhead, a drone relayed footage of a fleet of vehicles emerging from Harbour Tunnel, driving an alternate route before stopping one block east of the main stage. Police in riot gear and shields stood on the other side of the barricades as traffic from Sheung Wan to Stanley was diverted, shutting down most of Central. Star Ferry and the MTR were the only viable transportation moving through the city.

Kate made her way through the crowd. It was a long shot to find Kone amongst thousands and thousands of people, but waiting at the Peninsula for him to show up was a waste of time. Without the tracking signal, all she had left were her instincts.

After leaving Jake and Scarlett, she headed for the Embassy where Brad briefed her via satellite and reiterated that completing the mission was a matter of national security. She reassured him that once this was over, she'd bring Jake back to the States. Her instincts were to stay with Jake, to keep him safe. She worried about whether he'd be the same when he woke.

But he was also a distraction. Sorting out whatever feelings there might be between them would have to wait, not to mention her complicated relationship with Brad, which had grown more tense since he told her about turning Jake into a patsy.

For now, finding Kone and the Brethren were also secondary, at least for the next forty-eight hours. There was only a small window of time to find the right opportunity to neutralize the target. At the end of the briefing, she asked Brad for a favor, a hunch she promised would be repaid over dinner at their favorite spot, Real Food, in Pasadena.

Miles of barricades separated the enforcers from the demonstrators, an illusion of control. Sure, the mood was peace and love until someone lit a match. Kate knew how quickly a peaceful protest turned into an inferno. She tried to blend in, which seemed impossible as one of the few Westerners in a sea of Chinese. She kept moving, ducking, and dodging while avoiding getting too close to the police presence.

Electricity surged through the crowd. Cell phones lowered as a woman stepped onto the stage. Xu Li Ma was far from the normal politicalite. Casual attire. Not visibly charismatic. She seemed to be one of the masses, instead of being the one who led them all. A group of bodyguards lined the stage scanning the faces in front of them. She smiled and the crowd erupted with excitement at the sight of *their* candidate.

Eyes on the prize, Kate.

Xu Li Ma spoke and immediately exuded a tone of conviction and confidence. Each time she paused, the crowd applauded as if to place a period to a sentence that promised change. At the end of her speech, the streets rumbled with a cult-like chant that reverberated in their bones.

Kate texted Brad a recording, and a few seconds later her cell buzzed.

"We've been watching online. We're already on it."

"Any word on the DNA?"

"It's a match."

"That's why Maldone let him live." Kate ducked through the crowd. Her cell pressed firmly against her ear. "The question is, how are they related?"

"Don't you think POTUS would've told us?"

"It's possible he doesn't know."

"There was only one visitor since Maldone was locked up in San Quentin: Frank Harris."

"And Maldone told Jake he was the only one who was spared. Now you're telling me Frank Harris had a face-to-face? He must've known."

"I'll request access to the prison security footage."

"Brad, are you sure she's the right target?"

"Positive. Why?"

"It doesn't feel right."

"Stick to the plan, Kate."

"I'll call you later."

Kate hung up, preoccupied, until the barrel of a gun jabbed her aching ribs.

63

When I woke, the nightmares were gone, but the night was engraved in my soul. I wondered how often she'd spoken those words. How many had given their lives? How many more would be remembered in the pillars before this was over?

Fear is a good thing. Running from it is not. The voices rang in my ears. My heart swelled with an outpouring of love, evident by each lantern that was released to sea. No doubt those around me were alive because of him. Still, it was strange to be in a place where everyone knew him, except me.

I stopped and kicked a soccer ball. At first, the kids stared as the ball rolled past. Then one of them chased after it and kicked it back towards me. A simple act broke down a barrier. Soon the kids were surrounding me as I spun the ball on my index finger. They tried to do the same. I left them and walked through the community where I heard the whispers.

Lā sā lù.

A bell rang, and the kids darted towards a large cabin. Women were outside sweating over pots of porridge. Even though I'd never seen porridge, I was sure that's what the concoction had to be. I joined the line and tried to sort out my scattered memories. Scarlett waved me down with a concerned look. She dismissed a group of women and the two of us headed down a dirt path.

"What's wrong?" I asked.

"One of the children we brought from the warehouse is ill. We need to decide whether it is worth the risk to take her into the city."

We reached a cabin further down the hill and entered into a dimly lit space. A young girl curled up on a mattress shook uncontrollably as a woman kneeled beside her with a wet towel, gently wiping the child's face.

"The drugs and the conditions where they were kept cause many health problems." Scarlett nodded towards the girl. "She is either an addict or has hepatitis."

"Can't you give her a shot or something?"

"We do not have the right vaccine."

"What do we do?"

"We pray."

Scarlett placed her hand on the girl's forehead. I stayed back a few feet, unsure of whether to do the same. The voyeur in me wanted to get a closer look. Instead, I bowed my head and kept my eyes pointed towards the floor. When Scarlett finished, there was no miracle, no hallelujah chorus, and no bright light shining in the room. Nothing seemed different. And then everything changed.

The girl's eyes blinked as the color returned to her face. Life breathed easier through her body. What magical chant turned such pain and sickness into health? Scarlett smiled, more peacefully than I'd seen before. I thought of Sister Evelyn who performed miracles with a whisper or a touch. Nearly a hundred years later, I had witnessed a miracle with my own eyes. Scarlett was a healer, except she hadn't garnered the world's stage but the forgotten with a simple prayer.

"How'd you. . . do that?" I asked.

"I did nothing," Scarlett said in a hushed voice. "Jacob, prayer surrenders our will so God's power is released through us. He is the one who heals."

64

William and Timothy unpacked cords, wires, monitors, and hard drives. I stood off to the side and pictured a chair in the center of the room with no windows. Heat from a light burned down on my face. I swallowed hard as my reflexes fought the muscle memory of enduring water torture.

"You okay, Mate?" William asked.

"I've been in here before."

"Interrogation training," Scarlett said. "Each of us went through it."

I paced the room and winced at the breath that hit the back of my neck. I spun around, but no one was standing nearby. Scarlett crossed the room and dug into a large storage case. She retrieved extra clips of ammo and handed them to Bao, who stuffed them into a backpack, along with several flash bangs.

"What do you need us to do?" Timothy asked.

I put my walk down memory lane aside, and texted a photo of the check.

"Use the account and routing number to track down the bank. Access the funds and transfer them. You decide which bank. Then go through every frame of the video. Look for anything that we might've missed."

William entered a series of algorithms and countless icons appeared on the map. "Xu Li Ma is still active on SmarTone. Should have a location in a second."

"How'd you know the number?" I asked.

"We swiped it a week ago in Central." William paused. "She's in Mong Kok."

I turned to Scarlett. "Any word from Kate?"

"I have tried her cell—"

"You two will want to see this." Timothy pulled up a satellite feed. "Leung holds major shares in Mulfira Mining, so I searched through the records and found a mining facility in Sichuan." A few more clicks to the east and a separate window opened side by side with the previous screen capture. "Notice the images are not the same. The village looks to be destroyed. There is nothing in their reports that explains what occurred." He pulled the map further east. "And this spot here is not in any of the Mulfira documents."

"For now, we stay focused on finding Kone," Scarlett said.

"I thought this might be—"

"Tim, we play this out with Xu Li Ma, and then we look at other possibilities."

"Fine." Timothy's shoulders dropped. "You're in charge."

Another breath whisked across the back of my neck as I heard Frank's voice: *Jacob, train your mind to accept the pain. Turn it into strength.*

"If this goes sideways," Scarlett said to the others, "do not wait for us."

William reassured her, "We know the drill."

"We better go," Scarlett said to me. "Bao will take us to Mong Kok."

I wasn't much for speeches, but the words flowed rather easily.

"Thank you for honoring Frank. I don't remember much about him yet, but I believe in what he fought for—what we are fighting for—I promise, I won't let you down."

65

The train rumbled and screeched through a submerged tunnel beneath Victoria Harbor. I gripped the handrail and swayed shoulder to shoulder with Scarlett, Bao, and a mob of passengers. A door hissed. We shoved our way through the MTR station, up the escalators, and emerged street level on Argyle in Mong Kok. Bathed in neon it was the busiest district in the world.

When I first arrived in the city, the humidity weighed heavily, or maybe it only exaggerated how I felt on the inside. I didn't know who I was, and that carried with it the unknown, uncertain, and unanswered. There was no purpose when Lazarus was a dormant myth. With the serum flowing through my veins, I'd never wander aimlessly again.

I pictured Angelo Maldone locked in the cage at San Quentin. However, the words between us were muted. His icy glare was similar to Rimoldi's. I wondered if one day I'd return to those I'd forgotten, those who loved me when I was lost.

I held my cell to my ear, listening to Kate's voicemail. "Call me back." I was bothered being on the other end of unanswered calls. She pushed me to take a step of faith. I owed her for that. "Where's she staying?"

"YMCA on Salisbury," Bao answered, as if I knew exactly where that was.

We picked up the pace down Dundas Street as a van drove by broadcasting a digital commercial for Nike. Tourists bargained in jewelry, electronic and clothing stores while locals cursed their offers in Cantonese. Even more brand names were advertised on billboards hiding the low-rent apartments on the floors above. Street vendors were parked on every corner hawking fish balls, fried beancurd, and dim sum.

"Dundas is a popular red light district," Scarlett explained. "Mostly bars, nightclubs, and massage parlors owned by the Triads."

We dodged a double-decker and were lost in the flow of humanity. Bao slipped me an Associated Press lanyard with my driver's license photo and an alias. Michael Jordan.

"I remember that much," I chuckled. "No Kobe or Lebron."

Bao smiled. "Scarlett said you were obsessed with him."

"He knew how to improvise when the game was on the line."

"If Kate is right," Scarlett said, "you are about to do the same."

I pressed the audio com into my ear and made sure my shirt covered the Glock tucked behind my back. "I guess we'll find out."

At Kee Wah Bakery, I left them and crossed over to the Langham, a fifty-nine-story complex with a shopping mall, hotel, corporate suites, and Xu Li Ma's campaign office. I glanced over my shoulder to see Scarlett's eyes fixed on me.

I entered the building and took an elevator to the fourth floor. The doors opened into a small lobby. I introduced myself to a receptionist and flashed my ID. She picked up the phone and dialed. A young woman dressed in a dark pantsuit rounded the corner.

"Bianca Lee, campaign manager for Ms Ma." She shook my hand firmly. "Mr. Jordan, we do not have an interview scheduled with the AP today"

"I'm sorry for showing up unannounced," I replied. "It will only take a few minutes."

"Normally the office is off-limits to the press, but you are here. Please have a seat. I will see what I can do."

I found a chair and waited while the receptionist went back to answering phones.

"So far so good," I whispered.

The voice in my ear said, "All clear out here".

Bianca Lee returned and ushered me into a conference room. "Mr. Jordan, allow me to introduce you to Ms Xu Li Ma."

We shook hands and stared curiously at each other before the moment passed. Bianca Lee excused herself then poked her head back in the doorway. "Ms Ma has a lunch appointment in twenty minutes."

"You will have to excuse Bianca," Xu Li said. "She runs a tight ship."

"This won't take long."

"I have been interviewed by the AP a few times before. I have not heard your name mentioned though."

"I'm actually writing a story about your father," I said bluntly. "He was Secretary for Justice, and rumored to be affiliated with the Triads."

I knew I caught her off guard. I waited for her to respond.

"That was many years ago." Xu Li motioned and we sat across from each other. "Mr. Jordan, my father was not an honorable man. He was a corrupt politician, born into a family I have tried to distance myself from for many years."

"Do you know who killed him?"

"I was very young. May I suggest you contact the OCTB and request the file on his murder?" Xu Li eyed me closely. "Many in my family have tried to escape the Triads. However, dreams and aspirations of freedom have left many imprisoned. One must pay a steep price if freedom is to be achieved with the approval of men like my father. Despite what my opponents wish to believe, I am not the leader of an organized crime syndicate."

"Was your father one of the Triad Council?"

"I live in a city where seven million people are afraid of what is at stake. Many are lost. Helpless. Forgotten. Those are the ones who have paid the price because of the alliance between the Triads and my family. Until I have paid my debt, I am merely offering a bandage to a wound that grows deeper, a wound my father and the Council inflicted on far too many."

"What kind of debt?"

"Mr. Jordan, I assumed you were here about the election. I am afraid I cannot tell you any more about my father, or my family."

"Then tell me, is Alan Leung one of the Triads?"

"Alan is not a Triad. However, I will not doubt their influence in his campaign. You must understand that makes me a danger to the PRC, Triads, and anyone else who has chosen to side with my opponent. We are on the verge of a revolution, one that will not be contained. Last night, I stood amongst thousands who deserve to be free. I am willing to die for that cause."

"So you are not protected by the Brethren?"

Xu Li shifted uncomfortably in her chair. "May I ask how you know that name?"

"Confidential source," I lied. "Protectors of the underworld. Assassins for hire. Whatever you can tell me about them will be kept off the record."

"I will deny any of this if it is printed."

"Understood."

"The Brethren have protected the Triads for many years. However, I am not under their protection because I have separated myself from my family. I cannot say the same to be true of Alan Leung."

"Why are they protecting him if he's not a Triad?"

"Perhaps it is because the Triads need him to leverage their alliance with the PRC."

"Aren't you the one who wants to reopen the Golden Triangle?"

"What you have heard are simply rumors. While the Triads want to reopen the smuggling route, I have other plans."

"But you know the route within the Triangle?"

Xu Li Ma nodded slowly. "There are only a few left who do."

"Tell me what happened that night in Aberdeen, at the Jumbo Restaurant?"

She sat quietly for a long time and stared out the window. I was in no hurry. What she said next determined whether she could be trusted.

"My father was re-elected with votes paid for by the Triad Council because he was one of them. They gathered to celebrate, amongst other things. I can still hear the mahjong tiles shuffling and slamming against the tables. San Miguel flowed easily anytime they were together. As the night grew late, the rooms upstairs were off limits to the children. I left the dining room to escape the loud music and the drunken men who groped at anyone standing too close."

She paused as if deciding whether or not to keep going.

"That is when I saw him, an American boy." She glanced towards me, then back to the window. "I heard whispers, so I hid beneath the stairs. Children's feet passed over me, and I watched as other children boarded a boat tied to the side of the floating restaurant."

"What'd you do next?"

"I followed the boy upstairs. Where I found my father and the rest of the Council dead."

"What about the boy?"

"He stood in the hallway holding a weapon. I do not know if he saw me, or if he was a ghost. I followed him to the roof where he stood inside a room. I heard him say..."

"Mom," I whispered.

She gasped and turned her eyes towards me. "You have haunted my dreams for many years."

"Who was the woman in the room?"

"We were the only one's there." Her eyebrows furrowed. "When I found my father, I took his gun and followed you inside the room. I am the one who shot you."

"You're sure you were alone?"

"There was no one else. I fired six times, then left to find Angelo."

"Texting Tim," Scarlett said in my ear. "Standby. Keep her talking."

"Angelo Maldone?"

"He was in charge of the Council's security. He was always nice to me. It was not until I was much older that I discovered he was part of the Brethren."

"What'd he do when you found him?"

"Actually, his daughter, Emma, found me first. We went back to the roof, but when we entered the room you were gone. She told me to forget

WAKING LAZARUS

what I had seen and to never speak of it again. Now you have returned, alive."

"Until a week ago, I didn't remember anything about that night. I am deeply sorry for taking your father from you. That is one reason why I'm here, to ask your forgiveness."

"It seems we each have a debt to pay."

"I need to know the name of the Ghost."

"I will need something in return."

"What is it?"

"Protect what the Guardians have kept hidden."

"You have my word."

"After that night, Angelo disappeared, but Emma stayed to protect my family. She captured the children who tried to escape. Not long afterward she took her father's place as the Ghost. I believe the children she captured, are now her assassins."

Xu Li Ma pulled at a necklace around her neck. "I took something from you that night, something that belonged to my father." Her eyes welled up with tears as she slipped a medallion, hidden beneath her blouse, from around her neck. She placed it gently in the palm of my hand. "Forgiveness brightens the darkest path."

265

66

A moss-covered path weaved through Happy Valley cemetery where headstones jutted from the dirt. Jewish. Hindu. Catholic. Muslim. Protestant. Each religion sectioned off in death as in life. Trees offered a thin layer of shade from the sweltering heat as we searched the ascending terraces for the grave.

"Why doctor the video?" Scarlett asked.

"Motivation," I replied. "I never would've come otherwise."

"You think Kate knew about it?"

"I don't think so. She was as shocked as me when we watched it together. And we weren't the only ones who knew it existed."

Scarlett's cell rang. Timothy's face appeared on the small screen.

"The pixels are a near perfect match, but Will pulled out his bag of tricks. He found a series of pixels that were altered. Once he removed them, we found a second layer. In the original there is no chair. And no woman."

"She was added in?" I asked.

"Exactly." William yelled off screen. "Whoever did it was bloody good too."

"That means she could still be alive."

"All we know is that Xu Li told the truth," Scarlett warned.

"Who would have done this?" Timothy asked.

"President Palmer."

Timothy and William blurted in unison, "Holy…"

"He was the Secretary of State during the Program. He knows firsthand what I was trained to do. Tim, see what you can find on Emma Maldone."

"Got it," Timothy replied. "One other thing. I found a dozen accounts at Cayman National."

"How much?"

"Roughly 30 million."

"Can you transfer?"

"Top of the line security, Mate. Without the second password, we risk being flagged. One wrong move and the money will be frozen until the next ice age. Do you know the joint account holder, Mark Watson?"

"Convincing him might be tricky."

"What do you want us to do?"

"Monitor the accounts until I figure out how to access them."

"Will, have you found anything on Leung?" Scarlett asked.

"Still going through what we downloaded. So far everything is clean. He left his house earlier this afternoon for a scheduled rally in Happy Valley at seven o'clock."

"Was he alone?"

"Normal security."

"Okay, talk later."

Scarlett hung up and pointed at a weathered headstone, aged to the point that the engraved letters were hard to read.

IN LOVING MEMORY
NATHANIEL MARCUS SHAW
MISSIONARY AND BELOVED HUSBAND
OF EVELYN SHAW
HE LED ME TO CHRIST. FELL ASLEEP IN JESUS
AUGUST 19, 1910
GO YE INTO ALL THE WORLD AND
PREACH THE GOSPEL TO EVERY CREATURE
FOR I AM WITH YOU
ALWAYS.

"Why give you the medallion?"

"A sign of good faith. Or a chance to be free."

"Either way, Kate is after the wrong target."

I nodded. "We need to find her before it's too late."

"Bao will call as soon as he arrives at the hotel."

I ran my palm over the stone then moved around back where the moss was thicker. With the edge of the medallion, I scraped against the moss until I uncovered the bare stone. A few minutes of work and my fingers felt an indentation. I pressed the medallion into the spot, and a piece of stone slide down a few inches. I poked my finger into the opening and felt something smooth. I tugged at it until a thin, circular, hollowed, white jade artifact dropped into my palm.

I handed it to Scarlett. "Your fingers are smaller."

She slipped her pinky into the hole and gently pushed until a rolled up piece of paper slid out. She handed it to me and watched as I slowly unrolled it. For a moment, we stood quietly and stared at the torn edges.

"What is it?"

"A page from the diary."

67

An oasis of green in the heart of Hong Kong Island, the tight track at Happy Valley circled beneath the high stands that resembled a Roman amphitheater.

Alan Leung stepped off the stage to roaring applause from tens of thousands who filled the stands, many of which were the city's top one percent. On the infield, he was joined by the Ghost and waved at the crowd until he was ushered into a tunnel typically used by the horses and jockeys on race day.

"I'm paying you to protect me," Leung seethed. "Not to disappear."

"I'm making sure you get over the finish line."

"The polls show Xu Li is still ahead by ten points."

"Tonight, the odds will shift in your favor."

"I watched the rally last night in Central. The crowd was twice this size."

Outside the stadium, valets lined up ready to retrieve the fleet of Mercedes, Rolls Royces, Lambos, Teslas, and Porsches. Leung and the Ghost walked briskly as the crowd exited out of the stadium. In the opposite direction, about a hundred yards away, was the Eurocopter.

"Are you going to tell me who we're meeting?"

"Triad Council."

They buckled in and put their headphones on, which drowned out the engine and rotors. Leung flipped a few switches and lifted the copter off the ground until it hovered over the racetrack. From his vantage point, there were thousands below marching down Central toward Harbour Tunnel. It was a wave of people looking more like an army of ants that stretched for miles.

"Sheep led to slaughter by the Guardians," the Ghost said.

Leung banked hard at the tunnel where police in riot gear formed a blockade to the entrance. He glanced at the Ghost and noticed a smirk pursed her lips. He pulled the controls and the aircraft headed across Victoria Harbor with the Peninsula Hotel directly ahead. Landing on the rooftop was tricky with the cross winds, but he handled it like a pro. Kone was already there to meet them at the stairwell. He led them downstairs to the Penthouse.

"We have secured the asset," Kone said to the Ghost.

She squeezed his shoulder. "You are the one to see this through."

Leung heard the exchange. "Who are you talking about? Lazarus?"

The Ghost swiped a card at P7. "Alan, let's not keep our guests waiting."

Kone stood guard in the hallway while they entered the room. Inside was elegant, exquisite, with an American-Asian flare. Windows revealed a large private balcony overlooking the harbor. A buffet table lined with filet mignon, lobster, sweet and sour pork, chow mein, dumplings, and Peking duck ended with four bottles of Chateau Margaux 2009 Balthazar. One of them was already empty.

Leung followed the Ghost out onto the balcony, where four men were seated around an outdoor fireplace sipping wine. Leung knew them all. He never believed high-ranking government officials would be part of the Triad Council. Even more disturbing was the way they reacted to the Ghost. All of them stood and bowed as she approached. She was clearly more than an equal.

"Gentlemen, thank you for waiting," the Ghost began. "Alan was just voicing his concern over his opponent. I reassured him the tide would change. Of course, that depends on whether we are able to agree."

Leung found an empty seat and tried to grasp the power that

surrounded him. He was used to being in the room with CEOs who reeked of cockiness and ego. To be in the presence of these men was another world. He needed to find a way to level the playing field.

"Perhaps her words are a bit strong," he said. "I know it will be close—"

"You will not win," John Kwong, Chief Secretary, said. "Not enough votes."

"How can you be so sure?" Leung asked.

"Alan, let's hear what our guests have to say," the Ghost suggested. "We are here to negotiate. I suggest you tell Alan your terms so we can reach a mutual understanding."

"This is not your style," Kwong replied. "Highly unusual."

"We need to seize this opportunity that is before us. Alan will prove his loyalty."

"One hundred thousand shares of Mulfira Mining," Lam Chun, Financial Secretary, said. "Annually, for the next five years."

"You are out of your mind," Leung protested. "I do not control the company."

"Then this meeting is a waste of time." Kwong turned to the Ghost. "Perhaps we should speak in private."

"Alan will agree to the shares," the Ghost said. "Three years maximum. What else?"

"Twenty-five percent increase in government pensions," Richard Yuen, Secretary for Justice, said. "Funding for the OCTB will cease and the division will be shut down."

OCTB, the Organized Crime Triad Bureau.

"That's two," the Ghost said. "One more."

Max Tsang, Director of Imports and Exports, leaned forward. "We will reopen the Golden Triangle and you will funnel ten percent of the shale mining deal negotiated with the Americans directly into our smuggling operations."

"This is outrageous," Leung argued. "I will not be blackmailed."

"The election is yours to lose," the Ghost said to Leung. "Think of this as diplomacy."

"How can you guarantee I will win?"

"All these gentlemen need is your word."

Leung weighed the decision as he poured himself a glass of wine. He glanced at the Ghost, knowing she had manipulated him from the start. He held the glass up and nodded at the men seated across from him.

68

God's guardians on the earth of new and old
Protect a secret more powerful than altars of gold
A power unleashed through a covenant of light
Defends a faith that will not go gently into the fight

Blind unbelief ushers in trouble, war, and fear
A battle of profound love offers courage to all who hear
Yet when the skies are filled with smoke and fire
The end draws near and faith becomes dire

Amidst the darkness unchained in fire and strife
Our brothers' souls are reborn from death to life
Along a silk road ten thousand thousands return
To a story of mercy and love evil attempted to burn

We are guardians of the Light
And we will not go gently into the fight

"Abigail taught this to us."

"I only remember Doc reading the first part at his house. What does it mean?"

"It is a covenant shared with all who are rescued and with those who have joined the cause. Anyone who is a Guardian has rooted this message into their soul."

"So, there *are* more than just us?"

"In this war, we must be cautious who we trust. Kate has a purpose different than our own. She must only be told what we choose to tell. You must remember that. There are many who have sworn to fight until the end. In time, you will stand face to face with many of them. Jacob, you are the one destined to lead us."

"I'm not a messenger—or a savior. I don't even know if I'm a Guardian. Scarlett, you must know that once I find the Ghost, I will leave."

We reached the end of a narrow alley deliberately tucked away and stepped down the stairs below street level. Brick walls on one side, graffiti-covered on the other. Round oil drums served as tables. We slipped onto the stools as an elderly man asked for our drink order. I eyed the Cuban, a tobacco-infused tequila with grilled pineapple. Strangely, the urge wasn't as strong as it had been. Once the old man was gone, Scarlett picked up the conversation.

"Darkness surrounds us. Without the light, we will perish."

"You're talking about a religious war. I don't believe in religion."

"It is not about religion. It is about believing in what we cannot see. Hope. Faith. Courage. We have been called to protect the innocent from something far more dangerous. This war is our calling. It is why we were trained, and it is who we are."

"We're supposed to protect a weapon that has remained hidden for a hundred years, yet no one can tell me what it is. I'm not fighting for a higher power. But I will promise you one thing. Before this is over, the Brethren will pay for what they've done. All of them."

"Perhaps one day you will believe."

"Don't count on it. You can chase after a myth. That's not why I'm here."

"When you left with Abigail, I spent two years alone on the island. I was isolated, and that led to some dark days. When Frank returned, there was hope. I chose not to live in the past, but to fight for a future. I pushed the demons aside—all that I endured in the Program—and believed in a greater purpose."

"Frank kept secrets from all of us."

"He did what he believed was right."

"And that got him killed."

"The Program was a necessary evil. One that turned a smuggling route of drugs and slaves into an underground railroad used for many years to transport thousands from Macao, Manila, Phuket, Bangkok, Taipei, Tokyo, Seoul and many other cities. We have saved many in our quest to protect what has remained hidden."

"So, Xu Li Ma isn't planning on reopening the Triangle, she is protecting it?"

"She only knows us as the Guardians. We have never met with her in person, until today. When the Council was killed, there was much fighting within the Triads. Once my training with Frank was finished, I moved to an apartment in Kowloon on Waterloo Road. I shadowed the emerging leadership. Frank put the intelligence together so only he knew the end game. I can only assume that he knew Xu Li Ma was an ally."

"What about Maggie?"

"Frank called me the protector of secrets." Maggie's voice cut through the night. She carried three bottles of Vitasoy, which she set on the barrel. "Scarlett is right. We believed Xu Li Ma was on the side of the Guardians, but we couldn't be certain. Now it seems you have a secret to share with me."

"I didn't think I'd ever see you again." I stared in disbelief. "When did you get here?"

"I followed Frank's instructions and secured the diary with someone who could be trusted. Someone who cares deeply for you."

"Who? My mother?" I opened the bottles and handed them around.

"I'm afraid not," Maggie replied solemnly. "Jake, words cannot express my grief over your loss. Frank was a good soul." Her eyes softened. "Scarlett told me about the video. I know you have questions."

"Is she alive?"

"As you said yourself, Frank kept secrets."

"Why are you here?"

"Two weeks before Doc's death, Frank went to see Angelo Maldone in San Quentin. He had intercepted communication that the Brethren suspected you were alive. He went to Angelo to confirm this, which started a chain of events that finds us here. Doc was supposed to keep you safe. We did not know how close they were already. It seems they have been one step ahead of us from the beginning."

"Do you know about Emma Maldone?" I asked.

"I know she was there that night on the boat, and that she protected the Triads after Angelo disappeared. I searched through what little I have left—reading through the diary to be sure—there is nothing that will identify her now. But we must assume Xu Li Ma is right. Emma Maldone is the Ghost."

"Since Xu Li Ma knew about her," Scarlett said. "She might know how to find her."

"That is possible," Maggie replied. "Jacob, what did she give you?"

I removed the medallion from my pocket and set it on the barrel. I watched as Maggie studied it closely. She pulled out a black and white photo and handed it to me. "You will recognize Sister Evelyn and her husband, Nathan. Look closely at the broach on her blouse."

It didn't take more than a few seconds to know the broach and the medallion were the same. "Xu Li said she took this from me that night, that it belonged to her father."

"I read through what was written in Sister Evelyn's own handwriting of their travels once they arrived in China. They stayed in a village not far from here once controlled by the Triads. Each morning she stood in the streets and preached to the locals, which caused dissension with the local Triad Council leader, who happened to be a direct ancestor of Xu Li Ma.

Before the Triads could get rid of Sister Evelyn, a miracle occurred. Xu Li's great-great-grandmother was deaf, had never spoken a word since birth. She approached Sister Evelyn on the street as the villagers prepared to rid themselves of the American. Sister Evelyn prayed over her, and for the first time, the woman heard the cries of her family resonating in her ears. From that moment on, the Triads protected Sister Evelyn and Nathan as they traveled into the Mainland. When Nathan died from malaria, he was brought back to Happy Valley where the Triads honored him with one of their own gravesites."

Maggie held up the medallion. "Sister Evelyn was given this by Xu Li's great-great-grandmother. Rumors were it was lost during her travels in China. Those rumors were so strong that Japan attempted to retrieve it during the Battle of Hong Kong."

"We used it on Nathan Shaw's headstone." I slid the torn page from the diary across the barrel. "It opened a secret compartment that hid this poem."

"Doc traveled the world in search of this." Maggie retrieved the ultraviolet light and waved it slowly across the page. "This piece of paper is more than a poem. It is a map."

I looked for myself at a crude drawing beneath the words.

"Where does it lead?"

"Perhaps it is what so many have died to protect," Maggie said. "And why the Brethren are willing to kill in order to find."

"It is a sign that what we have believed is true." Scarlett sipped at her Vitasoy.

"How can we protect what we don't know exists?" I asked.

"If the Brethren discover this is in our possession, we are in far greater danger."

"So what do we do?" I drained my bottle.

Scarlett's cell buzzed. She read the text. "Bao said the room was empty. Only her backpack is there. He's bringing it with him."

"I will protect those on the island." Maggie handed the map back to me. "You two must keep Xu Li Ma alive until she can tell us more. A rebellion has begun. It is time for the Guardians to stand strong."

"Bao is waiting at the pier," Scarlett said to Maggie. She tossed ten bucks on the barrel. "Jacob, we better go."

69

Brad Cunningham downloaded a video onto a thumb drive and copied the IP address. A few hours sequestered in the Oval Office was enough to cause growing curiosity from White House staffers. He was on the inside. Better yet, he had gained the President's trust.

A secret service agent ushered him through a hidden door, down a maze of corridors and a flight of stairs that ended at a nondescript entrance. Cunningham placed his eye near a camera. A green light scanned his retina.

He entered the Situation Room, an intelligence center run by the National Security Council, Homeland Security Advisor, and the White House Chief of Staff. In the basement of the West Wing, Cunningham was at ground zero equipped with secure, advanced communications equipment.

President Palmer was seated at the conference table. His tie hung loose. His fingers tapped the Morning Book. It was clear the day had already been a grind. No firm handshake. No slap on the back. Straight down to business.

Cunningham found a seat and inserted the thumb drive in a slot built into the table.

For the next hour, they watched the interrogation of Robert Langston/Frank Harris. Brutal. Disturbing. Langston described the blueprint to the Program, how the children were recruited and trained, as well as who was assassinated on Palmer's orders.

It was damaging and criminal.

At the end of the video, Kone relayed specific instructions of when and where to deliver Lazarus.

Cunningham typed in an IP address and a screen appeared. A countdown clock. Twenty-three hours, thirty-seven minutes, eight seconds. Seven seconds. Six seconds.

"Black web," Cunningham said. "IP is encrypted."

President Palmer pointed at another row of screens on the wall that relayed a live satellite feed from Central to Mong Kok. "We're supposed to deliver him there?"

"Based on Kone's instructions. That puts him at the rally."

"Still no communication from Kate?"

"No sir. At this point, without a team on the ground, I'd consider her a long shot."

"Analysts put Xu Li Ma in the winner's circle, and we're supposed to hand over Lazarus as she takes a victory lap."

"Anything can happen, sir. Leung might break away."

"They've got us by the—"

"We need to consider the possibility that Kate's been neutralized. And that we won't be able to find Jake Harris in time."

"What are you suggesting?"

"Get ahead of this as soon as possible." Cunningham slid a document across the table. "We start by leaking this to the press."

President Palmer read it aloud. "Frank Harris, a prominent businessman, was kidnapped by an extremist group connected to ISIS in Asia. He was tortured and drugged. Without the knowledge of the Oval Office, a mission was attempted by a private security firm to rescue Mr. Harris. Unfortunately, during the rescue attempt he was killed. A video was released on the Internet and has gone viral. In that video, Mr. Harris confesses to absurd allegations under extreme duress. Lazarus was an alias used by the extremist group as code for the ransom demands and drop-off location. It is our belief that Mr. Harris said what he believed would keep him alive. However, in the end his life was tragically lost. Our thoughts and prayers go out to all who knew him."

President Palmer glanced up at Cunningham. "You are asking me to negate all that Frank has done for our country."

"Mr. President, whether Xu Li Ma or Alan Leung wins the election, if this goes viral and we remain silent, there will be no bridging the gap with the Chinese. You will be at their mercy, and they will force you into a deal much worse than Iran. Not to mention the possibility of impeachment."

"I need time to think this over."

"Your administration will be hit with a tidal wave."

"I understand what's at stake, Brad."

"We are out of options."

President Palmer pointed emphatically at the clock. "There's still time."

"Mr. President, the situation is no longer in our control."

"You want to turn Lazarus into a terrorist?"

"We go with the original story as a follow up to Harris' press release," Cunningham advised. "We tie him to the kidnapping and ransom due to his involvement in the Montrose bombing and the viral video. No matter how you look at it, we need to make him our scapegoat."

"You can't confirm whether he's with Kate, correct?"

"From my last conversation with her, there was no indication they were together."

"I won't leave Kate exposed if we do this. I'm the one who talked her into it for God's sake."

"We are both responsible," Cunningham replied. "Mr. President, if we don't hear from her by tomorrow night, we'll send in a team to locate her. I promise you, we will bring her back."

"I will hold you to that." Palmer slid his chair back. "Give me an hour. In the meantime, monitor the situation from here. You have everything you need. I've ordered all personnel to steer clear of this room for the next twenty-four hours."

"Understood."

Cunningham waited until President Palmer left the room. He entered a series of codes, and within seconds was connected to Hong Kong's Transportation Department, MTR, and street cameras. If Kate or Jake passed by one of the cameras, he'd know in real time. He checked to be sure his laptop was secured then typed in another series of codes. A screen appeared where he sent an encrypted message.

70

A floor lamp illuminated a corner of a rundown apartment where paint peeled from the moldy walls. A chair faced a window overlooking the streets below. Kone's shadow outlined against the glass. It was a perfect crow's nest.

A TV recapped Xu Li Ma's speech from the night before, edited in between the cameras that followed a growing sea of demonstrators marching through Central towards Cross Harbour where police in riot gear formed a line across the tunnel entrance.

Kate bit hard on a gag and yanked at the restraints that tied her wrists to a headboard. Her nose whistled from a deviated septum, courtesy of Kone. She wondered how long he'd followed her, and how he found her so easily. She didn't see him until it was too late.

He had prodded her with the barrel of a gun through the crowd into an alley to a waiting van. Then he punched her in the face and pulled a hood over her head. The next thing she knew, she was waking up in this room.

Kone crossed in front of her and answered the door. A shadow slipped inside and stepped closer to Kate.

"Not a sound," the Ghost warned.

Kone removed the gag. Kate sucked in a mouthful of air and glared.

"My father underestimated you," the Ghost began. "I will not be as careless."

"You were dead."

"A bit of movie magic," she smirked, "by someone within your circle."

"You're lying."

"Kate, you really must choose your friends more carefully." The Ghost glanced at Kate's cell. "It seems Lazarus is anxious to hear from you."

"You're dead to him."

"And yet you will be the stone that brings the castle down."

Kone walked over to a case on the floor. He opened it and removed a cutter. Kate listened as the blade sliced across the window. Next, Kone removed a sight, barrel, stock, and ammo for an M24 sniper rifle. Commonly used by the military in Iraq, Kate recognized it as the same model she trained with at Quantico.

"I was hoping our conversation would be more . . . civilized."

Kate mounted another flurry against the restraints. "You call this civilized?"

The Ghost moved swiftly, grabbed Kate by the throat, and cut off her air. "The wages of sin is death. You are only alive because I need him. I assure you, once Lazarus is in my grasp, your fate will be far worse than death."

Kone unfolded a titanium stand and set it close to the window. He secured the rifle in place and peered through the scope. She watched Kone casually enter the bathroom. When he reappeared, he held a towel and ice bucket.

"Sometimes Damas gets a little carried away." The Ghost removed her hand from Kate's throat. "For your sake, let's hope that doesn't happen tonight. Now Kate, tell me what you know about Lazarus."

When Kate didn't answer, Kone dropped the towel over her face and poured water from the bucket. She gurgled as the fear of drowning activated her survival instincts. Her heart pounded through her chest.

When Kone removed the towel, she coughed up a mouthful and tried to keep her wits about her. She was on her own, and that was going to get her killed.

The Ghost leaned over with a stare that sent a chill down Kate's spine.

Calculated. Controlled. Cunning. If she didn't think fast, she wouldn't make it through the next few minutes.

"You murdered your family." Kate's raw throat scratched the words out.

"They betrayed me." The Ghost paced the room. "Every last one of them."

Kate nodded at Kone. "And you turned children into killers."

The Ghost spun around. "I saved them and gave them a purpose."

"So that gives you the right to decide who lives and who dies?"

"The Brethren have evolved to be much more than assassins for hire. Now that I have the hard drive, even the worst in humanity will kneel at my feet."

"Then why do you need him?"

"Lazarus has something of great value."

Kate struggled to put the pieces together. "Did you know Frank worked for the Agency?"

"Robert Langston. Frank Harris. I am sure he's been known by many other names. But I assure you, I would've killed him myself if I had known he was CIA." Kone moved in but paused as the Ghost raised her hand. "My father verified he was who he claimed to be: an American smuggler from Sudan. Not a clue that he worked for the Agency or anyone else for that matter. You might say we shared a tragic love story. Or perhaps it wasn't love at all. He stole my children from me. Do you know how difficult that is for a mother? Of course not. Foster care, one-night stands, I don't think you'd understand. But it seems neither of us have had much luck with men."

"You don't know anything about me."

"I know more than you realize, thanks to my father. At first, I believed the Brethren were protecting him from the Triads when he disappeared before sunrise without so much as a word to his own daughter. Not until many years later did I discover his betrayal. Kate, I am the one who found him hiding in that miserable apartment."

Kate's brow lifted. What?

"Theresa didn't lead you to him. I did." The Ghost met Kate's gaze. "I gave you your greatest prize. Now it is you who will return the favor."

"Why kill Theresa?"

"Her death was unavoidable. I needed her as leverage against my father, to find out what he knew about the Guardians and their secret. Now it is only a matter of time before that secret belongs to me."

"Jake will never be loyal to you."

"He knows the way to the Silk Road." The Ghost resumed pacing. "Now, tell me about the diary."

"What diary?" Kate knew her bluff was weak. Kone was ready for another round, as if inflicting pain was a hobby. Kate added quickly, "Jake found it at Warren's house, but you already knew that. I'm sure Rimoldi was one of yours too."

"Believe me when I tell you, Neco was nothing more than a hired contractor. He was never one of us. Damas said you shot him, but not before Frank spilled the truth."

Kone returned to his crow's nest. The glow from a laptop cast an ominous glow on his dark features.

The water torture seemed to be on hold. Kate let out a miniscule breath. She needed to keep the Ghost talking and hope that someone was tracking the signal on her cell.

"Kate, what did Lazarus do with the diary?"

"He gave it to Margaret Johnson."

"The housekeeper?" The Ghost's eyes narrowed. "Where is she?"

"You'll never find her. She's disappeared."

"I will move heaven and earth, if that's what is required. You think you are here because Palmer wanted Lazarus to find the truth? Do you still believe the Program was created to save the lost? If that's the case, then you are more naïve than I thought."

"I've read the files. The Program saved thousands."

"C'mon, Kate. You're brighter than that." The Ghost paced the room, like a leopard circling its prey. "Palmer was the Secretary of State. He was the mastermind behind the Program. Frank was his protégé, the one who operated outside the rules of engagement. Frank picked the twelve because he needed them to find a weapon that has eluded the world for nearly a century. Now you are doing Palmer's bidding. Don't you see? We are hunting the same prize. Only one person has ever seen it with her own eyes. And there is only one left who knows the way."

"Sister Evelyn's diary—it shows where it's hidden."

"Her writings offer clues to its existence, but only Lazarus can take me there."

"Because he was the only operative who knew the routes in the Golden Triangle?"

"Now you're catching on — the Silk Road."

"He doesn't remember any of it."

The Ghost stopped in front of Kate. "We have ways to spark his memory."

"The extraction drug? That won't work on him."

"Don't take me for a fool."

"Even if he does remember, he will never help you."

"I have incentives: Rachel and Samantha."

Kate's eyes flared. "That's impossible."

"Everyone has a Judas. It seems you too have been betrayed by a kiss."

Kate leaned back against the headrest and closed her eyes. She wanted to scream, to rip her wrists out of the restraints, and strangle the Ghost with her bare hands. She didn't need a weapon. She'd made a promise to Jake. If Rachel and Samantha were in danger, she had already failed.

"You know, I feel much better after our little chat." The Ghost eyed Kate. "I feel like I've gotten a few things off my chest. Perhaps you missed your calling, Kate. I guess we'll never know."

Kone stepped over and tied the gag around Kate's head. She didn't fight. Instead, she sat quietly, plotting her revenge.

A few seconds passed before the Ghost leaned in close enough her breath brushed against Kate's cheek. "Third time's a charm, my dear."

71

Sweat seeped through my shirt as we continued a punishing pace through the city. Thousands and thousands of people filled the streets marching through Admiralty. Each one believing their voices and votes were going to change Hong Kong forever. We were the ones who needed to protect their voice of democracy.

Assembling a weapon in a matter of seconds was a cool party trick, but the depth of my instincts and training were unproven. I knew there was a risk that what happened at The Peak could happen again. Scarlett knew it too. Surviving the night might prove to be more difficult than either of us imagined. Chasing destiny meant running for as long as there was breath to breathe.

"Hong Kong Island is shut down." Timothy's voice filled my ear. Scarlett jogged as I tried to keep up. "All transportation is at a standstill."

"What about Bao and Maggie?" Scarlett was hardly out of breath.

"Already on their way. We also have a signal on Kate's cell."

"Where is she?" I exhaled and inhaled rapidly.

"Right where you thought she'd be," Timothy replied. "We tried calling. No answer."

"Are you tracking us?" Scarlett asked.

"You're near the tunnel. We might lose you once you go inside."

"Pick up the pace!" I yelled at Scarlett. "I'll keep up."

Timothy chuckled. "Good luck, Mate."

I knew it was wishful thinking, but it sounded good. Scarlett switched gears, and we were engulfed in the masses. I forced myself to move faster. A melody quickened my step. At first, I thought it was my imagination. Then I heard it surround me. I recited the poem from memory as the voices rang out in Cantonese. My sneakers hit the pavement at a steady rhythm.

Determination fueled the jaunt and left me gasping for air. Anxiety seeped beneath the surface at the thought that we might be too late. I thought of Mom. If she was alive, I needed to find her. At the same time, I wondered who tampered with the video. I heard myself call out to her, but she was never there. After all of this, I was still chasing her shadow.

Five miles in record time left me doubled over. Once we finally stopped, we stood in a place that parted the waters of Victoria Harbor. Each city block marked a return to the darkness that consumed my soul. I followed Scarlett as she worked her way through the crowd towards the front lines.

Resurrecting Lazarus was for the right reasons even though it may not have been the right thing to do. Anxiety subsided. Fear calmed. Resolve returned. No matter what the sunrise brought, tonight I was stepping into my destiny.

My mind flashed to the smell of burnt metal as my fingers rubbed the residue of countless rounds of ammunition. I crouched on a flatbed truck loaded with children not much older than I. My ears rang from the blood-curdling screams. Scarlett was beside me, and Damas crouched near the rear. Bullets ricocheted on all sides as we returned fire.

The vision morphed into nothingness before I emerged running through a village while an overwhelming stench of death filled my nostrils. Alone. I dropped to my knees, sure the end was near. When I looked up, I found myself kneeling before a door surrounded by a wall of granite. Vivid. Forever engrained in my soul.

In that moment, all I had seen and done in the Program returned with a vengeance. Training. Missions. Faces of those who were saved. And those who were dead.

I knew what the Brethren were after, and I was the one who held the key.

As long as Scarlett carried the belief and faith, I'd sink to the depths of the abyss to stop them from destroying the world. She was the only one who could bring me back.

"Jacob. Jacob!" Scarlett snatched me back to the present. "They are moving the barricades. Come on."

We were sardines amongst a wave of humanity. Officers stood to the side directing us into the mile long tunnel. Walking underwater, protected by concrete and steel, was surreal. The voices echoed off the walls and reassured me of our solidarity. My eyes met Scarlett's filled with determination. We were back in the battle—together—as if we had never been apart.

Red and blue flashing lights glowed ahead of us. An officer spoke into a megaphone and the crowd stopped abruptly. Riot police showed themselves and moved in formation. The crowd yelled in protest.

"What's happening?" I shouted.

"Keep moving—" Scarlett grabbed my arm— "or we will be trapped."

A canister hurtled overhead and gas filled the tunnel. Another canister and panic swept the crowd. We were being pushed in on all sides.

Scarlett squeezed my arm to keep us together. My eyes burned. She tossed me a shirt from her backpack. I held it over my mouth, and she did the same. A few elbows and punches later, we closed in on the riot police equipped with batons and shields. Bullets whizzed by my ear, but we kept moving. The officers swung and fired into the crowd. Several people nearby fell to the ground. I ducked as an officer swung at me. Scarlett dropped him with a swift elbow to the throat.

Ten feet from the line, Scarlett removed two flash-bangs from the backpack. She tossed one to me. I pulled the pin and threw it towards the officers. She kept to my right and followed. Two blinding flashes and an eardrum-shattering noise ripped through the tunnel.

Five seconds.

We darted towards the officers as they were disoriented, holding their ears, and stumbling backward. The crowd turned into a tidal wave, and we surfed them straight through the barricade.

We broke left and dove over a cement barrier. I breathed hard and hoped we'd gone unnoticed. Scarlett poked her head over the barrier as officers continued the assault on their citizens. The carnage was impossible to hide from the news helicopters overhead.

Timothy's voice cut through the static. "You two alright?"

"Barely," I answered. "What was that about?"

"Reporters are saying someone fired on the police. Standby. Will has been monitoring the police scanner. They're bringing in buses to transport the demonstrators to Argyle Street."

"They will take them to the old refugee camp," Scarlett added. "Tim, we need wheels."

"Mandarin Plaza is a block away."

72

Scarlett distracted the valet while I swiped a set of keys. We found the delivery van in an underground garage. With Scarlett behind the wheel, we drove the streets, avoiding as much gridlock as possible. We reached a standstill a few blocks from Xu Li Ma's campaign headquarters in Mong Kok. The energy of the crowd on the streets was magnetic, completely opposite from the aftermath at Cross Harbour Tunnel. Scarlett parked the van in a side alley. We proceeded on foot.

Timothy's voice guided us. "Signal is one block straight ahead."

Scarlett zeroed in on a high-rise apartment building wrapped in bamboo scaffolding. Music pumped through the streets from a main stage that fueled the chaotic celebration. Xu Li Ma's supporters were out in force, ready to cast their votes in the morning. Tonight, they reveled in what seemed to be an insurmountable lead over the PRC's frontrunner, Alan Leung.

"Signal is getting stronger."

"Maybe we should split up," I suggested.

Scarlett stopped in midstride. "We do what we do—together."

The crowd erupted as Xu Li Ma stepped onstage and waved to the crowd. A few hours ago it was the two of us, both searching for forgiveness. She gave me a gift and a burden.

I scanned the buildings and the people. If Kate was going to take the shot, now was the time. "She'll be on the ground. Easier to disappear."

Scarlett followed my eyes as Xu Li Ma's voice boomed in Cantonese. I understood every word as I kept my head moving side to side. I pushed forward, searching for any sign of Kate.

"An hour ago, the police reacted towards our brothers and sisters with extreme prejudice," Xu Li Ma preached. "Without provocation, they have attacked and beaten the very citizens they are sworn to protect. Tonight, we stand in solidarity with all who have been detained. We stand together on the brink of a revolution. Our past will no longer define us. Instead, our future will unlock our path together, to achieve the very democracy that is being threatened.

"We are fighting not only for our future, but for the generations to come. We will not be ruled over by corrupt politicians, the PRC, or the Triads any longer. Our war is against more than billionaire opponents, it is to preserve the freedoms we deserve as Hong Kongers. With the sunrise only a few hours away, we are on the verge of a new beginning…"

"You're ten feet away. She's right there."

I spun around in the middle of the crowd searching every non-Asian face. The more the crowd cheered, the more I blocked them out. I never heard the gunshot. I only saw Xu Li Ma drop on stage. For a moment the streets were eerily silent. Then the wailing began.

"We're too late," I whispered.

"Jacob, she is right in front of you."

A sea of people parted as I blindly ran forward. Kate slowly lowered her gun and dropped to her knees. Several bystanders noticed the weapon and swarmed her, grabbing and punching. I pulled the Glock from behind my back and fired in the air. That startled them enough to step back.

73

The thirteenth floor offered a clear view of the celebration below. Kone rubbed a triangle tattoo on the inside of his forearm, a sign of his allegiance to the Brethren. He peered through the scope then glanced at his laptop. Intel was being relayed in real time from thousands of miles away. The Ghost had set him loose to hunt in the New York of Asia. It seemed there were more than one target to choose from.

His pulse quickened once he caught sight of a van driving through the tail end of the crowd. His ears filled with chatter. *Eyes on Lazarus. Blue van. He is not alone. Asian female.* Kone knew it was Scarlett, which only complicated things. He followed the van until it disappeared into an alley. A moment later he picked up Jacob and Scarlett on the street.

From his vantage point, it would have been an easy shot. He leaned into the M24 and decided whether to pull the trigger. There was never any emotion in the act. That was the first lesson learned in the Program. Killing was always a calculated decision. One he had taken numerous times.

An opportunity to kill Jacob flowed through his veins, and it was tempting to settle a score with Scarlett. But if he disobeyed orders, he betrayed the others. He needed to follow the Ghost's instructions.

Kone turned his attention to Xu Li Ma on stage. He held her life in his hands. His heartbeat slowed as he controlled his breathing. He steadied himself and rested his index finger gently on the trigger. A few more seconds peering through the scope and he had Xu Li Ma in the crosshairs.

He exhaled and slowly pulled the trigger, discharging the bullet. He watched as the shot hit her directly between the eyes. She slumped to the stage as those around reacted in horror.

A shadow in the night, his eyes fixed on the security that swarmed the stage. A symbol of freedom and love was dead. He swung the scope across to find Jacob. He smirked as the crowd stepped away from the bait. The commotion served as a perfect smoke screen. He stepped back from the window, hidden in a concrete jungle, and disassembled the M24 before racing down thirteen flights of stairs without losing his breath. He disappeared out the back of the building and a few blocks away hid behind tinted windows of a 700 Series BMW.

Tires screeched as he hugged each corner, ducking in and out of traffic. He pressed the accelerator further toward the floorboard, reliving the moment the bullet pierced her skull. Neon lights glowed in the darkness as the thrill of the kill rushed through his veins. He punched the gas and disappeared into the mountainside.

74

I swept Kate up in my arms.

Scarlett kept the crowd at arms length, which wasn't going to last long. Security and police were already headed in our direction. Kate's body was heavy, her eyes bloodshot and dilated. I didn't know if she fired the shot. She looked incoherent, possibly drugged.

"Is Xu Li alive?" I asked Timothy.

"Doesn't look good. She hasn't moved."

"We will be next." Scarlett spun around waving her gun at the crowd, who were on the verge of attacking. "We need a way out."

Xu Li Ma's supporters inched forward as their celebration turned to rage. We fought our way back in the direction of the van. It was pointless. A man rushed me. With a swift blow, I sent him reeling backward. We were cornered on all sides. I fired another shot in the air, and the crowd stepped back enough for us to duck into a corner liquor store. Scarlett locked the door as the glass rattled from the banging of fists. A man protested from behind a cash register. We ignored him and moved down the aisle into a backroom then out an exit into the alley.

"Get to the side street," Timothy said. "Or you will be surrounded!"

I swung Kate's body over my shoulder. She groaned, "Judas."

Scarlett stayed in front as we moved to the end of the alley and out into the street. A mob had already gathered. Once we were in their sights, the chase was on. Overhead a spotlight from a helicopter beamed down on us. I spun around to see officers darting down the alley. With guns raised, they fired several rounds.

"We can make it," Scarlett urged. "Keep moving."

The mob and officers moved in force. Kate groaned again, her breathing labored. I wasn't going to let her die, not tonight.

"Forget the van, it's swarming with police. Cut left—now!"

Timothy was our eyes on the ground, so we didn't ask questions. We ducked into another alley and headed straight towards a dead end. I didn't know what would be worse, being shot, beaten to death, or watching that happen to Kate or Scarlett.

"Look for an entrance to the tunnels."

"They're closing in too fast!" Scarlett yelled.

"What tunnels?" I shouted.

"Head straight for the end of the alley. You'll see it."

A bullet ricocheted off the concrete. I leaned Kate against the wall to keep her steady and returned fire. I turned to Scarlett. "You need to get her to the Embassy."

"Not without you."

"I'll be right behind you." I emptied the clip as more bullets rang out. I tossed the Glock to the ground. "This isn't over yet."

Scarlett hesitated for a second before wrapping her arm around Kate's waist and fading into the darkness.

I turned towards the street and braced myself for the onslaught. I gazed towards the stars and said softly, "Surely, you have not brought me here to die."

I stepped out into the open beneath a bright light. As the crowd gathered, I raised my hands and walked forward.

Adrenaline turned to courage. Fear turned to peace.

I was dragged into the center of the street where the crowd struck me repeatedly. I dropped to my knees as blood dripped down my chin onto the concrete. I glanced up as the faces of Xu Li's followers glared with a righteous hatred. A dozen officers pointed their weapons at me. I interlaced my fingers behind my head and surrendered.

A woman emerged from the crowd and motioned for the officers to step back. She stared down at me with deep brown eyes, her hair pulled away from her striking cheekbones. I gazed at her and whispered one word.

"Mom."

75

Kate blinked several times before the white walled room became clearer. She reached over and touched the IV in her arm. The numbness in her body left her sluggish. She felt the wrap around her ribs as she turned her head to see Scarlett standing near the window.

"You are a hero." Scarlett had her back to Kate. "President Palmer told the world that you risked your life to try and stop the assassination."

"Assassination?"

"Your target—Xu Li Ma."

"I didn't shoot her. Did I?" Uncertainty rushed through Kate. She questioned her memory. Xu Li Ma *was* her target, but she never had a chance to follow through. She remembered the M24 perched near the glass, the water torture by Kone, and seeing the Ghost face to face. After that, everything went blank.

"You did not." Scarlett turned, looking like the weight of the world rested on her shoulders. "Your clip was empty. My guess it was Damas. He was always the best sharpshooter in the group."

Kate forced herself to sit up, wincing at the pain in her ribs. "I was shadowing Xu Li Ma in Central. Kone caught me off guard." She was angered that she admitted it. "He took me . . . to an apartment, I think. And the Ghost was there."

"Emma Maldone."

Kate nodded as she thought of who the Ghost was to Jake. "I don't remember anything after she left."

"We found you in the center of the crowd. They used you to get to Jacob."

A surge of fear struck Kate. "Where is he?"

"He is gone."

"Gone?"

"He sacrificed himself." Scarlett stepped closer. Kate noticed the redness in her eyes. "They took him. And we both know why. Millions of people watched it happen."

"I need to call the President."

"He issued a statement this morning in support of Alan Leung, who was sworn in as CEO yesterday. It seems the two of them are closer than we realized. Leung has arrested more of Xu Li Ma's supporters. Many of them are being held in refugee camps."

Kate was puzzled. "I'm sorry."

Scarlett handed Kate a tablet. She read the official White House press release regarding the kidnapping and death of Frank Harris by an extremist group. She cursed when she read the last two paragraphs naming Jake Harris as the FBI and Interpol's top fugitive on the terrorist watch list. Not only was he accused of participating in the Montrose bombing but also the assassination of Xu Li Ma.

"They released a video of Jacob at the hospital in Los Angeles. The world watched him being arrested in Mong Kok. President Palmer has publicly stated that he has asked Leung to release Jacob to US custody. He used Frank and Jacob, so before you call him you might want to consider which side of this you are on."

"That choice has already been made." Kate set the tablet down and leaned back against her pillow. "I promise you, we'll find him."

"Kate, who is Judas? You repeated that name."

"I intend to find out as soon as I'm back in the States."

"I'm leaving this evening for Zambia. Frank went there to find answers, so I am going to do the same. With what has happened in the last week, I believe there is someone there who will be able to help us."

"Scarlett, we are in this fight together."

"We found a map hidden in Nathan Shaw's gravestone. A key to what has been hidden for nearly a century. Jacob had it with him when he was captured. Our sources within the government have confirmed that he is no longer in police custody."

"Emma Maldone needed him because he knows where to find the weapon." More needed to be said, but now wasn't the time. "Scarlett, how'd we escape?"

"Underground tunnels built during the Battle of Hong Kong. They stretch throughout the city. It took hours to find a way out. By then it was too late. The city was locked down for twenty-four hours. I could not get you to the Embassy, so I brought you here. Jacob saved us. Now it is our turn to do the same."

Kate's eyes were opened. She had been played all along, perhaps long before she was ordered to protect Jake. She made a promise she intended to keep.

A nurse entered the room, checked Kate's vitals and blood pressure then left. When they were alone again Scarlett said, "You know he cares for you."

"He cares for us both." Kate pulled the IV from her arm. "Let's get outta here."

76

After a long flight, Kate walked out into the cold afternoon at Tom Bradley International Terminal. She gingerly carried her backpack and duffle. Six cracked ribs, a broken nose, dislocated finger, and emotional scars that would take months on a sofa to unpack. She waited as a red Camaro pulled up to the curb. Brad climbed out from the driver's side with a wide smile and hugged her tight.

Kate pulled away. "I'm a bit sore."

"Sorry. I'm just glad you're back safe."

Brad grabbed the bags and tossed them in the trunk. Then he opened the door and helped her into the passenger seat. Her body was stiff. She closed her eyes and took a deep breath as they left the terminal and headed toward the 105 freeway.

"You've been cleared by the Chinese government," Brad said. "Ballistics confirmed the bullet was not from your weapon. It was from an M24. Can you believe that?"

"What about the hearings?"

"The President's approval ratings went up twenty points once the press release was distributed. I guess the fight against terrorism still resonates with voters. For now, it doesn't look like there'll be any inquiry into the existence of the Program or Lazarus."

"So, he's running for a second term."

"Looks that way." Brad entered the freeway and switched lanes between traffic. "He asked me to head up the search for Jake Harris from the black site downtown."

"Brad, why would the President name Jake as a terrorist?"

"It's a safety net in case any more videos are leaked."

Kate sighed. "Any leads?"

Brad pointed to a manila envelope in the side compartment of the passenger door. Kate reached for it and pulled out a set of surveillance photos. She recognized the private airport at Kai Tak. She stared at Emma Maldone and Jake in a series of photos that captured them boarding a Gulfstream X.

"Kate, have you had any contact with him?"

"Nothing."

"I know you're still recovering, but I need you back."

She squirmed at his voice. "I'm not in any shape to do that yet."

"You'll be debriefed about what happened over there. Then you and I will build a team to track him down. I'm sure POTUS will make it right once we've got him back on US soil."

"I need time to think—and heal."

"You're the toughest woman I've ever known. I know you want in on this."

"I'm not so sure. Being there, with Jake, did something to me."

"Don't tell me you lost your edge."

"I just need time."

"At least think about it."

"Fine." Behind dark shades, Kate kept her eyes focused on the cars ahead. "Brad, I need you to tell me where Rachel and Samantha Harris are living."

Brad accelerated on the entrance to the 110 freeway. Kate waited for him to respond. It was a question she had wanted to ask since she opened her eyes in the hospital.

"I'm afraid I don't know," he said. "It's been sealed by POTUS."

Kate tilted her head back and closed her eyes. If she pretended to sleep, that might stop him from being suspicious. She stayed that way until the Camaro pulled into the driveway of her bungalow in Eagle Rock. Brad unloaded her bags from the trunk and set them on the front porch. He leaned in and kissed her on the cheek.

"You should get some rest. I'll check on you in the morning."

"Uh, listen, I'm going out of town for a few days. I'll call you when I'm back."

"Fair enough."

Kate waited on the porch as Brad backed out of the driveway and drove off. She looked at the peeled paint, and the brown grass. She held the keys in her hand but couldn't get herself to go inside. For a few minutes, she sat on the steps and listened to her voicemails. One from her realtor had news of a full-priced offer. This wasn't her home, not anymore. She'd take the money, put everything in storage, and set her operation in motion.

She loaded her backpack and duffle into the Jeep, gripped the steering wheel as she slipped into the seat then headed for the beach. If she took the canyon, she'd be there before dark.

The sun faded on the horizon as she stepped up to the door at the Malibu shack. She didn't have keys, but that didn't matter. A familiar face was there to greet her in the doorway.

"I was wondering when you'd get here."

Kate grinned. "Mitch, you're a sight for sore eyes."

"Sounds like you've had quite the adventure. C'mon in."

Kate entered the shack to the aroma of spaghetti and meatballs. It was the first sense of home she'd felt in weeks. She needed to get him up to speed, but that could wait. She was dying for a glass of wine and a home-cooked meal.

Mitch busied himself over the stove, seasoning the meat, piled up two heaping plates with a mountain of cheese and set them on the table.

"I thought this would be better than IHOP." He laughed. "You look like you've lost a few pounds."

"Not the kind of weight loss program I'd recommend. You've kept out of sight?"

"No one knows I'm alive, except for Powell and Chapman." Mitch dug into a pile of noodles. "It's actually not bad out here. Of course, I envisioned retirement on an island far away from all this."

"Technically, you're not retired."

"Listen, I've been following your guy since he returned from DC. He met with Mayor Osoria half a dozen times then spent a few days in Vegas. He met with Jake's ex, Rachel."

"He told me he didn't know where they were relocated." Kate dug into the spaghetti and responded with a mouthful. "He's been put in charge of tracking down Jake, and he's asked me to be on the team."

"What'd you say?"

"I needed to think about it."

"Staying close is a good way to know how deep he's involved."

"But finding Jake will be risky with Brad looking over my shoulder."

"That's why you need me."

"From the moment we met, I knew we'd get along. I'm still mad you didn't tell me you'd slipped out of the hospital that morning. I thought I'd gotten you killed."

"Like I told you, I'm an old dog with a few tricks left up my sleeve."

"I had DNA run on Theresa Maldone. She shared a ninety-five percent match with Jake, which means it's highly probable Emma Maldone *is* his mother."

"So, how do we find him?"

"You keep shadowing Brad, and I'll head to Vegas."

"Sounds like a plan." Mitch raised a glass of Pinot. "Here's to being a vigilante."

77

Scarlett reached the end of the market and turned down Akapelwa. She crossed the road and searched for a number. She had never traveled beyond the Orient. Since landing in Lusaka, Zambia, she had flown in a Cessna, bounced for eight hours on a bus, and asked for directions once she reached Livingstone. She walked the streets and saw firsthand the devastation.

Sleeved tattoos and fiery red hair with her Asian features drew attention from the locals. She kept her guard up and wondered if the woman Frank had searched for was as valuable as she hoped. Her fresh tattoo on the top of her hand itched. It was an exact replica of the medallion. A constant reminder of what it was she was fighting to save.

Nearly a fortnight had passed since Jacob disappeared. Maggie had yet to find any sign of his whereabouts. Kate called with news that she was going to see Jacob's ex-wife, Rachel. Scarlett had decided not to pass that piece of information on to Maggie. At times it seemed they were fighting different battles in the same war.

Children from the market followed her, running alongside, shouting their names. A girl grabbed her by the hand. Another touched the tattoos as if they were alive, while others played with a joy that was unexplainable considering the destruction that occurred. Scarlett was caught off guard by their smiles.

She hadn't been the same since Jacob was taken. She'd watched the news footage of him kneeling amidst the crowd and the woman who stepped forward. She had a face and a name to the Ghost: Emma Maldone. Timothy, William, and Bao were stalking the black web to find anything that might lead them to Jacob's whereabouts. Flying to Zambia was a long shot, but it was worth the risk.

Scarlett was near the end of a street lined with cinderblock structures. A blue metal gate marked the last property where shard glass lined the top of the concrete walls. She banged on the gate beneath a painted sign that read: HOPE HOUSE.

Before she left, Maggie explained the connection of the Hope Houses. Sister Evelyn had returned to Hong Kong years after Nathan Shaw was buried and started the first Hope House in Macau. From there, she planted these orphanages around the world, including Livingstone. Her desire to care for the poor, lost, forgotten, and hurting had long outlived her life on earth.

A young African opened the gate and greeted Scarlett.

"I am looking for Stella." Scarlett noticed that the girl was blind. "Stella Adams."

"Please, come in."

Scarlett followed the girl as she used a cane to find her way into the main building. Different country, culture, and community—the same need. If Maggie was right, she was about to meet a legend. Excitement balled up in her chest as she listened to her heart beat in her ears.

A woman entered the room. Bronze skin. Straight, sandy blonde hair. Arms muscular but toned. If Scarlett was fire then this woman was ice. Scarlett noticed the stitches over her eyebrow and the fresh bandage around her forearm. She was a fellow warrior. Someone who could help find Jacob. That is, if she agreed.

"My name is Scarlett and I have traveled many miles to meet you."

"How may I help you?"

"We both fight against the darkness only worlds apart."

Stella met Scarlett's gaze. "I'm sure whatever you have heard has been embellished."

"Damas Kone has caused much pain to your family."

Her eyes narrowed. "Why are you telling me this?"

"I am here to offer you justice."

"What do you want in return?"

Scarlett took a breath. "I need to build an army."

"Why should I trust you?"

"You are a Guardian." Scarlett pulled up her sleeve and revealed a lion tattooed on her forearm. "And so am I."

"I do not know you."

Scarlett stepped over to the girl who was blind and placed her hands over her eyes. She prayed quietly. When she removed her hands, the girl's eyes grew as large as her smile.

"Stella." The girl clapped her hands. "I see you! I see you!"

"I will lay down my life to serve you." Scarlett never looked away.

Stella's steel, bluish gray eyes flared. "If what you say is true, I will do the same."

78

A six-mile trek in a torrential downpour through the jungle led to a village in Sichuan, or what was left of one. I'd been here before, many years ago. I'd also seen this place on Doc's wall. The dampness and mud failed to cover the stench of death that remained. I was passing through, but I was not alone. A tracker was injected into my bones, a noose without a rope.

I unpacked a helmet, harness, and rope. That was all I needed to ascend a sheer granite wall that shot skyward ten thousand feet behind the village. I was stronger, lighter, and more like myself than the days before. I repeated the names I remembered, afraid that tomorrow those memories would fade too. Kate. Scarlett. Maggie. Timothy. William. Bao. The Ghost threatened to kill them all if I failed. And there were two others who remained elusive: Rachel and Samantha.

I climbed five thousand feet before pulling myself over a ledge with no fear of falling. I unhooked the harness, inched along the sheer wall, and free climbed another thousand feet. My fingers and toes gripped every crevice. With one hand, I held onto the granite, and with the other I removed the medallion from around my neck. I felt the rock for a camouflaged entry into the mountain. I knew what was at stake, what my actions would unleash. Once the door was opened, there was no turning back. I found the indentation, slipped the medallion in place, and turned the dial.

I surrendered to protect those I love. That one act will be the Brethren's undoing. For I am Lazarus—a Guardian of the light—and I will not go gently into the fight.